WESTMINSTER PUBLIC LIBRARY
D0098960

DISCARD
Westminster Public Library
3705 W 112th Ave
Westminster, CO 80031
www.westminsterlibrary.org

Memoirs and Misinformation

Memoirs and Misinformation

JIM CARREY
and DANA VACHON

Alfred A. Knopf
New York
2020

THIS IS A BORZOI BOOK
PUBLISHED BY ALFRED A. KNOPF

 Published in the United States by Alfred A. Knopf, a division of Penguin Random House LLC, New York, and distributed in Canada by Penguin Random House Canada Limited, Toronto.

www.aaknopf.com

Knopf, Borzoi Books, and the colophon are registered trademarks of Penguin Random House LLC.

Library of Congress Control Number: 2019954114

ISBN 9780525655978 (hardcover)
ISBN 9780525655985 (ebook)

Jacket painting by Jim Carrey
Photograph by Linda Fields Hill
Jacket design by Chip Kidd

Manufactured in the United States of America
First Edition

For my big brother John

For the name of a man is a numbing
blow from which he never recovers.

—MARSHALL McLUHAN

Memoirs and Misinformation

PROLOGUE

They knew him as Jim Carrey.

And by the middle of that December his lawn had burned to a dull, amber brittle. And at night, after the sprinklers' ten minutes of city-rationed watering, the grass blades floated in pooled water—limp and wasted like his mother's hair in the final morphine sweats.

The city of Los Angeles had been moving hellward since April, with bone-dry reservoirs and strings of scorching days, the forecasts reading like a sadist's charm bracelet, 97-98-105-103. Last week an F-16 had flashed like a switchblade through the ash-filled sky just as one of the gardeners on the Hummingbird Road estate collapsed of sunstroke and fell into seizures. The man fought as they carried him to the house, saying the Virgin Mary had promised him a slow dance for three dollars in the cool shade of the ravine. At night came the Santa Anas, those devil winds that sapped the soul, that set police sirens wailing as the sunsets burned through napalm oranges into sooty mauves. Then each morning a smoggy breath would draw across the canyons and into the great house, passing through air filters recently equipped with sensors to detect assassination by nerve gas.

He was bearded and bleary eyed after months of breakdown and catastrophe. He lay naked in his bed, so far from peak form that if you watched through a hacked security camera at this moment you might barely recognize him, might at first confuse him with a Lebanese hostage. Then, in a swell of facial recognition, you'd realize: *This is no ordinary shut-in watching television alone on a gigantic bed*, and as the bloodred Netflix logo glared from an unseen TV you'd say, "I know this man, I've seen him on everything from billboards to breakfast cereals. He's the movie star: Jim Carrey."

Just weeks ago, thirty seconds of home security footage was leaked to *The Hollywood Reporter* by some traitor in his extended personal-protection apparatus. In it Carrey bobbed facedown and fetal in his pool, wailing underwater like a captive orca. His publicist, Sissy Bosch, told *Variety* that he was preparing to play John the Baptist for Terrence Malick, who conveniently declined comment. The video sold for fifty thousand dollars, a sum just large enough to inspire that most sacred of animal behaviors—a spontaneous market response. After the fifth paparazzo scaled his backyard fence, his security team had it raised to fifteen feet, electrified, and fringed with razor wire, an eighty-five-thousand-dollar job including the city council bribe. Jim had since begun to hear the sizzles and squeaks of electrocuted wildlife as a sorrowful necessity, animal sacrifice to his godhead. And while some believed Sissy Bosch's John the Baptist story, most noted that it didn't explain Carrey's weight gain, or why some heard a distinctly Chinese accent in his moanings.

It was now 2:58 in the morning.

He'd been watching television for seven hours.

The binge had started with an episode of *Ancient Predators* featuring Megalodon, the super-shark terror of the ancient seas. Then came *Cro-Magnon vs. Neanderthal*, the story of how these early humans parted as cousins on the African plains, then re-met as strangers in Europe, only to begin a contest of genocide. Cro-Magnon had slaughtered without mercy, leaving famished Neanderthal orphans staring out from French caves into a blizzard, whose screaming whiteness, Jim knew, was that of total erasure. He was half French Canadian and learned from the narrator that he carried Neanderthal DNA within him; *he* was descended from these orphans. Feeling their doom as his own, he'd begun crying tears of desolation and then, unable to bear these, he'd hit pause with his grease-slicked thumb, freezing the screen on the tiny Neanderthal faces. For ten minutes he lay trembling, muttering "*Oh God* . . ." over and over until Netflix, greedy for its own bandwidth, reset to the main menu, casting its red glow over him and his guard dogs—identical twin, steel-toothed Rottweilers who both answered to "Jophiel." Their name was shared for the sake of efficiency in emergency, so that if one of Jim Carrey's many enemies broke into the house and he had only seconds to act, he could summon both with a breath.

Fearing this was the moment when he would discover his own long-standing nonexistence, questioning even the value of an existence as part of a species forever looping between horror and heartache, he wondered if the latest viral news story vexing his publicists was right. Had he actually died while snowboarding in Zermatt? He'd seen a YouTube video about how time behaves strangely in death, your final seconds distending, yielding rich washes of experience. What if he had died in recent days, arriving not in a hell or a heaven but rather a bedbound purgatory?

He'd heard stories about the Los Angeles morgue. Bored attendants taking gross pictures of the famous fallen, selling them to TMZ for down payments on houses in the Valley. He flipped to YouTube, whose algorithms, like reading his mind, offered a montage of celebrity death photos. A shot of John Lennon. Face puddled on a gurney. Splayed out for the crowd. If they could do this to John Lennon . . .

His mind now conjured an image of his own lifeless form, swollen and foul, the morgue goons standing above him, cameras blazing.

"Fuck . . . ," he breathed, unsure if he'd breathed it or not.

He'd gone to the bathroom, trying to reclaim existential certainty with a warm rush of urine through his middle-aged urethra. His heart was racing. What if it failed in his sleep and they found him in the morning, caked in his own excrement? What if the entire flight of paranoia that had brought him to this moment of feared death was a premonition of a future death, the Zermatt snowboarding disaster just fate's deft misdirection? No, if death should come, he'd look his best—crevice as clean as a whistle.

Thus resolved, he'd sat on his Japanese toilet and evacuated his bowels, wiped himself, and hopped in the shower, thoroughly sponging the orifice, then drying and powdering himself. He moved to the vanity mirror and kept going, trimming his wiry eyebrows, plucking the wolf hairs from his ears, rubbing bronzer across his forehead, his neck, around his clavicles in a broad swoop, so he looked like a Grecian bust.

Now he was ready for the boys at the morgue.

Here was a great star, they'd say. *A box-office god of the kind they don't make anymore.*

Now he was marginally less afraid.

He settled back into bed and began watching the first thing Netflix offered: *Pompeii Reconstructed: Countdown to Disaster.*

"This was the Hamptons or Riviera of the ancient world," said the host, Ted Berman, an off-brand Indiana Jones in a thrift-store fedora. Once again, Jim felt reality blurring into fiction as a digitally animated cloud of burning ash billowed up from Mount Vesuvius, the computerized notion of a camera's POV rose with it, high above the city, then stopped and panned into the volcanic crater, which suddenly seemed so very endless and all-devouring that Carrey cried out, "Security inventory!"

"Internal zones clear," replied his house, in the voice of a Singaporean opium heiress who summered in Provence. "You are safe, Jim Carrey."

"Defense barrier status?"

"Fully electrified."

"Let's do a voltage surge. Just to be sure."

The television's light dimmed as he heard a sound like a giant zipper being pulled around the property, twenty thousand volts of electricity surging through his razor-wire fence.

"Tell me I'm safe again," said Carrey. "And loved."

"You are safe. And loved."

"Tell me something nice about me."

"Your monthly water usage is down three percent."

"Flatterer."

The television regained brightness. The program resumed.

An earthquake had just rocked Pompeii, a natural phenomenon that the Romans had never experienced. Some thought it was the first act of a miracle and stayed to see more. Others were less sure, fleeing through the city gates.

"No one could have guessed," said Ted Berman, "that all who remained would die."

A succession of desperate moments with the documentary's main characters: a shipping magnate and his pregnant wife; young sisters born into a brothel; a high-ranking magistrate, his family, and their African slave.

Eyes tearing, Jim wondered: Was it wise to keep watching Pompeii, with the images of megalodons still fresh on the brain? With those Neanderthal orphans still paused in their French cave? Charlie Kaufman once told him that cinema's guiding illusion of distinct frames effecting fluid continuity was the same trick that creates the impression of time in the mind—that past and present are invented concepts, necessary fictions. Were he and the Pompeians just disparate squares of celluloid? Were they feeling the collapse of his world just as he was feeling the destruction of theirs? Was there only one pain? If this was true, then it must hold not only for the original Pompeians but for the actors playing them, people struggling for the next job.

To be seen. To matter.

Money was in charge now. Money had made them all indentured dreamers.

I don't have to be like this . . .

I could leave right now and just be happy . . .

But what would happy look like? At that moment, he couldn't remember.

An awful grief pulled him deep into the bed, multiplying his every pound a thousandfold. He summoned the strength to lift his thumbs and text Nicolas Cage, a man whose artistic bravery had always given him courage: *Nic? When you said the spirits of the dead are all around us, did you mean that poetically, or truly?*

But his exquisite friend did not answer.

Nic? again.

Again, no reply.

Seconds fell like loads of granite on top of him.

He considered abandoning Netflix.

He would eat the tuna Nicoise in his refrigerator, then go outside and maybe play-drown in the pool. He raised his head off the pillow, ready for action, but then stopped, suddenly sure that he owed Pompeii's dead a full and unbroken viewing.

He pressed PLAY.

Sets of unearthed remains were being digitally reconstructed by archaeologists from Frankfurt. Where, Jim Carrey wondered, would this technology be when he was dug up? What would people of the future conclude about him? Could they ever guess at what had writhed within his skull? His flayed father? His sweet-suffering mom? Might they one day reconstruct the ruins of the mind as well as those of the body?

The skeletons of the two sisters found in the Pompeii brothel had malformed teeth, the effects, the researchers concluded, of congenital syphilis.

"They were born with this social disease through no fault of their own," said Ted Berman. "Totally innocent and yet in constant pain."

The girls now received their close-up in a dramatized flashback, latex pustules bubbling off their eyelids as they gazed up toward Mount Vesuvius. In 1993 the Guru Viswanathan had observed Carrey's aura as "a glorious, radiant rose gold," and taught him to sense its shiftings within his transient form. Now he felt it arcing out toward the television as the syphilis twins cowered beneath the volcanic rain. He feared his soul was being taken from him or—worse—that it was fleeing.

Jophiel, affection! he tried to say, but could only gasp as, on the TV, Vesuvius's ash cloud blotted out the sun. Plunged into darkness, with a new appreciation for the word's impossibility, Carrey finally managed to bark "Affection!" and immediately the two Rottweilers clambered up to lie on either side of him, licking the tears from his beard.

"Deep affection!" cried Carrey, and the dogs (who had been trained to treat whoever spoke those words as a nursing mother and regard themselves as exactly six weeks old) moved from merely licking his face to nuzzling his neck, their muzzles so warm that Carrey might have confused the Pavlovian error for true nurture were it not for their steel teeth grazing the outline of his jugular.

He looked back to the TV: a shot of human bones on a steel table.

"Female remains," one of the Germans said. The camera zoomed in on a blue laser matrix completing the scan. "A wealthy woman. Perhaps eighteen years old."

The program cut to a flashback: the woman in her villa,

dining on a silk couch, a delicate beauty wiping her husband's mouth with a kindness that, Jim knew, was drawn from the actress's own way of loving.

The only truly selfless love he'd ever known, a giving without thought of taking, was with Linda Ronstadt in the rainy July of 1982. Sixteen years older, she'd sing him a Mexican love song, "Volver, Volver," a yearning lullaby that would settle through him as she held him to her sun-browned chest, running her fingers through his hair. "*Volver, volver, volver . . .*"

The words traveling forward through time to this moment: "Come back, come back, come back . . ."

But how could he?

He was not the bright-eyed boy she'd held. Had he killed that innocent kid, then dissolved the body in the acids of debauchery? He envied the doomed Pompeian man and his tender wife. He felt terribly alone there on the bed, Linda's voice whispering through him—

"*Volver, volver, volver . . .*"

As the laser matrix danced down the woman's skeleton, pausing over a set of bones scattered about beneath her rib cage, one of the Germans typed commands into his computer. On its screen, renderings of the bones gathered in a digital womb to form a tiny skeleton. A few more keystrokes gave it a shadeless layer of pink skin, a pair of tadpole eyes, a half-formed hand. A tiny finger plugged into a cupped mouth—

"She is with child," said the German. "Boy child."

And now new tears of abandoned hope joined Carrey's earlier tears of desolation.

"The cloud of superheated ash is collapsing under its own weight," explained Ted Berman. "And while the woman and her husband were safe from falling pumice in their vaulted villa, they will now suffer Pompeii's worst fate: thermal shock. As the air temperature reaches five hundred degrees, the woman's soft tissues will literally explode, her brain shattering her skull."

"*No* . . . ," said Jim Carrey.

"The baby's skull also explodes. Perhaps a fraction of a second after the explosion of the mother's intestines through her rib cage."

"*Please don't*," he begged.

And then, across his billion-pixel screen, the volcanic plume collapsed beneath its own mass, cascading down the sides of the digital Vesuvius. The syphilis girls, the magistrate, the young lovers and their child, all of them and their dreams, carbonized: flash-assumed into the death cloud whose blackness darkened the Hummingbird Road bedroom as it rolled across the digital Bay of Naples. Carrey moaned sorrow, closed his eyes like a little boy.

When he opened them again, Ted Berman was walking Pompeii's excavated streets in the present day. The camera panned across rows of plaster casts, bodies arrested in death, some with faces of abject terror, some guarding piled treasure with weapons, others tranquil, resigned. And finally: a husband and wife lying together, his hand on her pregnant stomach. And Jim Carrey, known for wild pratfalls and joyous mayhem—he curled into a ball and started weeping. Yes, he was a real mess. But once he'd shone so brilliantly. Oh, you should have seen him.

CHAPTER 1

A world before, he'd starred in a major summer spectacle, a movie that had effortlessly cruised to a $220 million global box office, with thirty-five percent of this fortune marked for Carrey personally, flooding into his financial reservoirs from distribution territories stretching, as was said, "from Tuscaloo to Timbuktu." That the film was, even by his own estimation, firmly in his second tier only made its success sweeter: the greater the impunity, the closer to God.

He'd filled with the love of the crowd as the blockbuster rolled out and on, opening in London, Moscow, Berlin. He entered Rome as a slapstick Caesar, walking a hundred-yard-long red carpet where he saw a publicist crouching right in his path and—gauging the moment like a cliff diver the rising tide—tripped right over the guy, going down spread eagle, head and shoulders walloping the carpet so hard that the crowd believed he'd died right in front of them. Lying there, Carrey thought of his uncle Des, shot and killed in a Bigfoot costume while on his way to prank a corn boil. Some lunged to help the star. Others just gasped. Carrey let their concern build before bouncing up like a coil and giving every subsequent interview with one eye crossed.

After, there was a dinner in his honor at the Quirinale Palace. A table for one hundred had been set by the president of the Italian republic. They'd all come for a brush with performative genius and watched, appreciatively, as at the head of the table, Carrey asked the veteran sommelier pouring wine into his glass if he could inspect the bottle. The man stopped and handed it to him. Jim sniffed the cork and examined the label, all of it just a setup for the moment where he plugged the bottle into his mouth and took a long chug before, with the face of a true connoisseur, declaring, "Wonderful. They'll love it." They did. They roared, all of them: the Swiss art dealer and the Three Men from Merck and the waiters watching from the kitchen, where the cooks were laughing, too. And the Camorra enforcer who had, that week, put two bodies in the Tiber. And the Swedish ambassador's husband. They laughed for this sudden relief from the burden of manners, and the laughter bound them across languages as they ate and drank on the marble terrace in the Roman night.

A twelve-piece orchestra played tangos, music that moved the owner of a dry-cleaning chain, a round woman, lonely in her late fifties, to decide, after three proseccos, that, having paid five thousand dollars to a corrupt senator's even-more-corrupt secretary to be here, there was no reason not to approach Carrey for a dance. She moved toward him like a heat-seeking credenza, and something in the boldness of her spirit swayed Jim Carrey. He waved away his bodyguards and took her hand, leading her out onto the colonnade. They tangoed passionately. She was surprisingly nimble, ready for every turn even though her fingers, greasy from the grilled branzino, kept slipping from his. He turned it into a set piece, feigning lover's frustration before taking her arm and throwing it over his shoulder, then pulling her close with eyes that said: *I'll never lose you again.* It had been so long since she was held. They spun like galaxies colliding, the whole orchestra soaring, the grifting crowd demanding crescendo and receiving it as Carrey dipped the woman in his arms and, seeing her lips pucker an invitation to kiss, licked her sweaty face from the chin up to the forehead, then stared at her like a happy puppy. This brought the whole room to its feet, love's caricature sowing want of its real form in the hearts of all present—even his own.

Soon he was back home in Brentwood, not a flicker of joyful mayhem in that famous face, only languor where so much raw charisma had recently shown.

The movie was falling from popular consciousness.

He felt his spirits fading with it, as if by unknown laws of human-industrial entanglement. He was lonely. And he was longing, truly if ridiculously, for the real version of that which he'd clown-played with the dry-cleaning *duchessa.* She'd given him a voucher for ten free shirt pressings, and taking it from his wallet he'd fixate, masochistically, on All That Might Have Been with Renée Zellweger, his last great love. She'd left him for a bullfighter, Morante de la Puebla. His heart had never completely healed, he realized, alone now on his Brentwood couch, numbing himself in television. He was clicking back and forth between *Engineering the Reich*, where Wernher von Braun was shooting men through the sound barrier as practice for the Apollo program, and *Vietnam Reunions in HD*, where a legless American hugged a toothless Vietnamese on the jungle hillock where each had lost his youth.

It was in the switching space between programs that Carrey glimpsed TNT's *Oksana*, and one of his mind's trillion synapses fired brighter than all others, demanding that he stay on the channel. There he saw a C- or even D-list actress, Georgie DeBusschere, as fully into the character of a Russian assassin as her modest talents allowed, torturing the Kyrgyzstani arms dealer whom she'd lured to a Bucharest safe house with promises of exotic sex. She'd drugged and bound him, then, when he woke, demanded the antidote to a flesh-eating virus currently thwarting her character's plot arc. Citing the virus's "rapid mutation rate" the man said he couldn't help her. She buried her power drill into his femur, then killed him with a judo chop to the nose.

Beholding Georgie in this moment of high violence, Jim's subconscious saw her eyes as his mother's eyes, her skin as his mother's skin, and her nose as his mother's nose: an error that filled his conscious mind with raw, candied rapture.

His early life was marked by the financial struggles of a beloved father, Percy, whose smile grew apace with the family's descent into poverty. His mother, Kathleen, sometimes channeled their decline viscerally, as her own imagined dying.

"The doctors say my brain is deteriorating at an incredible rate!" she would tell the family at the dinner table, her words filling young Jim with terror, fear that one day he'd return from school to find his mother lying brainless on the floor. Doctors prescribed codeine and Nembutal. She grew dependent on the painkillers, as so many have. He performed his earliest comic routines trying to make her feel better, a rail-thin seven-year-old entering her bedroom in his BVDs, pretending he was an attacking praying mantis, head crooked, pincers flailing, making her laugh against her suffering, which grew over time.

But the painkillers, over decades, took their toll. She'd lie there, rigid with arthritis, chain-smoking on the sofa of the North Hollywood apartment where Carrey had invited his mother and father to live with him when they ran out of money in old age. He'd come home from work on his first television series, NBC's *The Duck Factory*, to find her fast asleep on the sofa, stray cigarettes smoldering into the cushions.

Then the show was canceled and, running out of cash, he told them with deepest regret that they needed to go back to Canada, where at least if they got sick they could afford health care. He promised to send them money.

"You never see anything through, Jim," she'd told him. "You just never see anything through."

It was a crushing blow. Sometimes he'd dream of strangling her, then wake in cold sweats, guilty for his own imagined matricide, filled with a want of lost nurture that came back to him now, watching Georgie on TV. Who was this actress whose image stirred him so? What was this show? He pressed INFO: "*Oksana*: Subjects of an aborted Cold War experiment finally seek their truth."

Across twenty mind-rotting hours he joined them. He watched Georgie DeBusschere and her sisters battle to the

Moscow laboratory where they learned that they were all programmed killers, all hatched from the eggs of Soviet gymnasts fertilized with the frozen sperm of one Iosif Vissarionovich Dzhugashvili, better known as Joseph Stalin, raised by supercomputers on an unmapped Aleutian island. Awed by her beauty, he imagined her as a minor Kennedy, the only girl in a family of brothers. *They must have played touch football on the beach after clambakes*, he thought, watching her lay out a henchman with a roundhouse kick.

He couldn't have been more wrong.

She'd been born seventy miles outside of Iowa City, raised on a street of broken sidewalks. Her father was an alcoholic gym teacher. Her mother was a quiet and accommodating labor-room nurse. Georgie was one of eight children who fought viciously over bathroom time and frozen dinners. By her fourteenth birthday she had risen from the middle to the top of the pecking order, dominating her seven siblings—Cathy, Bobby, Cliff, Gretchen, Vince, Buster, and Denise—the family's increasingly strained resources making each child just a touch craftier than the one before.

She'd won a Rotary scholarship to Michigan State, where, assigned by a mainframe error to a graduate-level game theory seminar, Decision Making for Changing Times, she earned an A without even trying, finding the concepts came naturally. After graduation she went to Los Angeles, working briefly in print modeling before submitting an essay on Robinson Crusoe and a set of bikini pictures to the casting agent who landed her a contestant spot on *Survivor: Lubang*.

There, across the summer of 2000, she became loathed by

millions for betraying her best friend in the Gee-Lau tribe, a Mary Kay sales representative named Nancy Danny Dibble. Dull featured and acne scarred, Nancy had been cast for the strong response she elicited in focus groups: pure pity. The producers had planted her as a moral obstacle. For the contestants, the logical move was to dispatch her quickly, without regret. But what of the debt owed the weak by the strong? What of the viewers' delusions of morality—and the wrath that lived just beneath them?

Thinking to gain an ally on the cheap, Georgie shared her lip balm with Nancy during their first hours on the island as the castaways were ordered through seventeen takes of wading ashore. And while Nancy Danny Dibble may have never known a lover, she was a creature as erotic as any other. It's all there online, five seconds long, a voyeur's opera: compacted longing rushes through Nancy's eyes as Georgie applies the ChapStick to her lips. How long has it been since Nancy Danny Dibble was touched? "I need more," she says, and so Georgie runs the balm over her lips again. The gesture far exceeded whatever modest aims Georgie had for it, seeding a friendship that was cemented in episode 3, when, face lit by campfire, Georgie observed to Nancy that "Danny" was an odd middle name for a woman. The cameraman crouched low, his lens only feet from Nancy's face as she told how she'd taken it to honor the brother who drowned in the rainy spring of 1977, diving into a swollen Mississippi creek to rescue Dolly, a mass of dishrags and mop bits with purple button eyes, the only doll that Nancy had ever owned. Even in America, even from a casting pool of eighty thousand, this was no ordinary misery. Nancy's sorry aria soared until, with a feeble sob, she reached into the night like it might contain a wisp of Danny's hair. Georgie comforted Nancy, running her fingers through her hair, its Walgreens dye already fading in the sun.

"Georgie," said Nancy, "I'd-a liked if we were sisters."

"Nancy," said Georgie, as if the cameras weren't there, "we are sisters."

They pledged to win and split the money. But Nancy's misery proved contagious: handicapped by this woman (who also had arthritic knees, her very gait a show of weakness), the Gee-Lau lost a string of elimination challenges. Soon they were half the strength of the Layang, teetering on the edge of game-show extinction.

Ratings soared. Georgie DeBusschere's bikinied body became known to bankers and janitors, all in condos and projects. And why not? A million dollars was up for grabs here, enough money to grant that wildest of American wishes, escape from the lower class. Nancy Danny Dibble still believed Georgie would deliver them a victory. At night she dreamed herself driving a new, fully loaded Chevy Malibu through Jackson, Mississippi's finer suburbs, received by glowing housewives as a valued friend.

Georgie, however, knew the game was lost, and soon wanted just a warm bath. One night she walked up the beach, then crawled through the undergrowth to lie in a stream, where, bracing herself into the silt, she felt the edge of a dagger dropped by a Japanese corporal three days before Hiroshima. She worked the blade loose from the riverbed, tucked it into her shorts. The next morning, clenching it in her teeth, she swam deep into the cove, past the turquoise shallows, into darker depths where she encountered a full-grown moray eel.

How many watched Christ on the Mount?

Ten million ogled Georgie as she rose from the surf, the poor eel (the only innocent in this whole equation) slung around her neck, dripping black-green guts into her cleavage. She'd hunt again, and trade her kill for a favor after the next tribal merger. One of the Gee-Lau was sure to go, and while the Layang were likely intent on eliminating the strongest, Georgie bribed them toward the weakest, Nancy Danny Dibble. "Nancy's made us weak," she'd whispered. "She'll destroy you, too."

"I thought we were sisters." Nancy wept at the elimination ceremony, when the votes were finally read. "You promised! Say something!"

And here, as elsewhere, Georgie paid less for raw cunning than brutal honesty. The statement which viewers found so reprehensible was only made so for its cold truth—its unflinching appraisal of the crude gears that animate illusions of freedom. Georgie believed she'd done nothing wrong. She forgot the cameras and drew from the game theory she'd learned at Michigan State.

"All of life is a series of interlocking games, mainly meaningless, perhaps rigged," she told Nancy. "Some have rules we know; most have rules we do not. Are we being guided to some higher state? Or just forced from game board to game board for no end at all? The only way to know is to do what the games demand; I did only what the game demanded."

Nancy's cheeks glistened with tears.

The torches coughed up sparks.

And the Layang, sensing themselves in the presence of an advanced player, decided Georgie would be the next to go.

She quickly returned to Los Angeles, bent on turning infamy into celebrity. Represented by Ventura Talent Associates, she spent three years trying to become an actress, billed as the Eel-Slayer of Lubang, taking meetings for talk shows that never happened, winning roles in stillborn network pilots, unable to shake her *Survivor* anti-fame until, the greater horror, it was all gone.

She posed for men's magazines, each time wearing less, each time earning less. A gig as an auto-show bikini girl led to a job selling cars at Mazda of Calabasas, where, court documents allege, she once stole a used Miata. In time she married Darren "Lucky" Dealey, a rage-prone stuntman fired from leaping walls of fire for Rutger Hauer after assaulting a sound technician. Shortly before their first wedding anniversary he gave her a black eye; and she, in turn, sprinkled rat poison in his protein powder. Here was romance tragic even for a fading reality star. It was seven years, the biblical length of plagues, before fate showed her any favor; and even then, it was cruel.

Mitchell Silvers was a television writer and producer who as a USC undergraduate had obsessed over Georgie on *Survivor.* As an adult he abused power in service of desire, arranging through her VTA agent to meet Georgie at the Chateau Marmont. There, with a medicated lack of affect that she mistook for innocence, he offered to cast her on his upcoming TNT espionage series in exchange for sex in a junior suite. *It's just sex*, she told herself, *a means to an end*, *molecules bouncing around.*

Two months later, responding to Silvers's threats to abandon the project, TNT cast Georgie as the Russian assassin Nadia Permanova, a hard-bodied killer fighting central Asian warlords in the formfitting dominatrix gear that so beguiled

Jim Carrey, who as a young boy had fetishized the buxom Vampirella.

And who, as a man, watched slack-jawed as Stalin's daughters entered the Moscow lab where they found primitive hard drives containing every memory to be wiped from their brains across such lethal girlhoods, lost selves locked in magnetic tape. And finally, in a secret chamber, specimen jars containing human embryos floating in murky formaldehyde, the waste products of their creation. Georgie's character flew into a rage, smashing everything in sight.

And as the prop fetuses bounced across the concrete floor, Jim Carrey felt all the pain of lost love vanish. He felt himself, suddenly and surely, receiving nothing less wondrous than a message from the cosmos: Georgie, he knew, was his soul mate.

CHAPTER 2

Call it messy, call it madness; Carrey called it love.

He contacted Georgie through his publicist and suggested they share a night of self-discovery under the guidance of Natchez Gushue, a guru then popular among the city's spiritual seekers. Across the nineties Gushue had turned a Tucson AutoZone into a real-estate empire, at his peak swaggering around the city in a Stetson and fringed jacket, boasting of his royal Cherokee blood, asserting a spiritual mandate to reclaim his ancestors' land with a sprawl of Pollo Locos and payday lenders. Lawsuits describe him as delusional, profligate, only barely Cherokee. They say his empire was ruined by the same psychosis that found him, at the end, driving around Tucson with a loaded Uzi on his lap, ranting in word salad, high on methamphetamine. Natchez said that he embraced poverty willingly after receiving visions of Jim Morrison in a Cherokee Ghost Dance; that, if only more spiritually attuned, the Tucson police might not have mistaken his mystic tongues for word salad. He posted bail with cash he'd hidden in a fiberglass lawn armadillo, then fled north to California, prospecting for souls.

His first job was with Deepak Chopra, leading Quantum Encounter Workshops for corporate executives. But Natchez soon found fault with Chopra's teachings, perhaps because there was fault to be found, perhaps because he himself needed to be the alpha guru. He rejected Deepak's view of an eternal spirit as incompatible with the destructive nature of the universe. How, he asked, could Chopra deliver people from suffering through fantasy? No, it worked the other way around: the truth of cosmic brutality would unveil the truths of the self. Soon he was using meditation not to gloss over traumas but to induce them. One day he slipped ayahuasca to a group of Avis executives, then led them all in a visualization of the firebombing of Dresden that left four vice presidents curled fetal behind the Healing Pagoda.

Natchez was demoted to office work.

A yurt that housed the Sacred Gourd went up in flames.

Then Chopra cast Natchez out of his realm, a move that might have ended his career if he hadn't already found his first devoted follower in Kelsey Grammer.

Grammer, who in 2006 joined Gushue in meditations upon the Malibu mudslides where Natchez had helped Kelsey retrieve memories of his mother holding him in the moments just after his birth. Kelsey had seen every blue grain of her eyes, and in retrieving this image said he felt, however fleetingly, unconditional love. So was born another gospel in a country already frothing them from its mouth: *Gushueism*—a word at which critics often would exclaim, "Gesundheit!"—was a hodgepodge of extreme sports and regression therapy leading adherents not away from the brutality of man and nature but, rather, headlong into both. What his following lacked in numbers it made up for in status; Grammer had, over the years, seen to that. Small, illustrious groups often gathered on the ocean-facing patio of the Carbon Beach guesthouse where Natchez spent his days contemplating—he sometimes bragged—"the jagged edge of America's dream."

Jim and Georgie joined them as a Pacific hurricane hit Malibu, a storm that had killed hundreds south in Mexico; then, tired but still hungry, turned up the California coast. He found her even more alluring in person. He knew that past-life memories were sometimes recovered here and wondered if the same forces that were uniting him and Georgie now had done so before. Had they loved in other lives? Would they retrieve visions of those encounters? That would be something. He pictured them in timeless lovemaking, eons speeding harmlessly by as they burned through the positions of the Kama Sutra, and in this he grew so aroused that he failed to notice the half-stunned interest with which Georgie studied the other guests, his peers.

So this was it, she thought, standing among the A-listers on the patio. They all worked together, worshipped together. They shared agents and lawyers and gurus. It was a regular fame cartel. A rigged game, at least until someone brought you in.

"Are you excited?" Carrey asked her.

"Sure," said Georgie; then, noticing Gwyneth Paltrow in a pair of thousand-dollar heels across the way, removed her own scuffed pumps and placed them in her bag, taking the role of barefoot hippie girl as her strongest available option.

Paltrow was in pain. She had spent the past week yachting off Cannes with Brian Grazer, hosted by moneyed Moroccans speaking in hushed tones, trading wheat for oil; oil for assault rifles; assault rifles for artillery shells. They wanted film investments to launder dirty cash. She'd hated how this thrilled her.

"Feel nature's might, her majesty." Natchez sat with legs folded on a wicker sedan, belly bulging beneath a linen tunic three sizes too small. "We are breathing. We draw deep breaths."

"We are Orpheus entering Hades!" boomed Kelsey Grammer. "Explorers of the great within."

"And we remain quiet until the spirit moves us," said Natchez. "We are assiduously refraining from narration, from observation, from cross talk."

"Indeed we are quiet," said Kelsey, in a stage whisper. "We hushed, we blessed few."

Natchez could read his disciples' faces and, in the quivering of Gwyneth Paltrow's lips, sensed an inner journey had begun even before she spoke: "The Spence School. Manhattan. Senior year. It's early May and I really feel the spring coming on. A third-floor biology class, after school. Dust grains dancing amid columns of vernal light."

"Utterly sublime," said Kelsey Grammer.

"Cross talk!" snapped Natchez, then calmly, "Gwyneth. Continue."

"We all got frogs to dissect. I was reticent at first, but when the knife hit the flesh it's like I lost all fear. The blade seemed to guide me. So precise, so efficient. I finished the frog in a single class. So then the teacher, Mr. Libertucci, he gave me a cat. I finished that in two days, it was like some greater force was driving me to see how it all connected, to find out what makes it *meow*. So then he gave me a fetal pig." Paltrow's brow furrowed as her inner eye surveyed the past. "I'm seeing it now."

"Yes," said Natchez. "Dare forward."

"I'm seeing the tiny pig, in the wax-bottomed dissection tray . . ." Her face fell as she continued, "Eyes shut, almost like a sleeping child. And something's coming up from within me. I fight it, I have to fight it—"

"Don't fight it!" said Kelsey Grammer. "Be as the lotus."

"Goddammit, Kelsey!" snapped Natchez.

"It's an awareness that I'm not here for learning. I'm here, all alone after school, I'm here for the joy of pulling a blade through flesh," said Paltrow.

"Whoa, girl," said Goldie Hawn.

"I've been looking forward to this all day." She let out a deranged giggle. "The pig is an intelligent animal. A closer relative. A greater thrill, then, to dismember. Oh dear, I probably shouldn't be sharing this."

"You must!" said Natchez. "Dare forward!"

"I pull my scalpel down the abdomen," Gwyneth said, "I tear the fascia away, I'm in total control. I hack through the rib cage, its voided eyes looking at me."

"Its gaze," said Natchez, softly. "How does it affect you?"

"I feel guilty, maybe. Also lucky." A sudden light came across her face. "It's death's gaze."

"Death's gaze?"

"I want death to know I'm not afraid!" blurted Kelsey Grammer, tears of sudden realization rolling down his cheeks.

"Kelsey!" boomed Natchez. "Stop hijacking other people's epiphanies! Gwyneth, what happens next?"

"I cut its fucking head off!" exploded Gwyneth. "Okay? I'll tell Mr. Libertucci I did it to examine the vertebrae, but that's a lie. I did it 'cause I could. It's not enough to feel death's gaze. I want to do death's work. To deal death. I—"

"Lordy-lord," said Goldie Hawn.

"I stare into its fucking gaping pig eyes as I cut through its spine. And I'm sad, with each motion, to know I'm closer to the end. Because we're studying botany next. Guru?"

"Yes?"

"Is there such a thing as evil?"

"No, my dear," said Natchez. "Not on this porch."

Carrey squeezed Georgie's hand as if to say: *Have you ever seen magic like this?* She gave no response. She, too, had traveled back. Suddenly she was six years old again, her face pressed against the incubation chamber of the only sibling she'd ever felt close to, Denise, born two months premature. A fragile chest, beet red, begging small breaths from the world.

Denise now worked at a jewelry kiosk in a mall outside Iowa City, subsisting on minimum wage. A sadness for the smallness of her sister's life filled Georgie as Sean Penn lit an unfiltered Camel from the burgundy velour La-Z-Boy that was his recognized seat. The smell of cheap tobacco took Carrey back to the Titan Wheels factory, to working with his father and brother, all their money pooled for heat, gas, and food. He was sixteen, still a boy, and yet with a full-grown rage inside of him, an urge, so very natural, to destroy the factory that took them as no different and less precious than the piles of steel truck rims marked for buffing and blasting. He remembered slamming a pallet truck into the conveyor belts, again and again and again.

Below him, the waves crashed. And yet he declined to share this memory. He held Georgie's hand as the trauma gripped him, a panicked child. And her touch drained his pains away. For him it was further proof of her chosenness. For her? It was the start of a long journey into his hauntings.

"Animal-faced Pez dispensers," said Sofia Coppola. "Lined up on a Sonoma windowsill."

"Purple plastic testing containers warm with diabetic urine," said Goldie Hawn, "sitting on the kitchen counter of my blind uncle Warren."

"Strawberry-flavored codeine," said Sissy Spacek.

It had been six months since Sean Penn had shared any memory, and that had been only two words: "Bloodstained doilies." All came to attention as he spoke from the burgundy La-Z-Boy, never once turning from the storm.

"A bald child in a Ritz-Carlton swimming pool. It doesn't matter where. This kid's already outside space and time. His skin's almost translucent. He's six or seven. Head's still big on the body, and that amplifies the skull cavities, strains the muscles of his little neck and shoulders . . ." He coughed. "Something bulging from inside this little kid's chest, jutting at odd angles against the skin . . ."

"Fearless." Natchez regarded Penn as more peer than pupil.

". . . and it's a chemo port. Bandages. Surgical tape. What are they trying to do? Buy him a few more months. Weeks. Or maybe just a morning in a Ritz-Carlton swimming pool. Five hundred bones a night. Peak season. People trading coward glances as slowly they all get out of the water like he's some turd. Contagion. They ain't taking any chances. In ten minutes he's all alone there, turning weak circles, skimming his hands across the water's skin . . ."

"Did you fear the death in him?" Natchez whispered.

"Nah," said Penn, with a rasp. "I feared the death in *them*."

"Marvelous."

"I could use a glass of water," said Nic Cage, "I'm getting very thirsty."

"Follow that thirst," said Kelsey Grammer. "Dare forward, Cage."

"Next time you will leave the porch," said Natchez. "We have discussed the importance of respect and noninterference. Yet you do not learn."

And Grammer, chastised, quieted as Cage shared what would be the strangest memory of the night. "I see the city of Los Angeles," he began. "All in flames. Burning. I see flying saucers hovering above the canyons and—"

"What the fuck is this?" said Goldie Hawn.

"I'm saying what I see. Please respect my flow."

"Continue, Nic," said Natchez. "Please."

"I see these aliens with exoskeletons, like iron spiders, shooting death beams everywhere. A bowel-twisting firepower. Aw, man, all these demon-red death beams. Sky covered in smoke. The End Times sun, it's red like a, like a—" For a moment they hoped the memory would trail off, but then it came to him: "Like a baboon's ass."

"This is a memory?" said James Spader.

"When you put the bucket down the well and you bring it back up you don't always get water," said Cage. "Sometimes you get a wolverine that's been trapped down there forever and he claws out your eyes. So yeah, I'm seeing a big baboon-ass sun. I'm charging down the Pacific Coast Highway. Fires burning in the canyons, buildings reduced to smoldering rubble. I lead a band of Last Survivors and we—"

"He's grandstanding," said Kelsey Grammer. "Sheer narcissism."

"Continue, Nic," Natchez said. "Kelsey, hush."

"We fight these aliens. Come to kill us. Giant snaky guys. Skin all slick and glistening black. I lead the Last Survivors against these extraterrestrials who have come to annihilate humanity. Armageddon. They shoot us with these death beams, but the death beams, they don't affect me. Because my DNA? It's not like other DNA. Coppola genes are different. That's why I've felt so out of place my whole life. It's the burden I bear to save everyone and—"

"This is a plagiarism of *War of the Worlds*," said Kelsey. "Mule-fucked with the Christ myth, is what this is. He enters groups and he cannot help but sabotage for the sake of his own need to feel special. He did it in Goldblum's drama class—"

"Don't you Goldblum me."

"You made a farce of that workshop!"

"It was a Nouveau Shamanic experiment. A venture to the freedom that lies beyond the edge of annoyance."

"Hush, both of you," said Natchez. "Time runs in all directions. So, then, must memory. No temporal judgments here, please. Nic, continue."

Now Cage rolled his eyes back so only the whites showed, and no one could tell if he was being serious or not as, in a voice deeper than his natural speaking tone, he said, "The death beams, they bounce off me. Like peas. Everyone else?

Not so lucky. Flesh bubbling off their bodies. Death beams zinging and zooshing all around. This flesh-rendering heat. I can feel it down in my bones, can feel the marrow simmering." He clawed at his arms. "Now a big alien's coming at me. He's hideous. It's—Oh God, he's so horrific. I can't even—"

"You must!" said Natchez.

"He's got red eyes. A fat red stripe down his snaky body. He's got fangs. He's bearing down on me, bent to kill, there beneath the baboon-ass sun. I'm so afraid of my destiny, which is to fight this guy. Oh God, I'm so afraid . . ."

"Snakes beneath the baboon-ass sun?" said Kelsey Grammer, incredulous.

And Natchez might have banished Grammer to sit inside by the water cooler were he not so attuned to the battle raging within the man who, of all possible names, had chosen to call himself Cage. "Don't recoil, Nic. Dare forward."

"Okay. I'm going forward. Now it's even clearer. I have a sword of ancient steel, a relic of the Crusades. I left that out so far because it wasn't relevant. And I know, in my gut, it's the only thing that can kill an alpha alien. Which is my destiny. I close on him, lunging with my sword. But he dodges me. Rears up. Spits this black snotty stuff in my eyes. Oh God, I can't see. It smells so horrible, the alien snot. Ack, get him off me!"

"Fight it, Nic!" said Kelsey Grammer as Cage began to gag.

"He's coiling around me. Constricting me, like a boa . . ." Cage, tearing at his neck, trembling. "I'm losing my grip on my sword. I'm feeling my arms go limp. I'm looking into the alpha's red serpent eye and I'm feeling . . ."

"What do you feel?" said Natchez. "What comes over you?"

"Afraid . . ." Cage's lip curled, eyes trickling old tears. "Oh God, I'm so afraid."

"There, there," said Kelsey, suddenly pitying, laying a hand on Cage's shoulder with such kindness that Natchez forgave all his earlier trespasses.

"How very kind of you, Kelsey," he said. "How deeply empathic."

"Baby's gonna go," said James Spader, pointing to a little shed on the beach below, nearly submerged in the surf. As they rose to watch, Carrey and Georgie held each other's eyes for a second of deep appraisal. There was an excess of eagerness about him that she chose not to question. He emoted what he felt to be the golden light of love; she gave him her hand. Then they joined the rest, watching the structure torn from its foundation, smashed by the ocean, yielding inflatable alligators and flamingos to dance on the dark waves.

"Storms are getting stronger. Waters rising. The earth is growing angry," said Natchez. "Soon there will be nothing here but fire, water, and mud."

Thank God I found you, thought Carrey, staring rapt at Georgie's silhouette.

CHAPTER 3

Now two lives entwined.

The boy who'd fled Toronto's factories and the girl still fleeing Iowa's cornfields agreed that, the night being young, they should go to Carrey's beach house. They took his Porsche down the Pacific Coast Highway, satellite radio playing the seventh movement of Fauré's *Requiem*: "In Paradisum." While no classical aficionado, Carrey was moved by the music, sensing the majesty of the chorale as inseparable from the breaking power of nature, soundscape and landscape joined in the conjuring of the dead:

In paradise may angels lead you
On your arrival, the martyrs receive you
And lead you into the Holy City
Jerusalem—

An ecstasy overtook Georgie as she entered the film star's Malibu home, bought on a $10 million whim, a glass box of dreams.

She made twenty thousand dollars per episode of *Oksana*, an income secured after years of professional struggle and compromise. Yet when she had tried to buy a Laurel Canyon ranch house and gone to Chase for a mortgage, the loan officer rejected her, citing the famously short life spans of secondary characters on basic cable thrillers. She'd sat in her leased Prius, humiliated, ashamed—and enraged. Now she wondered at the blitheness with which money chooses some over others. Georgie had read of Carrey's breakup in the tabloids, had even watched Renée Zellweger receiving a bull's ear from Morante on the website of Pamplona's *Diario de Navarra*. She asked if he and Zellweger were truly finished, and he hemorrhaged.

"The Navajo elders joined our spirits, Renée and me. And after the breakup I felt like my spirit had been torn apart. I felt this wound I feared would never heal. But lately, Georgie, I've felt that wound closing. Lately I've felt whole."

"You have?"

"Yes. And guess what?"

"What?"

"Guru Viswanathan taught me to see all the colors of my aura."

"Oh?"

"Yeah. And after Renée it was bleeding out all its bright colors, just becoming this mucky gray. At night I'd feel an evil spirit in the house, this old woman with oily hair and a jaundiced face hovering over me as I slept, sucking all the color from my soul. I'd wake up screaming. But that's also stopped. You know how?"

"How, Jim?"

"It stopped when I saw you."

Here, Georgie knew, she'd found a rich, powerful star desperate to be loved. Desperate to believe. In Natchez Gushue. In Freudian confusion mistaken for destiny. In anything kinder than chaos. And gazing at his mother's eyes set in Georgie's face, Carrey marveled at the sheer benevolence of a creator who, working through local cable providers, would not only reveal but deliver her to him. Renée, he told Georgie, was only preparation for the true love now at hand. And Georgie, for all her later grievances, hurried to close the deal.

"Do you know what your aura looks like now?" she asked.

"Well, the colors vary from . . ."

"I can see it."

"You can?"

"Yes. It's a shining, golden light."

Whatever his later failings, it was she who kissed him first. Her own miracle, more or less, was also at hand, the journey begun on Greyhound buses crossing Iowa's endless nowhere arriving at its long-sought somewhere.

"Wanna go upstairs?" he asked.

She nodded. They went to the master suite. A slow montage of sexual joining suggests that, somehow, this love is different from all other loves. A dance of wanting bodies, the whispering of impossible promises. The storm's lightning pulsing against the gold-leafed painting that hung above the bed, an Orthodox icon of the Virgin Mary breastfeeding her superstar bambino, gifted to Carrey by probable murderers during the Russian premier of *Bruce Almighty*. Carrey gazes into Georgie's eyes—his mother's eyes—suckles her breast, his mother's breast, moves inside this near-total stranger like each thrust might restore him to the lost peace of the womb.

"Come for me, Daddy," she purred.

Within six months they had arranged for permanent karmic joining with a Melanesian spirit ceremony, held at Kelsey Grammer's home in the Malibu Hills.

Paparazzi choppers swarmed overhead, purchased by TMZ from the Marine Corps, still war painted black. Nicolas Cage served as Jim's Spirit Witness, breaking from the filming of *Bangkok Dangerous* to attend the wedding. His stuntman on the production had worked with Georgie's first husband on *Fast and Furious 3* and told Cage of their divorce: the poisoned protein powder, the Mazda Miata theft. He voiced his concerns just days before the wedding, when the two friends met at Cage's Bel-Air mansion for a Brazilian jiujitsu sparring session.

Stripped down to their briefs, sun low in the west, they circled each other in a black-sand dojo ringed with mastodon skeletons that Cage had won in Mongolian auctions. Carrey often wondered why they always fought at dusk. Was every moment in their lives just a scene demanding setting? Was the trap of persona everywhere upon them? The sun poured raspberry through the ancient rib cages, striping Cage's face in shadow and fire. Pleased with this visual effect, he made his plea.

"I'm frankly concerned, Jimbo. I say step back from this

one. I'm hearing some heavy stories about her past. Talking auto theft. Talking rat poison."

Georgie had already given Carrey her side. "Those are her ex-husband's lies."

"Even the mamba has its truth."

"Lumumba?"

"The mamba. It's a big snake. Look, I think the Renée wound has you falling for a knife fighter who may not mean you well."

"Georgie's taken my pain away."

"So would cyanide."

Taller and thus favored by the physics of combat, Carrey lunged at Cage, who fought dirty, gouging Carrey's eyes, saying if blindness was what he sought it was easily achieved. Carrey peeled Cage's hands off his eyes; Cage peeled Carrey's hands from his own hands. Vying bodies became vying fingers: Cage's thumb, unusually large from birth, dominated Carrey's pinkie, snapping the digit at its base knuckle. Carrey howled, surged with adrenaline, and threw Cage to the ground. They wrestled until their sweat-slicked bodies were covered in black sand, more suggesting aboriginal demons than millionaire actors. Finally Cage employed deception. He sighed, relaxed, feigned surrender. Then, just as Carrey relented, Cage crashed an elbow into his head, gashing the flesh of his eyebrow.

"You tricked me!"

"Only so you'd see! I'm looking out for you, Jimbo. In this scrapyard of dreams that we call home. This polluted meadow of bourgeois fantasy. This common grave of consumerist longing. This neon carrot dangling ever closer—"

"What are you talking about?" Carrey said, eye swelling shut.

"Celebrity, asshole. The iron maiden of a mass persona. The Torquemadan impalement of any chance at a true self. What if you're just a means to an end for this woman? Hey, only know what I hear. She's a knife fighter. Push comes to shove I'm hearing she would bury it to the hilt."

"I love her."

"Said the dopamine."

"I feel it in my soul, Nic, the place where Natchez was leading us. I feel a great peace. Renée was an equal. Everyone approved. Now she's with Don Alfonso. So where did that get me? We need to be loved and touched."

And, after pausing to appreciate just how perfectly the fiery sunset and mastodon shadow cleaved his face, Cage said: "We all suffer reverberant primal pains. Ancient men, getting eaten by vicious beasts? They wail inside us still. Why do you think we grapple here in this place of aged bones? Vanity? Boredom? Theatrics? *Wrong!* We battle ancient mojo in my black-sand shadow dojo! I just want to be sure you're going into this protected. With eyes open."

"There's no need," said Carrey. "Me and Georgie see each other's souls."

What was Cage to do? He'd played his best hand. He gave Carrey a kiss on the cheek, unsure if it was one of blessing or farewell.

Days later Cage stood beside his friend for the Melanesian Spirit Ceremony at Kelsey Grammer's house. Carrey's eye was still swollen half shut, his pinkie splinted.

Carrey's daughter, Jane, watched from the front row. He had her with his first wife, Melissa. She was a true child of

Hollywood, had once smiled before banks of cameras as her father pressed her seven-year-old hands alongside his in a square of wet cement in front of Grauman's Chinese Theatre. Growing up, more honest with herself than most, she wrote in her diary about celebrity's gravitational field—

The older kids want to be my friend just because of my dad. There are real friends and there are fake friends. I don't blame them but I see it.

She'd seen its toll on her father's psyche. The ego-distending adulation. The wrenching fears of abandonment. How the last box-office smash only raised the bar for the next project. Watching the ceremony, pregnant with her own child and, through that child, perhaps, filled with the hope of better things, she wished only for her father to be truly and lastingly happy with Georgie.

Who was a lonely bride.

Her father was deceased; her mother claimed sickness to avoid travel. None of her siblings attended. Her only guests were the Stalin girls. There was Oksana herself, played by Caprice Wilder, renegade child bride of a Greenwich hand-soap executive who drove to Los Angeles after 9/11 with only a meager alimony and the resolve to die famous; Olga, Oksana's loyal enforcer, played by Lunestra Del Monte—a woman named off of a MySpace plebiscite, she would later claim to have been a Kremlin agent in fact as well as fiction—and, finally, Stalin's youngest daughter, played by Kacey Mayhew, a former Memphis River Queen decrowned for making gonzo pornography under the name Ford Explorer.

Birds of paradise squawked from golden cages and a choir of Melanesian orphans sang as the newlyweds were showered with hibiscus petals. Carrey told *Us* magazine that his spirit felt unbound from his body, then felt Georgie's hand turning his face so the cameras could capture his unbrutalized side in a newlywed kiss.

All but one guest wished them well.

Katie Holmes attended with her then husband, a colossal action star whose real name, for legal reasons, cannot be given here. Hence, we shall call him *Laser Jack Lightning*. So there she stood beside Laser Jack: Katie, coal-eyed beauty, who had met Jim in the twenty-seventh chamber of Will Smith's backyard labyrinth two years before. Together they had found their way out of the maze, had, like Hansel and Gretel, grown close through shared peril. She noted a woodenness about Jim and Georgie's kiss, an ominousness in the speed with which the bride turned from her groom to the cameras.

Why, Katie wondered, eyeing them at the altar, *is false love so proud, and true love so fearful?* She smiled at Carrey with sad concern as he walked down the aisle, while Laser Jack flashed him a billion-dollar grin and a red-carpet thumbs-up.

Jim and Georgie's bliss was so great they made plans to enjoy it forever: at the Pasadena Longevity Center they had stem cells drawn and proteins synthesized for custom therapies promising to extend their shared life deep into the twenty-first century.

Age was just a disease, they were assured, curable like any other.

And yet bad winds were blowing . . .

Mitchell Silvers went missing from the set of *Oksana* for three days, returning in a semi-stupor, claiming he'd been abducted by an extraterrestrial television producer named Tan Calvin. But Angelenos have breakdowns all the time; Georgie, like most, just assumed he'd changed up his medications.

She had always wanted to visit New York, and that September, shortly after the Malibu ceremony, Carrey took her there for what might reasonably be called a honeymoon. They stayed at the Mercer in SoHo. Jim dreamed the neighborhood back to its 1980s heyday. He imagined all remnant graffiti the work of Basquiat, painters and poets and experimental musicians making love in the lofts, a lush, private fantasy of bohemia. For Georgie it connoted less artistic purity than brute arrival. *Mercer, Greene, Wooster,* she walked the streets without thought for their artistic or industrial pasts. The posh boutiques sang of paradise, and the paparazzi awaiting their exit from the hotel each morning, and following them through the days, made this, by far, the greatest role of her career, the mad rush of reality TV minus the sand flies and starvation.

Lunching on the sidewalk at Cipriani, she realized that all you had to do was sip water in the presence of Jim Carrey, eat salad with basic table manners, and, just like that, you entered social media's theater of a billion eyeballs. In centuries past, you had to kill on the battlefield or make a fortune in cargo shipping to join the aristocracy, but in Late America, miracle of miracles, you just needed to consume tuna tartare in the proper context. Her *Oksana* costars sent her heart-emoji-adorned links to shots of them on the sidewalk, pictures often taken only minutes before. Soon she was searching Getty Images for fresh visions of herself, meticulously planning the next day's wardrobe for the *Jim and Georgie Show.*

They ate dinner in a Chinatown restaurant, happy to discover they were still attracted to each other in overhead fluorescent lighting. They saw *Equus* at the Shubert Theatre, seated front row as guests of Daniel Radcliffe, who received them after in his dressing room, kindly playing along for a photo wherein Georgie, with outstretched, wiggling fingers, appeared to be casting a hex on him. Outside the theater they ran into Carrey's chief handler at the Creative Artists Agency, Gerry Carcharias, who invited them both to join him at the Christie's modern and contemporary auction the following evening.

It was a cool night, streets slick from a light drizzle. They dressed like for the Golden Globes, then piled into the Escalade, the car stereo playing *Sketches of Spain* as they drove up Lafayette, sidewalk lamps shining off the wet streets, Carrey telling Georgie that there was nothing more perfect than listening to Miles Davis in Manhattan in the rain, with her. Inside the auction house they sat with Carcharias and his second wife, Zandora, watching the rich capture treasures. A Warhol Monroe went for $50 million. A zebra by Damien Hirst, the great embalmer, fetched $25 million. Hockneys and Rauschenbergs fluttered between five and fifteen. Georgie struggled to conceal her exhilaration watching the paddles fly as a Russian oligarch battled Saudi twins for a Basquiat that went for $8 million. And Carrey's mind reeled as Gerry Carcharias bought a Hopper for $12 million, the agent seeming to have more disposable cash than any actor Carrey knew.

From what place had these dark fortunes been hatched?

Then a Frida Kahlo self-portrait went on the block, and Georgie gasped.

"You like it?" asked Carrey.

She'd always loved Kahlo's work, the feminine fearlessly encountering itself, the heroic struggle to escape from Diego Rivera's shadow. She nodded.

"Do you want it?"

"Stop."

"You do, I can see."

"Jim!"

And with this, sharing heated grins with Georgie after each successful bid, Carrey flew into pursuit, battling a Dallas oilman, a Japanese retail magnate, an agent of the sultan of Dubai, all chasing poor Frida from a million to a million two; from a million two to two million flat—where the Texan dropped out—to $2.2 million, where the Japanese retail magnate quit. Now it was just Carrey against the sultan's lackey, and he was Jim Carrey; he wasn't going to be bested by some hand-chopping despot.

"Do I have two point eight?" said the auctioneer.

Both met the challenge.

"Two point nine?"

Carrey raised his paddle like an ax.

"Three? Three point one?"

And there it was his.

Press captured the moment from twenty different angles, all showing Carrey glowering inappropriately at his vanquished foe, and Georgie in heaven, having received a gift worth more than her family's wealth going back generations. They made love against the window of the hotel suite, both staring out through the glass, and all the windows of the city staring back. Let them watch, both Jim and Georgie felt, let them share in this moment, watch us cum, let them feel the joined thrills of spiritual union and victory at auction. Each believed that the other's fevered pledges—"*I love you,*" "*I'll always love you,*" "*I've only loved you*"—were true, or at least not spoken to deceive. It was all too much to dream. And left Georgie so infatuated with Jim, and with the promise of a life filled with moments like this, that she told herself it was just a clerical error when, two weeks later, the Frida Kahlo arrived at the Hummingbird estate and, after unpacking it from its wooden crate, the art handlers gave her a certificate of sale which listed the piece as the sole property of one James Eugene Carrey.

CHAPTER 4

Then came the autumn of Mitchell Silvers's death.

An extraterrestrial subplot emerged in *Oksana*'s fourth and final season when Georgie's character, Nadia Permanova, encountered a wormhole in a Kievan sugar-beet field. She was guided through it by singsong voices, received on the other side by willowy light beings who gave her lucid visions of her past. She saw her five-year-old self slaying her own identical twin, wandering snowdrifts in stamina-building exercises, and finally she relived a medical procedure received on her fourteenth birthday as a frightened girl in a Red Army hospital, where a surgeon drew his scalpel beneath her belly button. The trauma of this memory sent her vital signs racing, forcing her abductors to end the encounter and return her to earth. The scene had enraged TNT executives, who were already developing a space franchise with a nephew of Ridley Scott. They gave Silvers a dressing-down, saying he'd be making DMV collision reels if any of Stalin's daughters so much as bought a helium balloon.

At home that night Silvers found an even-greater superior awaiting him, the intergalactic reality producer Tan Calvin. Calvin's people, Silvers had learned, were plagued by horrible body shame. The cosmos had given them so much: a cushy perch in a quiet stretch of galaxy, minds so powerful they'd moved from the wheel to quantum physics in a single century. But physical beauty had been denied them. They had, in response, mastered shape-shifting, donning appropriated forms to indulge escapist fantasies and to avoid traumatizing their colonized peoples. For Silvers's benefit, Calvin had chosen the form of a champion rower from Oxford's class of 1913, a man whose thick, wavy hair and alabaster skin had inspired poetry among his peers before a Krupp shell killed him at the Somme.

He laid a powerful hand on Silvers's shoulder. "You of all people would agree that what's good for the greater program is what matters. We require a new direction."

A black Beretta lay on the table. "Just a little more time," Silvers begged. "Give me one more season."

Calvin replied with a farting noise.

"Please," said Silvers, rushing to his dining table, crafted from a sequoia that was a sapling when Calvin wrote the Christ myth from scraps of pagan lore.

"I have ideas," he explained. "So many ideas!" He rolled out his final opus across the table, a plot-tree forest filling six feet of butcher paper, a thousand story lines that would send Joseph Stalin's daughters to distant galaxies, escaping all detection until massive Nielsen ratings had made Mitch mighty.

"It's not just you, Mitch. We're winding down the whole earthly production. We're moving on to the Inner Triangulans."

"Who?"

"It doesn't matter. Human things have long since jumped the shark. Extinction is destiny, that's never been a secret. I'm doing you a kindness, Mitch. Dark days ahead. Systemic collapse, fiery wrath. Toddler cannibalism."

"Toddlers?"

"As soon as their teeth come in. It's a crowded interstellar entertainment marketplace. Takes ever more to break through the clutter."

"Calvin."

"What?"

"Let me see your real face."

"I'd rather not."

"Please."

"I revealed myself once to a girl here a long time ago. I still regret it, I'm cruelly maligned for it. You people have such a narrow view of beauty."

"Please. I want to see—"

But both Silvers's curiosity and his will to resist were dissolved by a flash of Calvin's eyes. Then the condo's stereo switched on, Slavic wailings sadder than piss-stained snow gaining in volume as Calvin said, "Pick up the fucking gun, Mitchell."

Silvers palmed the weapon, face beading sweat; Calvin's tongue licked his perfect teeth just before he coolly instructed,

"Slowly, not a trace of fear in your being, you will rise from your chair and move toward the window."

Silvers obeyed, standing, walking into a brilliant light suddenly washing into the room: golden, calming, relieving him of the burden of himself. Whatever happened now was fine. Fated. Nothing bad could come from a moment that felt so totally good—

"Mitchell Silvers. Are you ready for your parting gift?"

"I am," Silvers said, voice breaking. "Yes, Calvin, I am."

And so he received his final frames of consciousness, false memories streamed into his mind so that he experienced them as his own personal history while describing them aloud.

"I see Georgie . . . ," whispered Silvers. "I see Georgie, she's so beautiful."

"Yes, she is."

"Her face, close to mine. I feel her breath on my skin, her lips so soft against my ear. She whispers. She tells me she loves me . . ."

"Let it take you."

"She loves me," said Silvers. "Calvin, I was loved."

"Yes! And now you lift up the gun."

Silvers obeyed, shedding tears of joy, raising the pistol to his head.

"She loved me."

"Bravo."

"I was loved!"

"Bravissimo!"

Then Mitchell Silvers's brains splattered across the windows where they'd cook for three days in the sun, generally admired by neighbors who mistook them for art.

CHAPTER 5

Georgie discovered the body.

It was a Wednesday afternoon; she and Silvers had scheduled a meeting to discuss a spin-off series. She left Brentwood in the silver Porsche at 2:07 p.m., taking Santa Monica Boulevard to Lincoln, then Lincoln into Venice Beach. At 2:24 she passed the condo's front desk, and at 2:28 she exited the elevator into Silvers's penthouse, where nature, ever thrifty, was hatching blowflies from his corpse. She gagged against the stench, then turned from Mitchell's body to the final product of his tortured mind, his unfinished symphony, the disjointed story lines for *Oksana*'s adventures in space. In suicide Silvers had derailed Georgie's hopes to finally be first on the call sheet, killing any chance for her spin-off. TNT quickly canceled *Oksana*. Stalin's daughters were left frozen at the end of season 4, discovering their father's corpse in the Moscow sewers, learning he'd ordered them all sterilized to keep his genes under strict control.

With her fortieth birthday approaching, watching this very fertility-focused last episode, Georgie felt a driving maternal urge. A desire, quite natural, to reclaim the right of motherhood she'd signed away in her domestic partnership agreement with Jim. She broached the matter one night as they ate ceviche on the back patio of the Hummingbird estate, the artificial waterfall running against jackhammerings of neighboring mansions metastasizing from great to gargantuan.

"Do you ever get lonely, just us?"

Jim pretended not to hear her against the hammers and the water. "What?"

"Wouldn't you like a little girl, a little boy?"

"I thought we discussed this. I thought we were clear."

"People change. I've changed."

"You can change all you want."

"But?"

"But you can't make me a father again."

"What gives you the right to deny me motherhood?"

"You did."

"When?"

"From the beginning. We had an agreement."

As he stared coolly through her, she thought of the Blueberry 9000, a Japanese sex robot she'd seen while googling, a steel-and-plastic woman complete with mouth, anus, and vagina, all imbued with advanced robotic clenching powers. It could sigh, moan. Scream. And it was only a matter of time, said one Tokyo technology reporter, "before cyborgs and humans dance in the fat and honeyed lands beyond the uncanny valley, sharing love as a feedback loop between all that was ever wished and all that has ever been"—words that had stuck with her.

"What am I to you?" Her hands were burning.

"Right now? Right now, you're someone who's going back on a contract, is what you are right now. Lots of women don't want children. You said you were one of them." His voice turned to pleading. "What are you doing?"

Callous, yes, but honest. This relationship was fueled by Carrey's deep need of maternal love, something Georgie was hard-pressed to deliver in the first place. How could she sustain the dynamic while nurturing a child of her own? And yet how could she endure it without one? She left the house, drove to stay with Lunestra Del Monte in Pasadena. For Carrey it was the opposite of endless motherly acceptance; it was indifferent abandonment. He begged for her return, by turns plaintive and enraged. Two weeks later, low on cash, she came back. But distrust had infected intimacy. He began counting her birth control pills and found sex so infected by anxiety that he couldn't maintain an erection. He turned to Viagra, and Georgie would lie beneath him, wondering, as Carrey struggled toward climax, if it might be nice to have a Japanese sex robot on hand to relieve her of the conjugal burdens that now seemed obligatory, mechanical, and even (she resisted the word) servile. One day she dug up their cohabitation agreement from his office drawer and felt a sudden nausea to read that there were three more years before a breakup scenario would yield her a dime.

And she felt no guilt at all, savoring sweet schadenfreude when the Fates delivered Carrey just a bit of the torment they'd long visited on her.

—

His two finest performances, in *The Truman Show* and *Eternal Sunshine of the Spotless Mind*, had been ignored by the Academy. Making *I Love You Phillip Morris* was supposed to change that. It told the true story of a devoted husband, Steven Russell, who discovers his homosexuality following a violent car crash, then abandons his family to pursue a life of fraud, cons, and hedonism. Sent to prison, he finds love with a fellow inmate, ultimately faking advanced AIDS so they can live together in Key West. Carrey had expended huge professional capital on its production, fighting to keep a scene of his character in the act of anal penetration, even defying CAA's mass psychologist, whose warning, "America has issues with sodomy," had all but predicted the *New York Times* review: "A star vehicle whose first gay erotic moment shows Mr. Carrey engaged in loud anal sex is asking for trouble."

Which it found.

The Bible Belt was written off from the start, but its capacity for vengeance was sorely underestimated. Carrey became the target of jeremiads from the pulpit of the Reverend Reggie Lyles Jr., a twenty-nine-year-old New Revivalist standing five foot seven in three-inch heels. His five-hour radio show reached three million people in America, and each week he raged against Jim Carrey's degradation of the American family, his promotion of adultery and divorce, his complicity in a gay cabal. Even after distributors abandoned the film, Reggie's acolytes, whipped into a fervor, pressed on with the crusade. Security feeds showed three figures arriving at the Hummingbird estate in a pickup truck one night at 4:13 a.m., wearing ski masks. They spray-painted GOD HATES FAGS on his gate, then turned to his security cameras quoting lines from Revelation: *And I stood upon the sand of the sea, and saw a beast rise up out of the sea, having seven heads and ten horns, and upon his horns ten crowns, and upon his heads the name of blasphemy.* They'd emptied barrels of bloody guts down his driveway, then—in a mad dash—befouled his swimming pool with the heads of the three pigs who'd provided the guts.

"Always pigs," Carrey's security chief, the former Israeli army commando Avi Ayalon, said, watching the bloated heads bob in the water. "Someone wants to send a message? They always go with swine. Filthy animals. Very intelligent. Did you know they eat their own?"

Security was enhanced across the estate. Avi moved temporarily into the pool house and, through Mossad connections, procured Jophiel, the steel-fanged Rottweilers that would, in time, be Carrey's only friends. The creatures came pretrained. "Kowtow," said Carrey, reading from the command list, "kowtow!" And as the Rottweilers whimpered at his feet, he smiled his humungous billboard smile; he felt the dogs were fully worth their hundred-thousand-dollar price tags, the warmth of the wish that money could bring death to heel. He and Georgie began savoring the nightly ritual where, per the training regimen, they'd hurl a lamb shank out into the yard—crying "Intruder!"—and watch the beasts tear toward it, rip it apart, clocking the response times.

While these dogs brought protection from marauding born agains, they offered none from the greater film industry. *I Love You Phillip Morris* ended its run losing millions. Now it was Carrey's turn for a lesson in powerlessness. He was nearing fifty, his fans aging, too. His talent was such that Hollywood could not replace him in its usual way, the kind of body snatching that saw Emma Stone swapped in for Lindsay Lohan, Leonardo DiCaprio taking over for River Phoenix. But, still, they could tame, control, punish. Disney and Paramount froze slated projects; a third, at Sony, was quietly killed. It hardly mattered that Carrey was still beloved, as his agents said, from the Ganges to the Andes, a reliable global draw. All across Los Angeles estimations of his industrial worth declined so steeply that his managers, Wink Mingus and Al Spielman II, arranged an emergency phone call to discuss what was then being called the Situation.

"We need to reaffirm the Carrey brand," preached Al Spielman II.

"We need something with penguins or polar bears," said Wink. "People love animals. People miss the days when they lived in jungles among animals and heard their own souls in the sounds of those animals. That's why *Ace Ventura* worked."

"I think it was the character they liked," said Carrey.

Wink Mingus said, under his breath, "*Ace Ventura* worked 'cause Ace Ventura loved animals. Just like people do. They saw their animal love in his."

"We need something four quadrant," said Al. "And fast." Then he sighed the sigh of his heart surgeon father, Al Spielman Sr., a sigh to suggest that while the situation was dire, heroic procedures might, just might, deliver a miracle. It usually bent Carrey to his will, but here, to Al's dismay, it had no effect.

"I've done nothing wrong," said the star, on his patio, Jophiel gnawing lamb bones at his feet. "Why should I make some stupid family film?"

"You wanna tell him, Deuce?" asked Wink.

"I do," said Al.

"Then do."

"You apologize so you don't end up playing lounges in Vegas," blurted Al.

Early gigs in Vegas had always sapped Carrey's soul. He'd feared growing old there, dying there. In nightmares he'd seen his own desert-aged face, an image that now returned: jowly with bleached teeth and hair plugs, whoring for the bingo crowds.

He froze, dread struck.

"I'd listen to him, Jimbo. Don't wanna end up back in Vegas, playing for the bused-in package tours. Old ladies clutching change purses."

The haunting deepened. A close-up on his orange spray-tanned face, a weary persona playing greatest hits on eternal loop for the casino crowds. Why was this vision so clear? Was this end somehow fated? He wondered all this just beneath his breath.

"Whatcha mumbling?" asked Wink Mingus. "Huh?"

"You think you're hirable right now, Jim?"

"If Robert Downey Jr. is hirable, I'm hirable."

"Downey never fucked a guy in the ass on film!"

"What's wrong with playing gay?"

"It's not commercial. Leads to confusion. A couple of my golfing buddies started asking about you."

"Oh yeah? Are they cute?"

A click on the line.

"Deuce?" said Wink. Silence. "Nice goin', Jimbo."

"I don't want to do some middle-of-the-road family movie, Wink. It amounts to propaganda for the wars. We're just distracting while—"

"Going into the underground parking. Gonna lose ya."

Then Wink Mingus was gone, too, and Carrey all alone with his fears.

He walked off the patio, across his lawn, up through the ravine to his cypress-wood prayer platform. There, sitting half lotus, Jophiel tight by his sides, he closed his eyes and beseeched the cosmos, "Guide me. Show me. Use me."

And, like so many of his prayers, this one was answered.

Two weeks later, on a clear night after days of rain, a 1988 Volvo 240 station wagon approached the Hummingbird gates, pale blue body rotted and rusty, riding low on its chassis. Georgie was asleep, Carrey alone in the living room, watching a YouTube video on the role of cheesemaking in the rise of Genghis Khan. Avi Ayalon heard the Rottweilers howling and checked the security monitors to see a man who hissed "*It's not safe!*" over and over, demanding, "*Open the gates!*" Carrey rose to study the night-vision figure. Hair oily and unkempt, cheeks gaunt, the eyes of a biting creature. Only his voice defined him as more than a straggling junkie, as Charlie Kaufman, the shape-shifting auteur who had written Carrey the finest role of his career with *Eternal Sunshine of the Spotless Mind*.

"Kaufman?" Carrey gasped. "Let him in."

Jophiel growled as he entered. Kaufman was tunnel eyed and jittery, hoodie pulled tight as he shielded his face from the foyer's security cameras, insisting they speak outside. The dogs followed them to the back patio, where Carrey and Kaufman sat on a teakwood bench beneath a sky of depthless blues, the night air sweet with mangoes rotting in the trees above. "You got a cell phone on you?" asked Kaufman. Carrey produced the gadget from his pocket. Kaufman snatched it from his hand, throwing it hard into the pool, hushing Carrey until it had sunk to the bottom.

"Christ, Charlie!"

"Oh yes. Be scared. These are vicious people."

"Who?"

"They got to my maid, Magda. She did some public-pissing films back in Berlin right after the wall fell. You know the drill. Squatting by the Reichstag, hiking up her skirts, a healthy flowing golden shower. Artful stuff. Even if it wasn't, Christ, Jimmy, she was just a kid! Trying to get by. Taking a pee. Reclaiming the odd square foot of history. And they used this past against her. Blackmailed her into poisoning my pet butterflies, Jan and Dean! I found them bobbing lifeless in their sugar water, I lifted them out with my fingers. So delicate. I kept blowing on them, Jimmy. I kept wishing my breaths could bring them back to life."

Kaufman paused, wiping tears from his eyes.

"Charlie, what's—"

"They fried my hard drives. Hacked my house so all the lights flicker and strobe and my stereo plays secret recordings of Richard Nixon confessing dreams to a shrink. You know what Dick Nixon dreamed? He dreamed of himself as a young boy leaping from a rusty swing set toward a distant Wabash freight train whistling songs of escape velocity, offering the promise of being anywhere but where he was. He leaps from the swing, he soars so high, little Dicky, seeming to fly toward that train, then falling toward the place where his shadow should be but isn't. The void. They're sending me a message. Making it very clear. These people? They'll disappear you. Make it look like a heart attack. A suicide. Hang you from a ceiling fan, pants around your ankles, your cock in hand, big kitchen spoon up your—"

"This is crazy talk!"

"I got people coming for me! I'm haunted by a monster!"

"Charlie! What kind of monster?"

"Krueger-esque! But no more hiding. I gotta tear him out from my nightmares. Into the light of day. Which is art. And you're the only guy who can help me."

"Help you what?"

"Strike him before he kills me!"

"Who?"

Shivering with the twin chills of fear and desert night, Kaufman dared to whisper his tormentor's name: "*Mao Zedong.*"

"Mao Zedong . . . the brutal father of modern China?"

"Shush!"

"But he's dead."

"Is he? Mao. Director of the largest, most lethal theatrical production ever conceived. Isn't that what a revolution is, Jimmy? The pageantry. The lights, the music, the costumes. Lavish set design on a massive scale. It's the ultimate mash-up of genres: romance, action-adventure, murder-mystery, thriller, coming-of-age. Fantasy. Mao, who promised to end all bourgeois privilege, then married a sexy Shanghai actress. Mao, who starved millions while lazing poolside, getting fat and writing bad poetry. And what's that telling us about hidden circularities? Why do these monsters yearn toward beauty? You ever go wandering alone at dinner parties? Say you've gotta pee, then explore all the rooms of the house? I do that all the time. You know how many Hitler landscapes hang in Hollywood's private collections? Behind false panels?

I count seventeen. Ever shave off a full beard? You just gotta try that little mustache before you're done. Next thing you're spouting fake German, goose-stepping around the bathroom. We've all got it in us, man!"

"Charlie. What's happened to you?"

Kaufman dropped his hood, then recounted his season in hell.

That autumn, acting on a therapist's advice that travel might free him from troubling dreams of his boyhood self in a cowboy outfit on a Coney Island carousel, he'd agreed to judge the Shanghai Biennale with Taylor Swift and Jeff Koons. Afterward they'd been taken on a tour of luxury condominiums across China's northern provinces with representatives of the Biennale's major sponsors: Louis Vuitton, Morgan Stanley, and the People's Liberation Army. In rural Henan, hiking on a sloped hillside, they were caught in the first spring rains, mudslides came roaring down all around them. Struggling to save her Pucci scarf with one hand, her iPhone with the other, Taylor Swift felt her big toe catch in the earth. She'd twisted and wriggled but couldn't free it from the muddy suction. It was trapped, she saw, looking down, in the eye socket of a human skull. Horrified, she'd gasped a perfect E-flat that hung in the air as more human remains surfaced around her. Rib cages tangled with spines, jutting femurs, grasping hands. All rising up from the liquid hillside.

She was far from Nashville now, wandered into a mass grave from China's great famine, the starvation of forty million caused by Mao's Great Leap Forward.

But large numbers of peasant dead were considered off-brand by Morgan Stanley, the Chinese government, and Louis Vuitton alike. A cover-up was concocted. Taylor Swift traded silence for the rights to bring her fashion line to the Chinese market with a runway show on the Great Wall; Koons was allowed to sculpt a gigantic Slinky on the steps of Beijing's Forbidden City. Kaufman had been offered generous film financing, but had alone refused cooperation. Cinema, he'd always believed, mimics life as a system of disparate images effecting unified experience through the magic of sequence and speed. For him the mass grave's surfacing was in all ways a haunting—a frame from the past usurping the present. And as the storm's wind wheezed through skeletal cavities, he'd heard an anguished voice speaking from beyond time, imploring him: *Remember us, Charlie! Tell the world of the monster who put us here. Don't let us be forgotten once the army bulldozers have plowed us back under!*

Back in Shanghai he stayed at the Peace Hotel, wondering how Mao's crimes would best be treated in cinema, jotting ideas down as they came. Horror seemed the right genre. Something like *The Omen*, *The Exorcist*. What if Mao's spirit was hatched—no, reborn? Yes, like a hungry ghost, refusing death, latching onto some equally gruesome modern entity? That was it. He'd popped a Xanax and gone for a walk along the Huangpu River, returning hours later to find his room ransacked, his laptop stolen, a new note scrawled on his pad, seemingly written in his penmanship by the Chinese Ministry of State Security agent already assigned to his containment: "Silence is golden."

He'd fled with just his passport—and a hit of inspiration making clear the scope of his project, and its required star.

"I need you, Jimmy," he said now. "You gotta be my Mao."

"Madness!" Carrey hissed. "They'll hang me for playing Asian!"

Kaufman had already addressed this. To take Mao head-on, as Daniel Day-Lewis might, would only arrive at the comic grotesque. But to channel him through the comic grotesque? Well, that might deliver the fullness of his horror. Kaufman's Mao would be re-spawned inside the mind of a tormented actor, "Jim Carrey," a star who, fearing his own collapse, explores the same dark appetites that guided Mao: the wish to be worshipped forever, to escape mortality by commanding history. A man who, convinced the character of Mao Zedong will be his *Raging Bull*, opens himself ever more to the tyrant's spirit, his lusts, his vanities, until he is devoured completely. Carrey was appalled, and yet—in Charlie's hands, who knew? It could be a masterpiece, his Oscar vehicle, something to make Tommy Lee Jones—who'd never given him his due and always called him a buffoon on the set of *Batman Forever*—croak of jealousy, that whiskey-soaked Harvard shit, God bless him.

Kaufman unfolded a worn treatment. Scratching out the opening sentence, he scribbled a new one in its place, and read it aloud: "Jim Carrey and Charlie Kaufman sit beneath a sky of depthless blues, the night air sweet with mangoes rotting in the trees above. The camera goes close on Carrey. 'How does it begin?' he asks, voice tinged with a tragic naïveté."

Carrey closed his eyes, head spinning; imagining himself playing himself playing Mao, he asked, "How does the movie begin?"

"With the hunger. A long crane shot, digital, rising over a soaring pile of starving peasants. Thousands. Millions. Tens of millions. Infants, children, mothers, fathers, the elderly, their final breaths, gasps, rattles, joined in singing an ancient harvest song. These are the innocents whose lives Mao devoured, feed for his demon dreams. Slowly, the camera cranes up the piled bodies, pulling back as it ascends, ever further, until the moment of maximum removal when we see this is all an inverted image set in Mao Zedong's milky, dying eyeball. He's on a steel surgical bed. Hooked up to respirators. An affront to the word 'alive.'" Kaufman lowered the script. "You're perfect for this! Who else could do it?" Clearing his throat, he returned to the page. "Time misbehaves in death. Minutes cough up centuries. Seconds excrete millennia. So it is here. We go from Mao's POV as the embalming team plug rubber tubes into his arteries, pump him full of formaldehyde. He's trapped in his own body. Not alive and yet undead. Tormented by something just beyond the flesh, something that here, finally, holds him in its clutches. Reckoning, he can't escape it. And as he shrieks inside himself like a man buried alive, the camera dissolves from Mao's bloated, gruesome, famous face to . . ."

"To what?" whispered Carrey.

"To yours . . ."

CHAPTER 6

Charlie Kaufman was living on the run. He'd fled his bungalow for the Saharan Motor Hotel, an old Sunset Boulevard fleabag where he'd guide Jim Carrey's spirit toward Mao's.

Carrey had stayed at the motel when he came to Hollywood in 1982, arriving with just six hundred dollars, a suitcase of clothes, and a secondhand copy of an apocalyptic bestseller, Hal Lindsey's *The Late Great Planet Earth*. The author claimed to have cracked secret codes in the Bible, and through them to have learned that nuclear annihilation was only months away, the end of everything at hand. Carrey had read it in a sun-warped plastic chair overlooking the Saharan's swimming pool, fetid water bobbing with cigarette butts and candy-bar wrappers, the haggled ecstasies of hookers and johns sounding from nearby rooms. Sometimes, lonely, he joined them. Sometimes he made his cruddy mattress wince with Tammy the peroxide blonde in the white leather miniskirt who worked outside the Comedy Store; sometimes with freckled Vicky from Montana who wished for soap-opera stardom while hustling the rush-hour traffic. Sometimes Vicky's fake Chanel perfume lingered on his skin as he read *The Late Great Planet Earth* above the motel pool, and sometimes, looking up, he'd daydream a thousand ICBMs streaking silver across the sky, could hear them all whistling down toward impact, and braced awaiting the moment when the motel's bricks and the book's pages and his own flesh would be vaporized, then blown out to sea by cleansing desert winds.

Vanishment, obliteration—strange imaginings for an aspiring star. But in his most desolate moments, when his jokes didn't land, when he feared returning home to Canada a failure, he'd wanted it so badly, anything to spring him from the stretching rack of dreaming.

But the missiles never flew, and the person of Jim Carrey only grew across the decades, soaring from blockbuster to blockbuster.

Those early days were far from his mind as he entered the Saharan that week. Kaufman greeted him in footed pajamas printed with fifties images of Tonto and the Lone Ranger. He gave Jim a squirrelly nod, turned to a figure splayed out on the bed, a paunchy man in a once-ivory linen suit, now splotched with sweat stains. The man drew three drama-teasing breaths, then flicked up the brim of his battered Panama hat to reveal a famous face in the morning sun.

Carrey gasped. "*Hopkins . . .*"

It is impossible to overstate the importance of Anthony Hopkins's participation in the entire Mao affair. He was the first of Hollywood's masters to endorse Carrey's dramatic talents, writing the star to hail *Dumb and Dumber* as a fearless exploration of "the savageries of class and the miracle of friendship." They had bonded at the 1998 Golden Globes after realizing they both inhabited characters through the spirits of animals: Carrey had based his Ace Ventura on an intelligent bird; Hopkins's Hannibal Lecter was a hybrid crocodile-tarantula with infinite patience. "The Menagerists," they'd dubbed themselves, and remained close. Kaufman had asked Hopkins to play the memory of Richard Nixon in the mind of "Jim Carrey" playing himself preparing to play Mao, a ghost inside a ghost. He'd accepted, offering to join in preparations. For Carrey his presence transformed the sordid motel room into a place of destiny.

"You once called me the Lewis and Clark of the dramatic wilds," said Hopkins. "But as old age brings sexlessness, am I not just as much your Sacajawea? I think so. The child I hold to my bosom is Art. My teat's milk is Craft. Let us, then, cross these frontier wilds. Let us find our fair Pacific, our . . ."

He yawned—then seemed to forget he'd been speaking at all. He held a glass of Burgundy, the crystal clouded with lip prints; Jim wondered what had brought Hopkins back to the bottle.

It was a woman. Hopkins had spent that winter directing *Titus Andronicus* at Yale's drama school, and there had fallen in love with a poet, Elise Evans, author of a Pulitzer Prize–shortlisted collection, *The Scarified Heart*. She'd lost her first husband, the mountain climber Chugs Stanton, to a Himalayan avalanche. Her second, an archaeologist, had left her for an older woman. She'd forsaken love as a biological ploy. Until Hopkins arrived. They'd spent that winter in her faculty suite, sharing warm baths as blizzards howled beyond the leaded windows. Hopkins felt his whole life had been a prelude to her touch, and with April's early blossoms decided the rest of his days should be just like these. He'd bought a sapphire engagement ring and booked flights to Mustique. At the York Street J. Press he was fitted for the ivory linen suit in which he'd hoped to marry her, sucking in his gut before a three-way mirror that refracted him into an infinity of bliss. Just a few more seasons together was all he'd wanted; in a flash of sunshine it had seemed so tauntingly possible. But his bones had betrayed him, femur and tibia grinding arthritically as he kneeled to propose, pain searing the joint, leg buckling beneath him. Crumpled before her, he'd begged the universe to go back just five seconds. His heart wilted as her lips touched his forehead, the kiss of a mourner, not a lover. Looking up he saw her eyes flooded with feared loss, tears trickling off her lips as she said, "*Oh Tony, I can't, I'm so sorry . . .*"

Damned fool, he'd cursed himself, riding Amtrak down from New Haven. *Goddamned fool, done in by your own creaky skeleton. How many loves does life owe anyone? None. So what were you thinking? That she'd nurse you into senility? Change your diapers? Goddamned fool!* he'd ranted aloud, causing at least one other passenger to believe Hopkins was berating him as they stood in the café car.

"There's much to accomplish," he said to Carrey now, half of him still lost in the pain of love's memory. "Let us begin."

So Carrey settled beside Hopkins as Kaufman flicked on

the flatscreen to play the first scenes of a carefully planned character indoctrination, footage from Mao's famine recently sent to him with a note that read, *You have friends in Taipei.*

Charlie had set the reels to slow motion, one-sixty-fourth real time, wanting Carrey to fully absorb every frame of Mao's murders. That day they lay on the king-size bed for six hours, watching hell on earth. Panning shots of starving people tending to crude blast furnaces, lining up for meager rice rations, patrolled by men with guns. Interiors of huts packed with children too near death to even eye the camera. On and on, a man-made hellscape. Carrey, who knew nothing of Chinese history, soon wondered why all these people were suffering.

"An earthquake? Flood? War?"

"Worse." Hopkins sipped his wine. "A dream. A grand design! Mao traded all the grain to Russia for capital goods, guns, the dangled hope of atomic power. He collectivized the land, made the peasants melt down their plows for steel. He wanted China to surpass Russia in wealth and stature. He wanted radios in kitchens and cars in driveways. Stalin engineered a famine to industrialize, so Mao did the same. He thought it a path to paradise."

"Utopia," said Kaufman. "More gruesome than Gomorrah."

"Yes," said Hopkins. "Mao promised a Great Leap Forward. Deliverance from feudalism! He never said how he'd get it done."

"What did he do?" Carrey asked.

"China was poor in everything except people," said Hopkins. "So he devoured them, taking lives as raw fuel."

Guru Viswanathan, we will remember, had once taught

Carrey to visualize the coloration of his aura. As Kaufman showed him what Mao had done while the millions died—reels of the despot dancing with silk-clad starlets at Shanghai garden parties, gorging on pork and whiskey, smoking his beloved cigarettes—he felt a spiritual pollution, a dimming of his rose-gold glow.

"He doesn't even care," Carrey gasped.

"Power never cares!" said Hopkins. "Watch how Mao lived while they died. Decadent parties, wild orgies, all raged in his villa while the masses starved."

And as Mao danced his lovers across the screen, fear roiled in Carrey's mind. Heath Ledger had lost himself to the Joker. Willy Loman had dragged Philip Seymour Hoffman into the void. Carrey regarded Ledger as an exceptional talent struck down too young. But Hoffman? Philip Seymour Hoffman? He could do certain things that Hoffman couldn't, but *Hoffman.* Just the name. His toes clenched. There was an artist. The unassuming excellence, magical. The depth of transformation. Hoffman was great, maybe in the line of Brando and De Niro. Hoffman, dead on the floor of a West Village apartment: the man had everything and still found this life so unbearable he numbed himself into oblivion. Carrey thought, now, of those early maps of a flat earth, water and ill-fated ships cascading off the edges, monsters playing in the margins, and he wondered if they were not geography at all, but renderings of the inner self. *Keep to the warm seas, stray not from trade routes.*

It was madness to conjure Mao's demons. And yet . . . the rewards. Hoffman as Truman Capote. Daniel Day-Lewis as Lincoln. The acclaim. Sweet fame, mother's touch, fellating validation. Now want of greatness overrode fear, blinding him to the misery on the flatscreen. He saw himself at some future Oscar ceremony wearing a sleek Armani tux, thin lapels (he'd have lost twenty pounds by then), the whole world marveling at his fitness while scenes of his Mao played on giant screens before a fawning Academy. He saw Tommy Lee Jones there in the audience, gaunt and gizzard necked, slumped in his seat, reduced to seething by the sheer power of Carrey's artistry. The dopamine hit just when, as often happens in the movies . . . there came a knock at the door.

"Who's that?" Kaufman slipped his hand under the pillow, grabbing the ivory-handled Colt revolver he'd hidden there. He'd been fascinated by this weapon since boyhood nights spent watching *Gunsmoke*. Caressing its cylinder, he saw, again, his boyhood self on the Coney Island carousel, watched by his spinster aunt Fiona, her every maternal instinct channeled onto him, little cherub Charlie, beaming as he drew toy pistols from his holsters, while he blasted away at Richie and Josh Kirschbaum, spoiled dentist's sons who mocked his secondhand winter coat, *bang-bang-bang*, carousel jingle scoring the slaughter and—

"Who's at the goddamn door?" Kaufman said, clenching the gun.

"Who . . . ?" Hopkins emptied his Burgundy. "Or *what*?"

"*Who*. A person knocks. A person is a *who*."

"But what does that person represent? What might that person bear? In drama as in life some people are *whos*, but most are merely *whats*. Geisel knew this well."

"Fine," said Kaufman. "Who or what is at the door?"

"Right now?" said Hopkins. "Rising tension! But in a moment, once I open the door, revealing the who or what behind it, well, Chuck, you'll see I've brought a touch of the ephemeral, the visceral, and, yes, whimsy, but also woe, to our endeavors. Hide in the bathroom, Jimmy. We don't want your famous face mucking this up."

"You're pretty recognizable, too."

"Don't worry," said Hopkins, "I shall make a mask of geniality."

And so Carrey shuffled into the bathroom, and Hopkins opened the door to reveal Lenny Weingarten, a thirty-one-year-old delivery boy for the Neon Dragon Bistro, bearing four Happy Family Meals sweating grease through paper bags.

"You're not Chinese," said Hopkins.

"I'm Lenny Weingarten."

"The website shows a fully Chinese staff."

"Those are stock photos."

"What are stock photos?"

"Pictures of people who sell their images to others without concern for context or truth." Weingarten had studied semiotics at UC Santa Cruz.

Now Hopkins, feeling himself the victim of false advertising, pressed a crisp fifty into Weingarten's hand and slammed the door in his face.

"You tried to get a Chinese guy in here?" said Kaufman.

"And what of it?"

"It's highly insensitive."

"You're the one casting a white guy as Mao Zedong."

"I'm casting Mao's spirit inside a white guy. And offering both as avatars of the über-demon, a raceless, genderless, devourer of generations. You're using the service economy to try and make an ethnic Chinese person bear witness to it."

"If it's all so innocent what's the problem?"

"We live in a crumbling multiethnic Ponzi-scheme society requiring a highly policed cultural environment to avoid outright chaos. That's the problem."

"*You* live in a crumbling multiethnic Ponzi-scheme society requiring whatever it was you said," said Hopkins, refilling his Burgundy. "*I*—am an Englishman. As for that Chinese delivery boy, he was a Jew. Would you have him out of a job?"

"What?"

"Anti-Semite!"

In the bathroom Carrey was already grappling with Mao.

At first the star tried to hedge, hoped to manage the role with safe impressionism, creating the tyrant only skin-deep. He contorted his eyes, stuffed his cheeks with toilet paper to effect Mao-ish bloatedness—but that only achieved an Asian Ed McMahon. Then he slicked back his hair with water, grinning maniacally—but that only sent McMahon careening into Ronald Reagan. The soul, an Esalen tantra instructor taught him, speaks through dance. So he began to move like Mao in the film reels with his Shanghai harem girls, undulating before the mirror, Reagan and McMahon falling away from his composition, clowning passing to conjuring. A harem. Intimacies with Georgie were still suffering from mutual distrust. Mao's grin coiled up through his own skin. He felt an erection stirring. And he enjoyed it—until, in the mirror, he saw a sooty haze about his person. His aura! The rose-gold glow completely gone. Now coal dust. He felt, again, the old impressionist's fear, that the throne of the self was not only empty, but not a throne at all, just a creaky barstool worn down by the weight of ten thousand asses. Where was Jim, in this moment? Who was Jim? What would a Jim even be if Jim was ultimately just the creation of a billion strangers' minds? Jim was the sense of Jim persisting from moment to moment. What, then, of these lost moments? Panicked, closing his eyes, taming inner chaos with the shiny rod of grammar—"I am Jim; Jim is me; me is I." But how could all these things be both different and the same? He sought grounding in pure reflection, but that wasn't him or me or I *there*. There was only Mao's specter, grinning, taunting. He tried scrubbing away the darkness with desperate splashes from the faucet, but Mao's grin only grew, wider and wider, like Guy Rolfe in *Mr. Sardonicus*, leaving him horrified at his reflection like some small boy in a grisly Halloween mask. The Neon Dragon Bistro's aromas wafted in, waking roaring hunger.

"Come, Jimmy!" said Hopkins. "Din-din!"

He returned to find Hopkins rummaging through the plastic bags.

"They forgot the fortune cookies," he spat. "The Huns!"

"They didn't forget," said Kaufman, fevered. "They just ran out of prophecies. We're at game's end, cowboys. All of us. With only one move left: complete annihilation. Of lives, of loves. Languages and species. Somewhere it's all already ended. All the words forgotten. This life is just a sloppy flashback."

"I'll take sloppy flashbacks over dead air," said Hopkins. "Let's eat."

So they feasted on shrimp fried rice and vegetable sukiyaki, TV flickering famine horrors: the withered elderly, children with distended stomachs, piles of dead sparrows fallen from the sky. Carrey ate with supernatural hunger, slurping lo mein noodles as the viewing climaxed in handheld footage of three men in extreme starvation, their every step an impossible task, sinew and skin, they moved like tragic marionettes.

"Dammit," said Carrey as his cheap plastic fork snapped in two.

"Use it!" cried Kaufman. "Eat with your hands! Feed the glutton!"

So Carrey clawed his fingers, snatching up greasy braids of noodles and stuffing them into his mouth. Hopkins cheered. "They starve while you gorge! Just as it was with Mao, dancing in Shanghai as the peasants ate their children."

Perhaps it was simply bad shrimp lo mein. Or perhaps Hopkins had spoken too soon, and his words (in distinguishing actor from subject) drove Mao's spirit from Carrey's plastic flesh. Carrey now experienced a nauseating tremor, an urge to flee this wicked séance. He tried wishing it away with the fire-breathing technique of Guru Rajneesh, which in the late 1990s had reliably purified his karmas and filled him with cosmic laughter. But tonight it failed him, each breath only spraying noodle mash across the television. The food stuck to pixelated peasant faces, blurring the space between worlds.

"I can't bear this anymore," said Carrey. "It's too much."

"I could call Johnny Depp," said Kaufman, waiting just a beat before finishing with cruelty, "We all know what Johnny did with Jack Sparrow."

"Enough!" said Carrey, with the double fear of not only playing Mao, but also losing him to Depp. "I'm trying, but it's terrifying. Do you know what it took to get my aura to radiant gold? Energy vortex visits. Malibu Memory Retrievals. Seven-day intensive Abraham-Hicks seminars. Georgie spends so much money on crystals. And right now? Right now my aura is like a toxic mist hanging over a poisoned creek with little kids playing in it, sweet, unsuspecting kids with cheap plastic toys. That's my aura right now, Charlie. Not to be unprofessional, I'm just concerned for my humanity."

"Humanity?" said Kaufman. "Humanity gets carpet-bombed in Baghdad so you can heat your mansion. Humanity dies slowly, cruelly, in Congolese mining pits so you can have a flashy new iPhone. Humanity gets pistol-whipped in the de facto penal colonies of South Central while you eat quinoa and ogle ass in yoga class. Humanity? It's a story people tell themselves to escape guilt while they capitalize off others' misery! You, you peddler of false escapisms! Big star. You lament your lost *humanity*? It's a little fucking late."

Then he hissed in Carrey's face with a breath so noxious that Carrey grabbed him by the throat, and then Kaufman (often slightly ill) spit phlegm in self-defense. Hopkins stood on the bed, pelting them both with shrimp lo mein, taunting, "You're worse than Sicilian street children!"

But the slur failed to injure as it had in his postwar boyhood. Hopkins lost his balance. He grabbed at Carrey, who was latched to Kaufman, and soon they all spilled to the floor in a cascade of noodles and profanity. They were now offensive even to their fellow Saharan reprobates, as an angry pounding on the wall was followed by the voice of a frustrated adulterer, "Shut up!"

"Sorry," answered all three men, suddenly still.

"Mao is sculpting history, which means using flesh," said Hopkins, picking a tiny shrimp from Kaufman's hair. "It's unpleasant business—but didn't Yahweh send the flood? Mao, too, felt he was justified. He, too, was creating a people."

"You gotta override your empathy," said Kaufman. "Can you do that?"

"I'm trying," said Carrey. "I feel very menaced. It's like he's taking hold of me. It's like he wants to consume me, you know? Along with all the rest."

"Let him in."

"I'm frightened, Charlie."

"You should be," said Hopkins. "Mao is hardly foreign to you. To any American, really. The death of religion. The holding of industrial quotas as society's highest aim? The crushing of human lives in service of the marketplace? The rule of super-empowered elites beyond all accountability? What is Mao but the father of modern capitalism? And, more, of celebrity's place within that capitalism? As a distraction. A diversion. As an ever-grinning knockoff god. Luke—he's your father."

"Where'd you get all that?"

"Dark nights."

Carrey's eyes went wide—this was a lot.

"Don't put *Star Wars* in his head," said Kaufman. "We'll get an Asian Jedi."

"Relax, Chucky Boy," growled Hopkins.

"Don't you condescend to me. You? You're just a reader of lines. A Howdy Doody. I'm the one who dives into the human muck to find them!"

"Oh, Chucky Boy," said Hopkins. "Spare us the bluster."

"I never bluster. And don't call me that."

"Both of you," said Carrey. "Stop it."

"Chucky-Chuck!"

"Call me that again." Kaufman, hand slipping beneath the pillow, he clenched the Colt pistol. "Call me Chucky one more time and you'll—"

"Guys. Stop, I'm ser—"

"*Who put the bop in the bop shoo bop shoo bop,*" sang Hopkins, merrily, "*Who put the Chuck in the Chuck-a-Chuck-a-ding-dong?*"

Fearing losing control of his own project, Charlie drew the Colt out from beneath the pillow, aiming it squarely at Hopkins, who lunged to disarm him. As they grappled, Charlie's soy sauce–slickened finger slipped on the trigger, firing off a round that grazed Carrey's shoulder. The blast left them all in shock, ears ringing. Touching the wound, Jim experienced no horror, little pain, only a giddy thrill and the warm-dawning realization that he'd never felt so alive. A twisted grin overtook his face.

"Mao's spirit is well with us," said Hopkins. "Let's call it a day."

He and Carrey departed, leaving Kaufman all alone in the sorrowful room.

For a while he just lay there on the comforter, calming himself with breathing. Then he reached for a small box on the bedside table, opening it with care. Inside, laid on tufted cotton, were the bodies of Jan and Dean, his beloved butterflies. Gently, he stroked their wings, imagining the moment as a scene from his masterpiece, how the digital effects team would bring the creatures back to life, how they'd flap from his fingers and flit across the room, wings shining in fluorescent light.

—

There would be no such peace, real or imagined, for Carrey.

Awaiting him at home was the script for Disney's Untitled Play-Doh Fun Factory Project. Usually he ignored such fluff, but this was different, marked as high priority, messengered from the Creative Artists Agency, a large-scale cultural-reprocessing facility in the California desert. Gerry Carcharias had attached a handwritten note:

Hey Jim,

Jack Black, Jude Law, Antonio Banderas, Katy Perry, Zoe Saldana, Wesley Snipes attached. Jackie Chan circling as well. Do you know what that means in Asia? Good chance to show you can play well with others. You're my favorite!

Gerry

Once he'd entered Rome in triumph. And now . . . a feature-length commercial for Hasbro? He dressed his shoulder wound, then climbed into bed beside Georgie, falling through garbled thoughts into a nightmare version of the memory whose retrieval he'd resisted under the guru Natchez Gushue.

Forty years ago, his family had lived in a fieldstone caretaker's house while working at the Titan Wheels factory outside Toronto. Now he was back there. It was winter, cold. Filthy snow at his feet. They'd taken jobs as janitors after his father lost the accounting position he'd held for thirty years, fired by his own brother-in-law, Bill Griffith, a man whose name, across Percy Carrey's struggle, became a byword for cruel fate. "Fucking Bill Griffith," he'd spit when his checks bounced. "Fucking Bill Griffith," he'd sigh to the mirror as he noticed his hairline receding.

In the dream Carrey approaches the sad little house, peers through its winter-brittle windows, and sees his mother, Kathleen, kneading onions and celery into ground chuck, a family staple bought at discount a day before its expiration from DiPietro's supermarket; its aroma, from a distance, often fooled him into thinking they were having steak.

He calls, she doesn't answer.

He turns from the house toward the factory's gray hulk, its floodlights cutting through the dusk. He knows that he's expected inside.

He walks shivering across the empty lot. He enters through the loading dock, punches the time clock, goes into the workers' locker room, pulls on his janitor's coveralls, laces up his steel-toed Greb Kodiak work boots, and tugs on his yellow rubber gloves. He finds his mop and his wheeled trash can and pushes them into the bathroom where his shift always begins, where the Jamaican workers would shit in the urinals to amuse themselves and torment him. He scoops out a slick turd with his rubber-gloved hand, scrubs the porcelain with disinfectant, gagging as he breathes.

He hears a playful jingle, like from an ice-cream truck.

It grows louder, beckoning. He follows it down a dingy corridor toward the steel doors that open onto the factory floor, where his father and brother work. But now they reveal something quite different from years ago. It's no longer the Titan Wheels factory—it's a Play-Doh Fun Factory, all machines candy colored, belching gusts of glitter that sparkle in the rainbow lights.

"Jimmy!" he hears his father's voice from above and looks up to see him trapped in a huge neon-pink funnel, his legs minced by giant blades painted with rainbows. They've chopped him up to the waist, but Percy Carrey is still beaming, a vision of Catholic martyrdom, eyes fixed on heaven.

"Fight it, Dad!" cries Jim, decades of anguish finding voice. "Why don't you ever fight it? Why'd you take us here? Why'd you just give up like you did?"

"The Fun Factory's not the worst place to work," replies Percy, with a shrug.

"It's chopping up your legs!"

"Don't fuckin' talk to fuckin' Dad like fuckin' that!" another familiar voice bellows from across the factory floor. Carrey turns to see his beloved big brother, John, trapped in a similar machine, also devoured up to his waist. "You're the fuckin' unhappy fuckin' one, Jim. Fuckin' you with your fuckin' insecurities. Your fuckin' suppressed rage and your needi-fuckin'-ness. It's pa-fuckin'-thetic. We fuckin' pray like mad whores for you. I swear to fuckin' God."

"You make me sound awful," says Carrey. "I'm happy. Enough. I didn't do so bad. Made some good movies. I have a good domestic partner—"

"Rub fuckin' that in my fuckin' face, why don't ya?"

"God you say 'fuck' a lot."

"What are you? My fuckin' mother?"

This would be their last exchange. John bucks up and down in the funnel before, with a final utterance of his favorite profanity, he slurries through the factory's tubing.

"Can you get me my smokes?" calls Percy as the blades gag on his femurs. "Could really use one."

"Why didn't you sue them when they fired you?"

"Good men don't sue, son," Percy says as the blades snap his pelvis. "Fucking Bill Griffith!"

"It's not Bill Griffith. You could have done so much more. You had talent. Why'd you let them take your life away? Why didn't you fight?"

Percy shrugs. "One day it just got dark for me."

"So you gave up on your dreams?"

"I didn't give up any dreams," said Percy, now short of breath. "One day you made me laugh so hard my teeth fell out. After that I was dreaming for you."

Suddenly ashamed of his anger, Carrey climbs up the funnel, straddling its rim, reaching for his father's hand. But the gears pull Percy down to his neck, arterial blood spraying everywhere, coating the funnel. Jim slips, scrambles, trying vainly to find a grip. But the walls are too steep, too slick. Down into the Fun Factory Carrey goes, steel teeth crushing his bones, the factory's cloying jingle soaring as it pulls him down to the knees, then the waist. Futile clawing, no escape. It chews him up to his shoulders. His neck.

Then blackness.

By its own twisted logic, the dream returns to the little fieldstone caretaker's house, the factory becomes the kitchen. He and his father are now ground human meat, sizzling in a gigantic frying pan alongside onions and celery, tossed by his mother's spatula.

"Mom! It's me! Turn off the stove!" screams Carrey. But his words are just the squeaks of bubbling grease.

"She can't hear us, son," says a clump of meat beside him. "She's in pain."

|| 83 ||

Carrey thrashed in the sheets, sweat-soaked, wailing, waking Georgie beside him. A month ago she would have woken him, would have held him and talked him back from the nightmare. Now, with their love touched by contempt, she only watched him flail and whimper, fascinated, even satisfied, to see the mighty star so helpless.

CHAPTER 7

Carrey woke to find Georgie gone, off to a screenwriting class she was taking with Caprice Wilder.

He had no memories of the Fun Factory; only a sense of submerged menace, from which he sought escape through a Buddhist teaching: that the mind is untrustworthy, a sewer of illusions. The problem with this, of course, is that, as all the world's minds are linked together, the sewer runs ever fouler, ever deeper.

He was just out of bed, standing in the kitchen with his coffee, when his publicist, Sissy Bosch, emailed, alerting him to a deep-fake video that had, almost overnight, gained such virality as to merit concern. Somewhere in the Korean peninsula a tech-savvy pervert had feminized Carrey's features, given him long raven tresses, and then spliced this new, female face onto the bodies of evidently incestuous lesbian twins. Their performance, in the subsequent HD video, had become a phenomenon through sheer exuberance, earning ten million views overnight. And tempting his hand beneath his bathrobe when, after clicking on the link, he saw his two digital female selves in fevered coitus.

How very smoldering his eyes were, in that heavy mascara. How pouty his red painted lips. How breathtakingly symmetrical, his four teardrop breasts. How coy, his gasps and giggles. Was this a pent-up transsexual drive finally given outlet? Or merely a particularly intense expression of masturbation's guiding narcissism? Despite Sissy's fears of brand catastrophe, he had no worries about copyright infringement, authorship, ownership. He watched, transfixed, fascination overriding all concerns for the strangeness of this new dimension; he dreamed himself alongside his female selves as they rode each other through pornography's Persepolis. Far from wanting to sue anyone, Carrey longed only to pass through the screen. To caress and be caressed, to meld with these female versions of himself in some ultimate feat of completion. How effortlessly they would read the language of one another's faces. Nothing to hide. No need to perform.

I'd be totally understood.

It had been decades since film had captured him so entirely. He forgot his coffee and lusted into the screen, jackhammering away at himself in the laptop light, and he might well have climaxed but for the biting thought that suddenly consumed him. If these South Korean lesbian Jim Carreys could get ten million views overnight, did it even matter what he, the actual Jim Carrey, did or didn't do with his talents? He'd fought all his life to build and control a public persona. And now he'd not only been drafted into amateur porn but was performing in duplicate without pay of any kind.

As if sensing this surface fracture of the self, a pop-up ad offered him a hot deal on numbness: a commercial for the loveliest fast-food delicacy he'd ever seen: the Wendy's Honey Butter Chicken Biscuit. Its deep-fried surface was shot in dreamy HD, buns supple and crusty. He wanted only to eat these biscuits, to drown them in the two new dipping sauces whose names—*Zesty Barbecue, Honey Mustard*—were sung by an off-screen gospel choir as they drizzled across the frame.

He raced to his Porsche, salivating.

As he tore down Hummingbird an inner voice assured him that two of the Wendy's breakfast biscuits would set him right.

But at the drive-through window another inner voice rose up from somewhere altogether more dangerous and desperate—

"Give me five of the Honey Butter Chicken Biscuits."

It wasn't comfort he was seeking here. It was stupor, a complete if fleeting escape from thought and emotion. He devoured two of the sandwiches, slathered in Zesty Barbecue, while slow-cruising down Sunset, and another pair in the Saharan motel parking lot, heavy with Honey Mustard. Then he shuffled past the pool, entered Kaufman's room, and plopped down on the bed to eat his final biscuit. He had one tub of each dipping sauce remaining and, as he peeled off their foil covers, was drawn into the ancient tug-of-war between sweet and savory. Wanting to extract all possible pleasure from this last hunk of heaven, he dipped it between the sauces, enjoying both taste experiences and (initially) a dramatically enhanced sense of personal freedom. Would the next bite be Zesty Barbecue or Honey Mustard? Across all wild creation, only he knew. And what smug assurance that brought him until the instant when, in his very hand, the biscuit changed course to Zesty Barbecue while, only a second before, with all certainty, he'd chosen Honey Mustard. What force separated a person's actions from their will? What caused Jim Carrey at 10:03:28 in the morning to usurp the biscuit-dipping plans he'd made a mere half second before?

Was it fate? Chaos? If so—what, or who, was he?

He chose to choose the sauce he didn't want, just to prove that he was real.

"*Eat it, assclown . . .* ," he muttered, lowering the biscuit down toward the Honey Mustard with slow stealth, like a cat about to pounce on prey.

"Everything okay, Jim?" said Kaufman, watching.

And Carrey gave him eyes that said nothing could ever be promised.

"We're nearly there," said Hopkins. "Mao's task, you will recall, was to demolish the past. To remake China as a dignified global power, no opium den of colonial exploitation. This goal was gruesomely pursued, but at length, as we see every day, it was achieved."

With a click of the remote he began the day's viewing.

A slick state propaganda film on color stock garished across the flatscreen, footage of Chinese military and party officials gathering in the Gobi Desert, wearing special glasses like midcentury teens at a 3-D drive-in. Carrey lay in a lipid daze, a person watching reels of people watching, their anticipation fueling his own as a Mandarin voice began a countdown, "*Shi, jiu, ba* . . ." At zero came a burning flash, then a gnarled junior mushroom cloud.

"China's first nuclear explosion," whispered Hopkins. "Mao's seat, finally, at the table of nuclear powers. The equal of Truman, of Stalin. Feel his triumph as your own, Jim."

Then came the obligatory nuclear wreckage reel. Carrey was enthralled, a toddler at a monster truck rally. Makeshift huts vaporized. Shock waves snapping telegraph poles. A cage of baby goats, fur so soft he wanted to adopt them all. He connected, cozily, to their latching, infant eyes—until they were carbonized. Then soldiers charged into the detonation site, a thousand sacrificial extras striking poses for the cameras, heroically oblivious to the poisoning radiation. Carrey's mind flashed images of their eventual flesh-bubbling ends. He lost all Maoist indifference; he mourned these men who, like him, had once been fresh and new, had picked up feathers fallen from the sky. Then all his chakras curdled with the grand finale: a scene inspired by Hollywood Westerns, a thousand riders and horses wearing gas masks and UV visors, tragic cavalry galloping into ghostdom. He felt a horrific peril. At what point did the portrayal of evil become evil itself?

"Turn it off!" he howled. "I don't want to exploit this. I don't want to even try to understand it."

"It's the birth of modern China," said Kaufman. "And, with it, modern capitalism."

"It's a crying slaughter."

"Wussy," spat Hopkins. "Buck up!"

"I'm not a wussy."

"Then play on!"

"I mean it, Tony. I'm gonna puke."

"It's that gross breakfast you ate."

"It's not the Wendy's . . . ," said Kaufman. "It's the actor. Stuck on his own trite moral vanity. We should have gone to Johnny Depp. Or Bale. Bale's not afraid of anything."

"Call him! I don't need this evil inside of me."

"But, it's already there," said Hopkins. "Shrieking out from ancestral memory. Two million years of rape and murder coded into your every cell."

"I'm feeling unwell right now."

"That's Mao making himself at home."

"Oh Christ, Tony, I'm so afraid."

"Have courage," said Hopkins. "One more push."

So began the final rite: footage from Mao's greatest caper, *The Cultural Revolution*.

For three hours they watched Chinese youth rising up by the million, riding trains across the countryside, marching through cities. Students burning books, toppling statues, even razing buildings whose aesthetics dared to evoke any time before Mao's. Filling up city squares, inflicting abuse and brutal struggle sessions on perceived inheritors of privilege, believing, madly, that crimes in the present could cure wrongs in the past. Half the population, it seemed to Carrey, was lost in a cultish fervor, the rest cowering in fear.

"Anyone can rejigger an atom bomb," said Hopkins. "But to possess the minds of millions? To make them your willing zombies across a whole decade? That's real magic. By 1966 Mao was old and paranoid, fearing plots against his rule. His wife, Madame Mao, was once a famous Shanghai actress. Now she became his partner in conquering Chinese culture. They ordered every film released in China to feature him as its mighty hero."

"Really?" said Carrey.

"Even more. They had every printing press churning out his image, deep into the billions. Crowds hailing him in every town, chanting his teachings and waving his picture."

"Isn't that appealing?" asked Kaufman.

"It's how it was for me after *The Mask*," said Carrey, wistfully. "I had my own action figures. Millions of them, hauled around the world by speed-popping truckers. My face—my face!—it was gigantic, pasted on endless billboards. Even the Maasai knew me, I'm not sure how. I was on safari in Kenya with my daughter. They gave me a tiny bow and arrow and invited me to shoot up termite mounds."

"That movie stayed in theaters forever," said Kaufman. "I saw it three times."

"So did I," said Hopkins. "And so did Kenneth Branagh."

Carrey wanted back there. He wanted it so badly, to reclaim that adulation. That power, that industrial heat, and a reprieve—however long or brief—from stardom's gray afterlife, the dim-flickering realm of John Barrymore and Bela Lugosi.

He hung on Hopkins's words like keys to salvation.

"Only the young, Mao said, could save China. And only by destroying his enemies. He became, for them, greater than the Beatles and the Stones and the Hula-Hoop combined. They joined him en masse, heeding his edict to eradicate, crushing all opposition. Imagine that kinda power, Jimmy?"

"Any studio head who gives me shit gets sent to an Orange County labor camp," said Carrey, eyes suddenly gleaming. "Flog all the lawyers in the town square. Bring every critic to heel. Hang the paparazzi from their own camera straps; I shall admire their lifeless bodies as my parade moves past, see them dangling from every palm tree in the Palisades."

"Yes! Now make it Mao!" commanded Hopkins. "Say it: '*I, Mao Zedong, command the world!*' Give me a rural Chinese accent while you're at it."

"I, Mao Zedong, will the . . ."

"That's you impersonating a Chinese person! A cop-out! I want Mao's spirit speaking through you!"

"I, Mao Zedong . . ."

"Deeper!" Hopkins grabbed Carrey's groin. "Yes, feel it in your nutsack!"

"I, Mao Zedong," boomed Carrey, *"can will the end of all things!"*

Carrey rose and strode to the window, peered through the slatted blinds out onto the courtyard swimming pool. He recalled, it seemed at random, his first stab at fame, decades before, aged eighteen, standing in line with his father, Percy, outside Toronto's NIB, the National Institute of Broadcasting, a hustle promising to make a network anchor of anyone with eight hundred dollars and a free afternoon. They saved up their cash, drove seven hours to wait forever with three hundred other suckers: cross-eyed stutterers, would-be weathermen with facial tics, souls devoid of charisma, sadder than a scene from Lourdes. Years later, when he got famous, the NIB took out full-page ads in the *Hollywood Reporter*, sending congratulations, claiming to have given him his first break by suckering him and his dad out of their cash. He remembered how they had laughed at their own conning, broke on the cold city sidewalk.

Is there a dormant anarchic urge in all of us, a violent child waiting to be born?

Now the monster overtook him.

Carrey stepped onto the terrace and imagined, gathered down below, a sea of Mao's youth brigades cheering his name, calling him down onto Sunset Boulevard, clogged with thousands more of their kind, freshly bleached minds. Scenes from *Cleopatra* infect the fantasy as they hoist him onto a jewel-encrusted litter where his two lesbian female selves kneel by his throne, dressed like Egyptian slaves in leather collars and gold chains. They coo in semi-orgasm as Carrey gives his minions an adequate if hackneyed command—"To glory!"—that sets off the frenzy.

His youth brigades rampage across the city, a giant human fist, all actions willable by his whims. He dreams them out to Burbank, surging through the gates of Walt Disney Studios, ransacking the office suites, burning every last trace of the Play-Doh Fun Factory project before (in a stirring close-up shot) ripping Walt Disney's head from its cryogenic freezer and tossing it among them like a beach ball. Carrey preens and claps, his only concern whether to watch Disney's head decompose in the sun or toss gold coins to the acrobats who soar and tumble for his delight.

Then his acolytes topple the statues of the Seven Dwarfs, finding beneath them a secret underground laboratory filled with mutant Mouseketeers, a colony of lab-rat Funicellos and pharma-chimp Cubbies. There's a fine line between a mouse and a rat, a finer line still between a rat and a bat. Through abominations of genetics these children ran the whole spectrum, looking up from aluminum feed troughs of Pez and raw chicken to hiss at the sunlight, their fangs bared, their skin translucent from years belowground, faces caked with filth. Once liberated (but are they really free?), they join the Carrey brigades as a spear-tipping horror, gnawing off the faces of the LAPD riot troops, clearing the way for the rest to come charging up Rodeo Drive, toppling all the luxury cars, firebombing the fancy boutiques, news choppers hovering above, the well-coiffed reporters all weeping for their own crashing housing values as the horde turns down the Avenue of the Stars, toward CAA's headquarters. There they pause, all eyes fixed on the master. Carrey raises a powerful hand, gestures grandly, slowly, toward the building, then, with a nod, says, "Spare no one." His faithful bear down on the Armani-suited agents who scurry like vermin to the roof, where, surrounded, Gerry Carcharias pleads, "I'm so sorry about the Play-Doh Fun Factory. I should never have tried to package a great artist like Jim Carrey into that gross headcheese. Forgive me!"

"Nuh-uh," says Carrey.

"Please!"

"Afraid not."

Carcharias grovels, but Carrey plugs his ears with his fingers and begins making gibberish sounds against which his minions toss poor Gerry Carcharias from the roof, then unfurl a gigantic silk banner into the wind, a field of deep Chinese red printed with an image of Jim Carrey's face so perfectly morphed with Mao Zedong's that there is no telling where the one man ends and the other begins.

CHAPTER 8

Charlie Kaufman hopped a flight east, believing that a Taiwanese billionaire, still "miffed" about Mao, was eager to finance his project.

Before departing, he encouraged Jim to immerse himself in radical Marxist message boards, to perfect Mao's accent with coaching from his friend Cary Elwes, a master of dialects whose great-grandmother, the noted linguist and reputed SIS triple agent Lady Winefride Mary Elizabeth Elwes (wife of Gervase Henry Elwes), would scold him in Cantonese when he was a small boy. Further, he asked the star to gain at least thirty pounds, to arrive as close as he could to Mao's emphysema by chain-smoking. And, perhaps most injuriously, to visualize and refine the death scene from Kaufman's film treatment.

So it was that each morning, in place of healing mantras, Carrey would lie in bed, clear his mind, and, with all of his actorly prowess, fuse his being with that of the dying Mao. Acutely aware of his breathing, eyes closed in dark prayer, he soon could feel the embalming tubes plugged into his veins, could hear the teams of physicians whispering around him. Some days, tears of self-pity would stream down his cheeks as he imagined the final shot from Kaufman's pages, Mao's eyes dissolving into his own, joining tyranny and celebrity. Then, more or less satisfied, he'd move into his favorite part of character preparation: the weight gain.

Georgie blessed this whole enterprise, half hoping a lauded Mao turn would fill his inner chasms, half just for the amusement. At breakfast she'd watch as Carrey ate grilled cheese and bacon sandwiches, slabs of French toast soaked in maple syrup. Many nights he'd dine at the Little Door in West Hollywood, guzzling vintage wines, pleasing himself with escargot and foie gras as a warm-up for bacon-wrapped filet mignon with sides of truffle fries and *gratin dauphinois.* Some days, with Maoist gut-greed, he'd eat five, six, seven Wendy's chicken biscuit sandwiches, no concerns for body mass now, unquestioned commander of his dimpling fingers. Gone was the Honey Mustard Conundrum, and with it the old, uncertain Jim Carrey. Now he was himself, yes, but also Mao, realizing, more and more each day, that raw appetite had always been the link between celebrity and tyranny. Then he'd waddle down to the pool, both Jophiel scampering at his sides, licking traces of sugar and grease from his face and fingers as he sat by the water's edge, gladly taking their hunger for love.

Heart and belly full, he'd paddle out lazy laps, imagining his swimming pool as the Yellow River, recordings of great Communist speeches playing from all the outdoor and underwater speakers. America's brutality made slightly more sense as he heard the words of Trotsky—

"Everything that should have been eliminated from the national organism in the form of cultural excrement in the course of the normal development of society has now come gushing out from the throat; capitalist society is puking up the undigested barbarism."

Sometimes he'd let the pool jets massage his back, pondering Marx.

"In bourgeois society capital is independent and has individuality, while the living person is dependent and has no individuality."

One day, his whole abdomen cramped after a lunch of Frito pies. Struggling toward the side of the pool, fearing for his life, he wondered what his legacy would be if he expired then and there. And in this moment of crisis Carrey joined so many millions in having Mao's thoughts transform his view of the self and the world.

"The overthrown bourgeoisie tries by hook or by crook to use literature and arts to corrupt the masses."

What, he wondered, desperately climbing from the water, was Play-Doh as a toy but a corrupt and failing capitalist-imperialist society fetishizing its own excrement? Dumbing its children down from birth, taunting them with what they could expect in place of real dreams, real lives, in exchange for any chance at real souls: crap. What, then, was the "Play-Doh Fun Factory" but a foul celebration of exploited labor? He knew factories. No one had fun in factories. They sweltered and slaved, hunched and harried, people reduced to things, manufacturing so much meaningless plastic shit that made no one happy, poisoned the oceans, corrupted the food chain.

The modern world was a burning bus speeding toward a cliff with a maniac at the wheel. And he was not apart, but complicit, a hyperactive child making yuk-yuks in his seat, keeping everyone laughing, distracting them from certain doom.

Faster, faster, no more room to brake—

Suddenly Disney's untitled Play-Doh Fun Factory project was the devil's work, and it offended him now as a matter of revolutionary principle. Wink Mingus, Al Spielman, and Gerry Carcharias, suddenly they were all class criminals, deserving whatever they might get. Suddenly he knew that Mao could not live in him without destroying Hollywood, and that this campaign must begin with Disney's Play-Doh project.

More and more, his representatives were calling, pestering him to join the toy-based abomination against Kaufman's assurances that funding for Mao was just "one card game" away. As if stepping into the role of Madame Mao, Georgie suggested they use her fortieth birthday as a trap. Together they planned a Chinese-themed party in the Hummingbird backyard, the grand estate become a stage on which Carrey's Mao Zedong would deal Disney's Play-Doh Fun Factory project a mortal blow.

On the night of the party Carrey's maple trees, planted to evoke his Canadian home, were all festooned with Hunanese cherry blossoms that had been FedExed overnight. His swimming pool was stocked with a higher class of surface-feeding carp, gold and amber bodies sparkling in the sunlight while a Chinese string quartet played harvest songs. Greeted by tumbling acrobats upon arrival, the guests simply believed themselves the lucky recipients of a generous star's love for his partner; a man who had, for his own reasons, on a pricey whim, decided to transform his Brentwood estate into a regal Shanghai villa.

The Disney executives floated about the lawn of bantering A-list guests, bathing in overheard conversation.

"I'm in love with you," said Quentin Tarantino, to Georgie.

"With me?"

"Yeah. From *Oksana.* The scene in the sewers. Stalin, what a dick. You and the power drill. How'd you sneak all that blood onto basic cable?"

"Mitch was into swapping reels at the last minute."

"An anarchist."

"Yeah, that's what got him. That and the whole extra-terrestrial arc."

"Was he a believer?"

"I hope so. He once left the set for a whole week, walked eighty miles into the San Gabriels to take a meeting with a guy he thought created the human species."

"I've watched every episode."

"Of *Oksana*?"

"Yeah. I love all that Soviet shit. The fucking Nazis killed twenty million Russian men in World War Two. That's why the women are so beautiful. The survivors got to be picky as fuck. The women think they're over the fucking hill at twenty-four, and they start putting all that silver makeup on. And shit. It still haunts them, man. It's why they're paranoid. It's why they sent that Turkish guy to kill the pope. I've been noodling around that, the Turkish guy and the pope. The Vatican's got two flying saucers. Howard Hughes said he got to sit in one, and that was before he was all fucked up. Hey, did Stalin really jizz in Dixie cups—or was that just a conceit?"

"Dixie cups?"

"Or not Dixie cups. Whatever fucking cups the Russians had. Commie Dixie cups. The whole bastard daughter thing. Your origin story. Fuck, I love you."

Los Angeles, a city built on golden sun and grand prizes, required strong belief in magic. Slight derangement was the first stage of the human filtration process, and she read it on his face as he spoke, the unhinged exuberance that had turned a video-store clerk into a legend and which now, by momentary contagion, showed her that the whole path here had been worthwhile. Quentin Tarantino knew her . . . Quentin Tarantino was her fan.

"Seems likely in that he was a maniac." Tarantino was in full stride. "Crazy people love to play with their spunk. Soviet Union. Uncle Joe. Mother Russia. I've been circling the space. Noodling. We should have a meeting."

"A meeting?" Georgie asked.

"I got my eye on you. There's this part. Dunaway-esque. Brilliant. A she-devil that'd eat her own young, a killer instinct that comes in handy when werewolves take over her mining town. But they're not just fucking werewolves. They're a metaphor for economic predation in the wake of the collapse of the industrial economy!"

"Sure," she said, unsure whether or not to take him seriously, but happy, for the moment, to believe that a real career might finally come to her. "It's fun to play the heavy."

"I don't play, honey," he said; then, with a wink, took his leave to pursue a passing tray of hamburger sliders.

Across the yard Nicolas Cage assailed Natchez Gushue.

"A Stone Age ax and a saber-toothed-tiger skeleton are coming up for auction in Shanghai. Seeing them triggered some crazy visions. Or memories. Or whatever. I think I've lived many lives, Natchez. I think I've been saving humanity for a while now."

"I look forward to hearing about it. You should come by the bungalow."

"But it's urgent."

"I'm really just here to enjoy the party."

"You know how big a saber-toothed tiger is? Imagine two of them, one on either side of me. I wear a furry loincloth, my torso ripples muscles; I'm seven percent body fat at this point. I carry this giant Stone Age ax. Then, wandering these wastelands, I encounter, oh God, this vision, it's so awful. It's—"

"Aliens?"

"Have you dreamed this, too? Their spaceship is sleek, black, small. Like a scout mission. Their bodies poised to strike like giant pythons. My sabertooths attack, eager to defend me. The aliens kill them with their red plasma beams to which, once again, I'm immune. Only now, I have no fear. I go fucking berserk." Nic's eyeballs bulged. "I'm hacking away at them with my ax. Guts squirting everywhere."

"Shall we get another drink?"

"I slaughter them, Natchez. I kill them all, or at least the guys on the ground. The spaceship lifts off. As it rises, this voice comes out of the air. It speaks to me."

Natchez sighed, a cocktail-hour hostage. "What does it say, Nic?"

"It says, '*See you in Malibu when the clock ticks no more.*'"

—

There was dinner in the garden, a long table set for fifty, adorned with plum and lotus blossoms. Anthony Hopkins was given a place of honor beside Carrey. Hopkins watched as the star stuffed his face with his bare hands, devouring chunks of suckling pig, indifferent to the plum sauce smeared across his jowls. Then a piece of gristle flew out of Carrey's mouth, landing grossly on the lapel of the white suit that Hopkins hadn't cleaned since the day at Yale when Elise declined his proposal. He could take no more.

"You're borrowing from *The Grinch*," he leaned low and scolded, enraged that the jacket would now require cleaning. "Pick up your fork and eat like a head of state."

Carrey froze with a fried piglet's ear dangling from his craw, his own insecurities feeding the rush of an undeniably Maoist rage. First, he was livid at Hopkins for dressing him down in front of his peers. In ego defense, he decided Anthony was jealous of him. Of his talent, his youth. But then paranoia bubbled up within rage. What if Hopkins was secretly against him? Trying to make a fool of him? What if others were involved, coconspirators? What if this was the story they'd use to detract from his performance? *Carrey wasn't Mao*, they'd say. *He was just the Grinch.* That's it, that's what they'd use to deny him his due when awards season came. Bastards. He scanned the table, reading every face for signs of betrayal. And then, just as quickly as rage had turned to paranoia, paranoia turned, as it does, to want of triumph. A colossal will formed within him, a determination to show Hopkins and everyone else that he was not only a fine actor but the finest of his generation. He'd planned to give a dinner toast laced with Marxist criticisms, comments against American capitalism, vampiric imperialism, just edgy enough to scare off the Disney execs, his class enemies, the same who'd crushed his father, who'd have broken him in the Toronto factories if he hadn't escaped. Now he decided to make the air truly unbreathable for them. He rose from his chair, bone-dry desert wind rustling the leaves of the maples, an impish grin taking hold as he raised his wineglass.

"America is a failing fascist Ponzi scheme."

The table quieted, silver forks settling on porcelain.

He imagined himself a great dragon, spewing fire—

"It doesn't take care of its sick, doesn't care for its poor. Doesn't protect its children. Abandons its veterans and its elderly. America's very God is a fraud, invented by marauding settlers to justify native genocide, a savage deity blessing a savage people, forgiving the napalming of babies in Vietnam, the starvation of five hundred thousand Iraqis in our own lives. And who at this table lost five seconds even thinking about that? No, we drown that out with our positive personal affirmations. We don't even look after our own. The people who work fifteen hours a day doing our makeup, hair, and wardrobe have to invoice the studios six or seven times before they get paid. They beg while someone siphons interest off their money. And whose fucking idea was a fifteen-hour day in the first place?"

Wink and Al watched aghast, hoping this was all a bit, wondering when Carrey would switch to family-friendly impressions. Carrey looked down the table of gathered stars, his peers: Jack Nicholson, his close friend Noah Emmerich, Dame Helen Mirren, Brad and Angelina. And, just as Mao would have, leveled charges while holding out the chance of redemption.

"Once, we were artists. Pure! But we, all of us, we became

a distraction, compromised for the sake of fame, comfort, the approval of strangers. We spend our lives pursuing something as empty as 'relevance' and they use our fear of losing it to corral us. Dirty Malaysian money. Saudi money. We'll take it all. What went wrong? We sing and dance not to entertain but to distract people from the crushing gears of a capitalist machine that has no ideals save for greed and violence. And let's not kid ourselves, Hollywood is the best PR firm the gunmakers ever had. What a sick culture."

"But what about artistic beauty?" asked Cameron Diaz.

"When you can perceive beauty there's no excuse for serving ugliness. For aiding cons, inflaming desires, promising everything and delivering nothing. It doesn't matter what you put on TV because people are so frightened and lonely they'll watch it just to hear human voices and feel like they're not alone. They're so beaten down all they need is a soccer tournament every four years and they stay in their place. This is not a society. This is a system of soul-murder. And history will not be kind to us for our complicity, because we know better. The executives"—he nodded Maoishly to the Disney team—"they can say they were serving their god Mammon, but we artists can't. We're all East German playwrights now, complicit with the regime! And there will come a time of judgment. We're destroying the planet. This cannot last."

Leonardo DiCaprio, who had long shared these feelings, raised his martini Gatsby-style and cheered, "*Global warming is a fever meant to kill a virus!*" He was so enthralled by Carrey's bravery that he accepted it when the star, now veering deep into Mao, continued in the slightest Cantonese accent.

"The American citizen is so lost he doesn't realize he's a factory pig. Drugged and poisoned from the cradle to the grave. Chained to impossible debts. Never ever free. Liberty? Bah! This is a land of invisible fences, we're all prisoners watching Capra on movie night. But nothing lasts forever. Europe's monarchies sent their sons to die in the trenches of the Somme just as surely as we drove Chiang Kai-shek into the sea. You think America will be different? You think this era, one not of consumption but of gluttony, will last forever? It will not . . ."

"We're going six thousand miles an hour around the sun and nobody's driving this bitch!" said Gary Busey from the woods, where, for his own reasons, he was halfway up an eighty-foot pine tree.

"There will come another crisis soon," continued Carrey. "The capitalist scheme will collapse, the people will reclaim their rights. There will be violent unrest. Ask yourselves, Which side am I on? That of the people, or of the billionaires and their running dogs whose heads, I promise, will end up on sticks. The revolution begins now. The death of false gods!"

His peers cheered him madly. Carrey was Mao as he'd seen him on YouTube, standing before the Chinese Communist Congress, receiving endless flows of love, the adulation making him something more than a man: a vessel of longing, of dreams. Georgie gazed at him fondly, for the first time in weeks, then nodded to the waiters. They hustled into the kitchen and came out bearing the coup de grâce: two large cakes, half life-size, one of Mickey Mouse, one of Minnie, each impaled on a jagged chocolate-bark pikestaff, raspberry filling oozing down into puddles from their open wounds.

The guests roared even louder. If not exactly at the call to violent revolution—this was, after all, a gathering of millionaires—then at his very gusto, his defiant ballsiness.

Jane Fonda, recognizing this all as a performance, made sharp whooping sounds unheard since her photo ops with the Vietcong. Through gritted teeth, with a raw sexual hunger, Lara Flynn Boyle said, "I wanna cut him."

Meanwhile Kelsey Grammer, who had been warming up his vocal cords with soft humming through most of Jim's speech, raised his glass to ejaculate lines from Shakespeare. "Let Hercules himself do what he may! The cat will mew and dog will have his day."

"Dammit, Kelsey!" said Natchez Gushue. "Allow the man his moment."

"What?" protested Grammer. "Does he get to just suck up the whole evening?"

Carrey knew now, totally, that he had it within him. The magnetic Maoist stuff. He wondered, with perfect grandiosity, if the Mao was not just prelude to a greater historic role. Ronald Reagan had won the White House, and Reagan was just a wooden day player compared to him. The Disney executives, fearing proximity to this kind of trademark sacrilege, rose from their seats, faces twisted in careerist fear, and fled the patio as the actors photographed the grisly cakes, sending them viral.

"What did you do?" said Wink, who couldn't look at the confections for too long without risking memories of Nicaragua. Carrey glowered at him, smugly satisfied.

"Sick fuck's getting off on this," said Al Spielman II, who as a pillar of the business community was appalled, but as stress eater was eyeing the raspberry filling that oozed down Minnie's breasts from the gaping wound in her head.

"He's lost his mind," said Wink, pulling Al by the arm to follow the Disney executives, assuring them this was just "some Andy Kaufman shit" that Jim had cooked up, that in time they'd tell their grandkids about it, and a couple of disturbing cakes shouldn't interfere with business.

No sooner had they left than a great rumbling sounded from the Mojave, a noise like the grinding of vast metal plates. People had been hearing it all summer. Jaden Smith, who had recently become a flat-earther, offered his theory that it was cosmic wind vibrating along the planet's edge like the reed of a clarinet. Gary Busey, now at the very top of the pine tree, pointed toward Orion and shouted out a different view. "Sure, the earth is a planet orbiting the sun. But what they keep from you is that the cosmos *itself* is riding on the back of an iguana swimming in the *opposite direction*! I jumped off that old lizard a long time ago."

"Fools," scoffed Lara Flynn Boyle as the sound came again. "It's the crumbling of the wall that keeps the real from the imagined."

And right she may have been.

Georgie quieted the guests for the special entertainment she had planned as much for her pleasure, and needs, as for Carrey's. They all milled toward the house, ground lights dimming, making a stage of the patio. Then, from inside, came a zaftig blonde whose stage name was Helena San Vicente but who, to all eyes, was the perfect reincarnation of Marilyn Monroe. Quentin Tarantino wondered if this was a hologram as she began her two-song set, starting with "I'm Through with Love," ending with "Diamonds Are a Girl's Best Friend," her every swooning note and gesture honed just so, as if the spirit of the dead siren was summoned and guiding her. The crescendo bound them in wonder, her sequined bustier falling to reveal a tasseled bra, the bra falling, in turn, to show her ample breasts adorned with rhinestone pasties, Helena flaunting her assets excitedly, mesmeric proof of something utterly great living beyond politics: artistic immortality.

"Some men are following me," said Monroe in her first moment on film, inviting a million popcorn-chomping American rubes to fill in whatever flavor of sex fantasy that crossed their minds. And after this they couldn't look away. They'd visited their worst upon Monroe, had taken her life while she was young. And yet here—boulder rolling from the tomb, not blocks from where she'd died—here she was. Monroe, returned, a Technicolor Venus, an undying persona come to bind them. To resell them on the absurd hope that they, too, if luck was kind, might live, in whatever pale way, forever.

Where normally only a handful of guests would stay after dinner, nearly everyone remained, dabbing their tongues with MDMA, popping magnums of champagne, crowding to devour the cake flesh of Mickey and Minnie Mouse, some scooping with their hands, Quentin Tarantino cutting off Mickey's entire left ear and happily giggling as raspberry filling gushed from the wound. Songs from the forties and fifties played across the house speakers—Tommy Dorsey, the Andrews Sisters, Count Basie, Ella Fitzgerald—midcentury rhythms casting innocence on them all, strangers taking strangers as lovers, coupling off among the shadows of the great estate, a pairing that found Georgie drinking champagne with the young Monroe impersonator, studying the girl's face like appraising a painting, gauging the degree of real beauty versus mere affect beneath all that foundation and concealer, trying, even, to place the origins of her voice.

"Where are you from?"

"West Hollywood."

"And before that?"

"Oopsie!"

The girl splashed champagne down her cleavage, letting out a giggle. And Georgie, between the spill and giggle, decided that, more than just an apparition, this Monroe was an answered prayer. With predatory swiftness, she pressed her mouth to the girl's chest, felt the body acquiesce as she licked the sweet wine from her cleavage. Then she took her by the hand and led her down to the Jacuzzi where Carrey's Mao was already floating naked. Georgie watched Helena's eyes as she unzipped her Versace gown, letting it fall it to the ground, feeling her beauty affirmed by the younger woman's gaze.

"Come swim."

Then Helena disrobed again, now with slightly less confidence, feeling Jim's and Georgie's eyes on her as she lowered herself into the water.

"Mr. Chairman," said Georgie, with a grin. "May I present to you the great Marilyn Monroe."

Helena giggled breathlessly, sidling up to him in the water jets. Her voice went tiny and girlish as she whispered into his ear, "I like a man with nukes."

"You can kiss him," said Georgie as Helena leaned close to Carrey, her face so true to the real Marilyn's that he perceived no difference between the dead woman and the girl in the hot tub, his inner voice reeling to think that here, in his arms, whether natural or paranormal, was what Mao must have always wanted but never had: the greatest sex symbol ever produced by the West.

—

In the master bedroom wet bodies fell on fresh sheets. Georgie took charge of the encounter, guiding Helena by the hips as she rode the father of modern China.

"Tell me I'm a good girl," moaned Helena.

"That's Mommy's good girl," Georgie said, holding her by the throat.

Carrey watched, marveling at the genius of it. Could the Hollywood Foreign Press, or the Academy, for that matter, ever grasp the fearlessness and brilliance with which he'd realized this role? Then a draft of Maoish paranoia: Charlie Kaufman would try to take all the credit; auteurs always pulled that shit. Should he even thank that ingrate from the Oscar stage? Protocol would demand it. But what was protocol to Mao? And what, at the end of it all, would Mao mean to Jim Carrey?

He would have lost himself to the existential tailspin but for Helena's nipple in his mouth, washing all care from his mind.

He came with a whole-body squeal.

Afterward, they lay there in the bed, covered in one another's sweat, breathing in common time, all happy with the encounter. But Helena's happiness was greatest.

She'd grown up in the small town of Grand Lake, Colorado. Her stepfather was a violent drunk. After school, to avoid going home, she'd go to the town library and watch old movies on VHS, starting at random, soon tracing the American feminine from Doris Day to Norma Jean Baker, whose invented self, Marilyn Monroe, had stopped her cold. What an awesome power this woman had, this constant state of vulnerable arousal that reduced men to pliant things. She'd freeze and study frames. She memorized hours of dialogue.

At night she'd worked checkout at the Safeway. Once, during a late shift, it was snowing so hard out that when she caught her reflection in the big plate-glass windows the night became a scene from a classic film. And she was the star, perfectly framed, a small-town dreamer set inside a snow globe. There were countless theaters of viewers watching; she felt the warmth of their attention. She pushed out her bust, threw her head back, heard their applause and the whistles of soldiers as they fell under her sway. She knew, in this moment, that she was bound for greatness. On a brown-paper grocery bag, in sparkly purple ink, she wrote sacred declarations.

I WILL

1. Be successful actor beloved by the worldwide media—
   a fenomenon [*sic*]
2. Marry famous movie star have kids
3. Have TWO HOUSES and A HORSE STABLE!

And here, naked beside Jim Carrey, whose films she'd always loved, admiring Georgie's blond-wood vanity piled with red Cartier boxes, she knew her dreams were coming true.

CHAPTER 9

Twice that next week, invited by Jim and Georgie, Helena had returned, parking her Hyundai outside the gates, wondering how long it would be until they gave her her own security code.

Georgie hadn't planned to continue past the initial encounter, but upon consideration had sensed further opportunity. She'd be free of Jim's increasingly Mao-sized sexual appetite, and young Helena, whoever she was, would have a fun thrill, a taste of magic in the canyons.

But she'd set two ironclad rules: Jim was never to see Helena without her permission. And Helena was only to pass through the Hummingbird gates as Marilyn: "I mean right down to that fucking wig." This last part was critical, allowing

Georgie to feel she was bringing a cartoon, and not a rival, into her bed.

With these terms agreed upon, the games continued to everyone's pleasure. Sometimes Georgie played at porno director, commanding them through positions, feeding them both lines. After the third visit, an afternoon tryst, pitying Helena the task of wiping Mao's mess from his stomach, Georgie left them to go sit in the steam room. Helena then lay on his chest, both of them bound in postcoital panting, their eyes playing across the panoramic landscape photo he'd hung over the fireplace: Hunanese peasants, Mao's people, all crouched and farming a mist-covered valley.

"What's the picture?"

"That's my home."

"Tell me what it's like."

"Well . . ." He studied the scene. "It's misty? It's an incredibly mist-rich place. And the people? They're all mist farmers."

"I'd like to go there with you."

"I'll take you there."

"Promise?"

"Of course. For the spring Mist Festival. They'll love you. We'll go up the river together on my barge, they'll receive you as a goddess, everyone waving, showering you with flower petals."

"That's so beautiful . . . ," she said.

They stared at each other for a long moment. And then, not breaking their gaze, he belched, a long and low-winded belch, with a look in his eye that said, *What do you think of that!?* She burst into laughter, appreciating the sudden gastric comedy which left her feeling that she'd glimpsed a special side of him—that they'd just shared a true and unguarded moment, and that, across the coming years, many more would follow. She was hungry for more of this intimacy, realizing, excitedly, that this would be the first time between just the two of them, without Georgie there. She grabbed him, whispering, "I want you. I want you without her here . . ." And then they were at it again, joined in this thrilling discovery, a gray area unforeseen by Georgie's rules. This, she decided, was what it must feel like, the real thing that she'd never known.

Not just fucking, but something more.

And just as *The Helena Show* was getting old for Georgie, she answered her phone to hear a woman say, "Please hold for Quentin Tarantino."

Their conversation at the party, he told her, had turned his noodlings into concepts. Those concepts had gotten together and "fucked without a condom," giving birth to something beautiful.

A revenge story.

"Isn't it about time a woman assassinated a president?" he asked.

"Huh?"

"Oswald. Booth. Hinckley, almost. How come men get all the fun? I don't mean a good president. I mean some twisted soulless fucker. Twenty, thirty years in the future. Some glutton asshole who stole the election and all the misogynistic lackeys who surround him are too corrupt to do anything about it. Until my girl decides she's gonna storm the White House."

"Who is she?"

"She's fucking karma, man!" blurted Tarantino, manic. "She's uncut estrogen with an attitude. She's gonna even the score for women everywhere, incinerate the whole cabinet, then snap the pig fucker's neck as payback for two million years of women, and I'm just gonna go out on a fuckin' limb here and say it—everyone knows they're smarter and tougher—having to suck and scrub for their male inferiors. She's the wrath of motherfucking god and her name is Lilith, the first woman before Eve, okay? So we get the whole fucking Bible thing, which is public fucking domain, and if the censors get up in our shit we'll tell 'em to go suck the devil's fuckin' dong!"

Georgie was stunned. She knew how he'd revived the career of John Travolta. How he'd elevated Uma Thurman, made Bruce Willis hip again. Was it really happening? she wondered. Her own moment of exaltation?

"I can't talk about it on an unsecured line. We've already said some of the trigger words. Even 'trigger' is a trigger word. Fuck. I'm out in Palm Springs. Can you get here next week?"

"Of course."

That night she watched *Kill Bill* and *Jackie Brown*, more in a dream than for research, attention shifting, often, from the images before her to the ones spawning in her mind, of herself as Lilith the Avenger, killing evil men with sprays of gunfire, snapping their necks without remorse.

That week she was on the treadmill before the sun came up and adopted a special ketogenic diet, shedding five pounds in six days. She practiced Krav Maga with Avi Ayalon, summoning ghosts of her past to fill her character's beating heart with rage. She seethed at Mitchell Silvers, at Lucky Dealey, even at Carrey. All of her life had been preparation for this moment, she knew, and therefore all worthwhile.

It was perfect.

But the day before she was due in Palm Springs, standing in front of the medicine cabinet mirror—she saw a wrinkle.

A new wrinkle.

Just beneath her nose.

An offense to her beauty, a mark of decay, and one that, after twenty years in Hollywood, she knew exactly how to deal with. She visited Dr. Marcus Mendel, the chief preservationist for Hollywood's elite, and arranged for the usual filler treatment.

"Just this one line," she told him. "Fill it up. Give me the Restylane."

"The Restylane's gonna leave you red," he said, then, as per his coaching from a recent pharmaceutical marketing seminar, launched into a pitch for a newly FDA-approved and significantly higher-margin product, Vividerm. "Your body processes Restylane as a foreign agent. Vividerm is totally natural. Made from real cultured human collagen."

"Where do they get it?"

"I believe it started with a car-crash victim." He paused, a moment of reverent silence. Then, casually, "Apparently the raw terror of collision lets loose a flood of magical hormones. The Swiss captured them all. We're lucky to be living in these times."

"Vivi-derm?"

"Ashton Kutcher was one of their first investors."

He brushed his fingers across his forehead. It was strikingly smooth.

"I switched last week. There's no more plastic look. See?"

He swung the examination-room magnifying glass in front of his own face, resulting, at once, in a macabre distortion—a great, leering globule of Marcus Mendel—and incontrovertible proof. It was like the plump thigh of an infant, Mendel's middle-aged forehead. No redness. No swelling.

Not the faintest trace of a needle.

"It's natural."

"Natural?"

There weren't even any pores.

"The body assimilates the Vividerm."

Medical miracles happened. That Vividerm would arrive in this moment was luck beyond belief. Proof that her career resurrection, at Tarantino's hands, was destined.

"Give me the Vividerm," she said, with a shrug, like taking the latest iPhone over the model prior. Mendel sat her down, stuck his syringe into the wrinkle, pain-prick promising youth.

"What about the crow's-feet?"

"I wasn't going to, but okay."

"And the forehead?"

"Just a tiny bit."

That was it. In and out, Mendel giving no instructions for aftercare, because Vividerm, latest fruit of an age of wonder, required none. She was back at Hummingbird by early afternoon, packed her overnight bag, loaded it into the Porsche, and drove into the desert.

After she left, Carrey ate a lunch of two grilled sandwiches and a small bottle of ketchup.

Then he walked to his gym and climbed into his hyperbaric chamber with a tube of Pringles, the pressurized oxygen brightening his senses as his headphones played a recording of Mao reading from one of his famous speeches, People of the World, Unite and Defeat the U.S. Aggressors and All Their Running Dogs. Carrey knew it by heart now, he mouthed the Mandarin words in perfect time, almost like they were his own: "U.S. imperialism is slaughtering the white and black people in its own country. Nixon's fascist atrocities have kindled the raging flames of the revolutionary mass movement in the United States . . ."

He was in there for an hour, rewinding and repeating; posturing and gesticulating so madly by the end that, viewed from outside, the nylon tent resembled a hatching cocoon as the Carrey-Mao crescendoed: "U.S. imperialism, which looks like a huge monster, is in essence a paper tiger, now in the throes of its deathbed struggle."

He heard a buzzing at the front gate.

Twice more, staccato, impatient.

He fumbled from the hyperbaric chamber.

He plugged his nose, blew three times, depressurizing his skull as he passed through the kitchen. Again, the buzzing of the gate, now longer, demanding.

He feared it was the born agains, again, thought to call Avi Ayalon. Or what if it was Charlie Kaufman, returned from Taipei? What if the deal had fallen apart? Wink and Al were livid at him for blowing Play-Doh. They'd seize upon the crisis. They'd crowbar him into something even worse. Because they could. Because the actor, however exalted, is always labor, and if there was one thing he'd learned from being Mao in recent months, it was that capital preys on labor, fangs in the worker's neck. He'd fight. He'd mount a revolution of his own, crush the corrupt system that had welcomed the money of bloody-fisted oligarchs who robbed their own people. He'd take the project to Soderbergh and they'd self-finance, break the town. Advanced sales to the Balkans alone would pay for the budget. And more. They'd start their own studio, finish what Redford started; they'd defend the integrity of working people everywhere. Maybe it was all the oxygen crammed into his brain by the hyperbaric chamber, maybe pure fervor, but he could smell it now, again, the sweat and ozone-scented air of the Titan Wheels factory, could feel the starving-child hunger that had never left him. Yeah, that was it. He and Soderbergh, or whoever, they'd restore the dream of Charlie fucking Chaplin.

The buzzing again, extended, demanding—

And it wasn't Kaufman.

On the kitchen security monitors Carrey saw Helena San Vicente, come to surprise him in tight blue denim, a white blouse, Monroe from *The Misfits.* He'd told her there would be no visit this weekend, that Georgie was out of town. She stared expectantly into the street-facing security camera, eyes green in night vision, blond locks like magnesium flares. Why was she here, uninvited? What was that but at best a power grab—at worst a whiff of crazy? But to the powerful, madness is itself an aphrodisiac. Those tits. The sweet demon-green, night-vision tits. A mighty Lust Faction rose up in the Parliament of his Mind, shouting down all forces of caution, of reason. He had no choice.

The gates swung open.

—

Carrey slammed Helena against the foyer wall.

Unbuttoned her shirt.

Pulled down her jeans, her lavender panties, fumbling beneath his belly to free his erection, then he took her from behind. She climaxed, he followed.

"I want more," she cooed.

He led her to the master bedroom; she walked just a pace behind him. Without him seeing, she wet her hand with both their cum and, spreading her fingers like a Balanchine dancer, dragged them along the walls, through the drapes, finally streaking across the glass panes of the French doors. Wanting to last all night, he took two Viagra from a bedside table where he kept his medicines, then made a request.

"Can we do the Marilyn from *Some Like It Hot*?"

"The only clothes I brought are lying in the foyer." Her eyes wandered to Georgie's closet. "Maybe Georgie has something?"

Carrey assented with silence.

She moved across the room, opened the door, suppressed a gasp. This closet was bigger than her bedroom in the apartment she shared with three others. Georgie had an apparent infinity of shoes, all lit like art on built-in shelves. Three long racks heavy with red-carpet dresses that screamed out to be touched, worn—appreciated. She parted the silks and chiffons, fully expecting to see, beyond them, a Polynesian beach.

"Ya findin' it okay?"

"Yeah."

She opened the drawers of the bureau, diving into an ocean of colorful silks, each a month of rent, not the knockoffs or the thrift-store buys that she owned. The black negligee flowed like a liquid over her body. She strapped on a pair of thousand-dollar heels. Were these things hers by right of fate? Always awaiting her arrival? She stepped out into the bedroom, transformed—but it wasn't enough. Suddenly Carrey turned directorial, eyeing her like Hitchcock did Tippi Hedren in his games of cast and capture. He pointed her to Georgie's vanity, stood behind her there, staring in the mirror, eager, hungry.

She brushed on foundation, but it wasn't what he wanted.

He took the pancake concealer, thick and greasy, and layered it across her face before painting her lips red and dotting on the famous mole. Then, on her forehead, he caught a shiny knot of scar tissue, a flaw he'd never seen before.

And as Monroe had no such thing, he dabbed at it with the concealer, wanting to erase the girl from the apparition. It was too thick. Whatever it was, it had healed badly. He dabbed again, soft but determined, allegro, and as he did Helena San Vicente returned to her twelfth birthday, her stepfather, drunk, his eyes darting to her friend's growing chest. Afterward, when she summoned the courage to confront him, he threw her into the rough brick fireplace whose edge gashed her temple. Doctors would ask questions. So she got a Band-Aid, a mumbled half apology; she lived for a week with that throbbing pain in her head.

And now it returned, in phantom form. She felt a searing heat around the scar. Her pulse, now, it raced with traumatic memory. She dug her fingernails into her palms, hoping to ground herself with this other pain, to continue . . .

Helena winced as she lay on her stomach, her negligee hiked up, Carrey lapping at her from behind. It was no different from the foyer, but now it felt wrong. Her muscles tightened. Her limbs screamed to curl into a ball. She squirmed out from beneath him, retreating against the headboard.

"I don't like it like this."

"Like what?"

"Like I'm Marilyn Monroe."

"I know you're not Marilyn."

"You do?"

"Yeah, you're Helena San Vicente."

"I'm not her either."

"Then who are you?"

Her voice faltered; he sensed that she was barely sure: "Celeste."

"Celeste?"

She had come to believe Georgie didn't love him, and she knew, deep within, that she could. She had imagined the life they could live together, and now described it, offering him her dreams like paper flowers to a volcano.

"Have you ever thought about moving to Santa Barbara? You'd like it. It's so nice up there, I know they have water restrictions, but they're still zoned for horses. This wig is too hot." She was unhooking the hair clips, working her fingers beneath the cap. She pulled it off, placed it on the bed. Her real hair was tawny brown, a pixie cut. He stared at it with jagged horror, seeing her no more as an escape from his being but as another of its menaces, a frightened, broken child arrived here in his bed with dreams wanting financing, either with his dollars or his days, and not a milligram of birth control between them. He was quiet, scanning the seconds for exits.

"I love you," she dared; dangerous words in this place.

"Jesus Christ," said Carrey, realizing the scope of her

delusion. Best to be very clear. Then, with crushing softness, "Love doesn't play any part in this, honey."

"Not with her, it doesn't. She doesn't love you."

"Who doesn't?"

"Georgie. You can tell just by watching."

"Don't bring her into this."

"She brought me into this."

"We've already broken the rules, Helena. Please . . ."

And in a voice suggesting that the meek shall inherit nothing more than their own pain, she protested, "That's not my name."

His phone vibrated on the ottoman; their eyes raced to its glowing surface, and each saw that the caller was Georgie. Carrey took the phone, walking into the hallway. Celeste listening as they talked, his voice suddenly tender. Then she turned and saw herself in the plate-glass bedroom windows, striking herself, again, not as a lost person, or a person in pain, but as the star of a film. It was okay. There were millions watching, she felt it, it was all being guided by a narrative hand that wouldn't have brought her here or given her this magical wardrobe change for nothing. Crying at cosmic benevolence, she realized this was the scene where she'd prove her love by showing that she couldn't live without him. Where he'd realize he loved *her*—

Carrey ended his call, and rather than return to the girl in the bedroom decided he could do with a shower. He'd get her a car, suggest she leave in the gentlest tones, he decided, running the water. He'd find the words to give her a soft landing, tell her it was no one's fault. Eventually, if necessary, he could change his cell-phone number, her texts would go to whatever lucky lotto winner received the old one. He toweled himself dry, stood at the vanity mirror applying his nightly beauty regimen, a twenty-minute production: eyebrows trimmed, bronzer dabbed, pimples concealed. Finally, putting on a friendly smile, he reentered the bedroom to find his prescription bottles emptied out on the nightstands, and Celeste's eyes rolling back in her head as she seizured on the bed, bloody saliva running from her mouth into the platinum wig, the act, at last, complete: she was a perfect Monroe bleeding final dreams into the Brentwood night.

At the Palm Springs JW Marriott, Georgie booked herself a Pilates class for the next morning, wanting to show up with full energy for Tarantino.

Her face had felt hot, a little puffy, after the injections. Her cheeks and forehead were flushed, but she ascribed that to the dry desert air. She slept with a cold gel mask on, cucumbers chilling in the fridge for the morning. Then she woke to find herself joined to an unenviable and, at that point, undiscovered demographic: the one person in ten thousand who exhibits a massive negative response to Vividerm.

Her face, her very instrument, was transformed into something like a rain-soaked catcher's glove. There was bruising and swelling where the needles had pricked her. And a general palsying about her mouth, her cheeks, her eyelids, one drooping, the flesh like cheap plastic, unable to convey any trace of emotion into the world. Not of her horror. Or of the guilt. That she had done this, was now more trapped than ever in the self which, with this audition, she had been hoping to transcend.

She called Mendel. They had a screaming match, and an

uneven one, as Georgie, all bruised, felt pain in speaking, and the dermatologist was, in his own eyes, an artist beyond reproach.

"You said there would be no reaction."

"I said it was totally natural."

"You said it was better than Restylane."

"For most it is."

"Not for me."

"Well, then you should have stayed with Restylane."

"Fuck you."

"Pardon?"

"You fucker."

She raced to CVS and bought cortisone, Benadryl. But the pills just made her sleepy, and they did nothing against the Vividerm. It was in there, deep down, setting off a flood of histamines.

Her lunch with Tarantino was set for 2:00 p.m.; she called to try and push it back a day. His assistant said he was leaving for Washington to scout locations in the morning and warned that he'd cleared a full afternoon for her, that he rarely did this and took his time very seriously.

She couldn't let this get away.

He was staying in a suite at the Ace Hotel. She drove there panicked, cursing herself for being so easily suckered, her mother's voice rising now from her lips, berating her, *Of course you fucked it up, you fuck up everything.* She moved the sun visor to hide herself from other drivers, berating turning to self-help as the hotel approached, her own voice now assuring her, *You can do this, he's an artist, he'll understand.* He'd taken suites by the pool, was there with his casting agent and a personal assistant, a young blonde who lost her artificial grin as, seeing Georgie, she gasped with raw fear of contagion.

"I'm having a reaction," Georgie mumbled.

"No! You look great!" the girl replied, with counterfeit warmth, taking her out by the pool to a table bearing muffins and croissants, coffee and tea, an HD camera.

Beyond it, reclining in a lounge chair set toward the sun, was Quentin Tarantino, making explosion noises and giggling as he flew a drone low over the pool, buzzing the spa-goers and watching their reactions in real time on his laptop.

"Quentin," said the assistant. "*Quentin!*"

He landed the drone, then turned, straining to see Georgie as she approached.

The sun was behind her, she came into view only gradually, so that she became, across the seconds, a figure of mystery. Then he saw it: the bruised face, swollen and glossy with cortisone, fixed at all emoting centers, transmitting none of the pathos he'd fallen for on *Oksana.* He realized what it was—a plastic surgery mishap worthy of tabloid commemoration. He'd seen it before. What was it that made people do this? He pondered this question as they bridged the moment with formalities, taking delivery of green juices, each praising the calming desert air. But her eyes followed his as he studied her skin, looking for the exact points of injection. Part of her hoped it all might work for his envisioned fight scenes. Part of her noted how his belly tested the buttons of his shirt, thinking it total bullshit that a man could get away with that.

"So, you wanna read?"

"Sure," she managed.

"Carly, can we get her the pages?"

He looked to the camera on the table, picked it up, pressed RECORD, and held Georgie in the frame as the assistant brought them scripts.

Tarantino said, "Let's go to page seventy-two. *Siege of the Treasury.*"

She flipped through the script, came to a page filled with capitalized carnage, the words almost attacking her from the paper: DECAPITATED, DISEMBOWELED, SKINNED ALIVE, FACE CLAWED OFF. The Benadryl was hitting her hard. She struggled to remember her character's name, then even to find the lines.

Quentin had the handheld camera rolling, red light aglow, moving it across the tray of pastries. She considered her face going viral, a mudslide of views and clicks burying everything she'd done in her life up until that moment. It had taken all her wiles, all her cunning, to claw her way to this lowly perch. She couldn't contemplate the rainforest floor.

She felt a sudden vertigo, a falling, as Tarantino directed—

"Keep it grounded. But remember. This bitch is hackin' dicks off."

Georgie looked down to the page, saw the character's name—Lilith.

Quentin read the action: "Interior. Night. U.S. Treasury. Lilith rushes past the printing presses, Uzi blasting, throwing grenades. She's vengeance and velocity, shooting up the guards. Their blood sprays across the sheets of money, tens, twenties, hundreds."

"I like this," said Georgie, appalled to hear her own mumbling, knowing it was all being written into silicon forever.

"She makes it into the office of Treasury Secretary Saperstein," said Tarantino, then pushed the camera right up in her face. "Okay, now read."

Georgie looked down, seeing the name: *Treasury Secretary Saperstein.*

Her face wasn't totally paralyzed, more swollen and drugged. But this—this was a tough one under any circumstances. Her eyes raced ahead. Flowing pages of Tarantinian genius, vindication, quotes from scripture, predeath bons mots. These were the lines and this was the role she'd dreamed of, that she'd lived for. And yet she couldn't make it past this horrible motherfucker's *S*-heavy name—

"Thhheck-wa-tawwy . . ."

Tarantino zoomed closer, half grinning. Power through, she told herself.

"Thhheck-way-tawwy . . ."

She took a drink of her green juice, trying to pass this all off as a dryness of the throat, a very normal actor's challenge. She tried again, no use. Her lips were in full mutiny. And then it got worse; she felt the green juice trickle down her chin, saw Tarantino's eyes follow it down onto her linen blouse. Los Angeles is a city of lucid dreams, built on a desert, illuminated by wonders but plagued by fears of sudden erasure. And these now overwhelmed her.

She broke into tears.

Tarantino passed his napkin.

"Truth is, I'm still figuring out what I want to do with this part," he said.

He turned to his young assistant, flashing a grimace across his well-creased, middle-aged face, one the assistant knew meant *Show her the door.*

Then, back to Georgie: "You got a lotta heart."

She went to the hotel and packed her things. Drove home two hours through the desert, wanting Jim's arms, needing him to tell her it all would be okay.

She'd later remember that the house had been too tidy. The bathroom was indictingly immaculate, no toothpaste on the sink, fresh hand towels on the rack. And the bedsheets, usually only changed on Wednesdays, were freshly cleaned and pressed. Housekeepers on the weekend? Never. Then, in the hallway, she saw a twinkling speck on the rug. She leaned down, picked it up: a glittery acrylic fingernail, a tiny talon, cotton-candy pink.

Half filled with hope, half with dread, she went into the office off the kitchen, locking the door behind her. Sat down at the desktop. Saw the software icon for Brentwood Home Security Systems, clicked on it. Inside were folders storing video feeds of the past days. She fast-forwarded through the footage of the Hummingbird Road gate.

Hours and hours of it.

Then a woman's figure came into grainy form.

Pause. Zoom.

She saw that it was her chosen sex doll, Helena San Vicente.

The gates swung open.

She watched the young Monroe impersonator enter.

Switched to the foyer camera.

Saw Carrey grabbing her, the lusty meeting, their disappearance into the master suite. She sped across the hours, then slowed as the street-facing cameras flooded with ambulance lights. Paramedics rushed inside the house. A space of dead minutes. Then out came Helena, body jostling on the gurney as they carried her into the ambulance, limp flesh flaring green in the night-vision camera.

But this tryst wasn't so surprising to Georgie, and it wasn't the sight of a girl on a gurney that most horrified her. It was the speed and the ease with which a life could be consumed here, the acid realization that she was, herself, already at some point along the way in this process. That her dreams would not come true here.

She stepped out into the living room to see him in the flesh.

He flashed her his trademark genial grin, but his puffy eyes betrayed him. Then he burrowed back into his hot-fudge sundae and the afternoon's viewing, a History Channel documentary, *Mysteries of Atlantis*. The narrator described a set of ultrapowerful crystal orbs thought to have given the ancient Atlanteans access to nearly limitless energy and also, most appealingly, supernatural powers. A group of explorers believed that erratic electromagnetic readings suggested these power spheres were located in a trench off the Greek island of Santorini, but couldn't afford the advanced submarines required to recover them. Watching, Carrey wondered: Was all his previous stardom just preparation for some greater spiritual-historical role? Was the cosmos speaking to him through the television? Presenting him with his true fate—something far beyond make-believe?

He loaded up a spoonful of vanilla ice cream, twisted a slick of fudge around it, then poked at a maraschino cherry for a bit before losing patience and plowing the spoon into his craw. Sweet sugar settling over him, he resumed his wonderings.

Was the cosmos tasking him with using his personal fortune to recover the power spheres of Atlantis from the deeps off Santorini? The power spheres, said the narrator, may have lifted the Atlanteans from their craggy island into realms of pure energy. They didn't die; no, they became eternals. Light Beings. Would that happen to him, once he led his recovery team? What a relief. At last, he'd be free from the burden of becoming. He'd be pure energy, shining out into forever. He couldn't wait to crew up and was scrolling through his contacts for Philippe Cousteau's number when his phone vibrated with arriving emails, the surveillance files, sent to him by Georgie, with herself cc'd. Didn't notice her standing in the hallway. He looked up at her bruised, swollen face, his eyes popping.

"What happened?"

"You're asking me what happened?"

"Huh?"

"I'll tell you what happened to my face if you tell me what happened to your fuck-toy."

"What fuck-toy?"

"You don't remember?"

"Honey, we should call you a doctor."

"Check your fucking emails, Mao."

He unlocked his phone, saw the newly arrived files, opened them—

Saw Helena on the gurney. Felt his earlobes burning, felt, within him, the Parliament of his Mind split into a Victim Front, which charged Georgie with bringing the crazy girl into their lives in the first place, and a Catholic Shame Party, which told him he'd committed sins of the flesh, nearly destroyed all he'd built, that he must repent or meet the Lake of Fire. And each agreed on his first words, which were:

"She's okay. She didn't die. She—"

"Ha," said Georgie. "Then that makes it all okay."

Now the Victim Front rose up, refusing to take this taunting, needing to make certain things very clear. "You're the one who found her!"

"Excuse me?" Part of her had been expecting an apology.

"You brought her into our home. You set up the rules you knew I'd break."

She sensed that this might have been true, and grinned in sensing, also, that the point no longer mattered, it would never need settling.

"You fucking set me up!"

"You won't need to bear my treacheries anymore."

"Georgie, I'm sorry . . ."

"Don't be sorry." She walked toward him, took his shaking head in her hands, stroked his hair like he was a child on the first day of kindergarten as she explained, "I'm gonna give you a better deal than you'd get with any lawyer. And I hope you're smart enough to take it."

She patted him on the cheek, then walked from the room. He followed her out to the foyer and watched, throat dry in surrender, as she disarmed the house alarm, then lifted the Frida Kahlo self-portrait from its place above the piano.

"Vividerm," she said.

"Huh?"

"It's what happened to my face. See? I keep my end of things."

Then she carried the painting out the door, laid it in the trunk of Jim's silver Porsche, and pulled out of the driveway. She went to the Viceroy Hotel in Santa Monica, booked herself a room with an ocean view. There, sitting out on the small balcony, with Frida as her company on the patio chair opposite, she sipped a dry rosé and thought of all the bright days to come.

CHAPTER 10

That week, as the tabloids ran news of Jim and Georgie's split, Carrey, Wink Mingus, and Al Spielman II gathered on the Hummingbird estate's back patio to discuss the various crises now facing them: a public split with Georgie and the rumor of a scandalous affair, a deep insult to the Walt Disney corporation, and—only recently learned—the growing concern of certain high-ranking persons in Beijing.

Wink Mingus carried two hundred pounds of warrior muscle on his six-foot-seven frame. He'd worn his hair in a greased ponytail since his days as a Green Beret sowing havoc across Central America in the 1980s. There he'd commanded his men to paint the Panamanian dead as human voodoo dolls, had dropped them into the Vatican embassy courtyard from helicopters to scare out General Manuel Noriega after George H. W. Bush, with classic American whimsy, had changed his designation from puppet to pariah.

But combat trauma had left his nerves frayed. His left eye blinked uncontrollably, leading many lunch partners to wrongly feel he was letting them in on special secrets, and earning him the nickname Wink, which generally delighted him; he'd never much liked being an Eddie.

"Christ, Jim, we've done so well together," he said, surveying the Hummingbird grounds. "Look at all we've built. A lot of people think you're crazy right now."

They're scared, thought Carrey, ashes flurrying down on his forearms. *Of me. Of the business. Their own loss of power.*

"You've angered the gods, Jim," said Al. "*Phillip Morris*. The Mickey and Minnie cakes. The fucking girl. We've got ourselves a real cock-up."

Gerry Carcharias was dialed into the meeting from the Amalfi Coast, and—just as Carrey was about to demand how Al knew about Helena—Carcharias's voice came crackling through the speakerphone, saying, "Jim! It's Gerry. We want to talk about how we can help you. You know people are still very hot on you over here at CAA. Wink and Al are doing one heckuva job and . . ."

Carrey's interior went riptide, his own raw survival instincts rushing against a fading flow of Mao's paranoia, and against them both a sensation of drowning as he struggled to recall how the old Jim would have managed this situation, then a horrible panic as he realized he didn't know. And that he didn't know other things either. Religion, according to Mao, was just a drug fed to the masses. That had seemed a valid point when he read it in character. Did Jim now agree? Had he lost God in the mix? Or had the holy father walked out on the performance? As Wink's and Al's lips moved, he searched frantically for pieces of memory that might define him—

I remember riding a two-wheel bike at the age of three in Aurora, Ontario, pedaling down the street to all the neighbors' amazement.

I hated cauliflower as a kid, it made me gag but not anymore.

I got spanked a lot. "If he gets out of hand, just hit him," they'd say.

My parents told everyone, "Feel free to beat him if you need to," joking but not really, anyone who looked after me was allowed.

My aunt Janet used an old piece of Hot Wheels track—

Eleven years old getting drunk every weekend down on all fours puking into a bucket while giving my brother, John, and his friends a half-conscious thumbs-up, waking up naked the next morning on the cement floor of Marty Capra's rec room; they'd all stripped off my clothes as a joke—

Sneaking into the drive-in movie theater at thirteen to watch The Exorcist.

Winning the Halton County Speech Contest, my father in the front row, cheering so loudly the top plate of his dentures fell to the bottom of his mouth and, and—

My sister Pat inviting me to eat the cake batter she's mixing, but really it's wallpaper paste and I gag on it, our laughter—

Losing my virginity age fifteen to a skinny blond girl who was twenty-five while Styx's Grand Illusion *played on the Panasonic in quadraphonic sound and—*

The flow of memory gave way to a torrent of impulses.

Run into the canyon.

Shit my pants, see how long it takes them to notice.

Break Al's fat little finger—which was now pointed at Carrey's chest, the churlish man saying, "People once loved you, Jim."

"Loved?"

Al had been raised in the tony suburb of Scarsdale, New York, the only son of Al Spielman Sr., a pioneering heart surgeon whose favor he had always sought but never received. He'd graduated from Columbia, his father's alma mater, with high honors, then gone into politics, working as a Carter White House staffer during the Camp David Accords, a promising career ended when he bought three grams of heroin from an undercover D.C. police officer. Family connections spared him jail time, but his political life was over. He fled west in 1983, at first trying his hand at stand-up comedy, then, in failure, becoming a manager, modeling himself after the great Bernie Brillstein, building a stable of talent that would lift him to the highest echelons of Los Angeles society.

"The guys at the Riviera think you're nuts."

Carrey clenched his jaw, imagining Al slandering him at the snobby Brentwood golf club.

"And so do some guys in China."

"China . . . ?" Carrey, hands now tingling, sensed not just a plot but an imminent boom lowering. Did they know about Mao? Had Georgie told them?

"I'm not sure I follow."

"We're quite sure you do."

"We know all about Mao!" blurted Wink. "Jig's up, Jimbo!"

"Kaufman swore me to secrecy."

"Kaufman!" spat Al. "Kaufman was getting played the whole time. There was never any billionaire in Taipei. His whole reality was fabricated by the state! They had him from the get-go."

"It was a mindfuck, Jim," said Wink, winking. "They have everything. Including a treatment now guaranteed to never see the light of day. An abomination opening with a dying Mao and a long shot of forty million starving peasants, suffering, miserable, poor, sacrificed people who"—he was red-faced now—"would lose us the entire Asian market! You've gone crazy, you know that?"

"That's what everyone's saying," said Al.

The suggestion that Carrey was somehow insane had long been used as a tool of manipulation by his handlers.

The touching of this wound enraged him now.

"I need you guys to go."

"Let's all just settle down," said Gerry Carcharias. "Let's do a deal. Eh, Jim? Like old times. We let this whole episode go. Pave it over, make it a speed bump. And then you, as a favor to us, you take all the passion, all the fearlessness, all the unflinching artistry that you brought to the character of Mao. And you bring that to the possibly even-more-challenging character of Morris Simmons."

"Who's Morris Simmons?"

"He's your ticket back into the American heart," said Al. "He's the lead of *Hungry Hungry Hippos in Digital 3D.*"

It would be a massively budgeted, heavily digitized summer spectacle, and more: the start of a franchise based on a beloved 1980s tabletop game in which small children imitated an animal feeding frenzy. CAA's data scientists had declared it a surefire juggernaut, their research suggesting deep affinities awaiting monetization across all demographics. Several A-listers had lobbied to star, but data from the vital five-to-ten age bracket had argued strongly for Jim Carrey, soon to be reintroduced to America as a winning father figure through a massive marketing campaign.

"Read him those Kenny Lonergan pages."

"Don't read to me like I'm some fucking child."

"Hear us out," sighed Al.

Working under his pen name, Mitch Branchwater, the acclaimed playwright Kenneth Lonergan had produced a three-page treatment, which Wink Mingus now pulled from the front pocket of his cabana shirt. He cleared his throat and began—

"Meet MORRIS SIMMONS, forty-eight, Chicago advertising executive. Proud resident of the upscale suburb of ROSEDALE. He is fired from his ad agency after losing its biggest account, THE MERIWETHER COMPANY, makers of 'Satellites, Latrines and All Inbetweens.' If no place for Morris at Meriwether, no place for Morris in world. BIG PROBLEM."

Most of Carrey, still ready to die for his art, fantasized leveling Wink with a blow to the head. A smaller, somewhat needier part marveled at Wink and Al's very professionalism, their coordination, and was tempted by this promised restoration to his former commercial heights. This was enough to sedate him as Al opened his own copy of the treatment, continuing:

"Each morning MORRIS pretends to go to work but really drives to a neighboring town, MECKLENVILLE. Spends days hiding in Mecklenville Public Library, reading children's books, the books his mother once read him. One day finds a book called *INTO HIPPOPOTOMA*. Can't put it down! Tries to check it out. But librarian says it's not a library book. She doesn't know where it's from. So it's his. STRANGE. One day driving home finds OLDER MAN (think Sam Jackson) in three-piece suit. Just standing by his mailbox. Guy has a letter, gives it to Morris, says: 'Tell me, Morris: Do you remember how to dream?' Morris asks how he knows his name but guy vanishes into SWIRLING RAINBOW. Morris being watched by NOSY NEIGHBOR (heavyset) from whose perspective he's been talking to THIN AIR. Neighbor's face says: Guy's gone totally crazy! Morris opens letter, written in MAGICAL RAINBOW INK, saying he's won a safari to LAND OF HIPPOPOTOMA. Same place he's been reading about in MYSTERIOUS LIBRARY BOOK."

"What a curious coincidence," said Al.

"I'm already hooked," said Gerry Carcharias.

"At night," continued Wink, "he reads to his children ZACK and MOLLY, from *Into Hippopotoma*. It tells the story of Hippopotoma's founding by THE HIPPO QUEEN (think Dame Helen Mirren), who rules benevolently over the hippos. Morris tells kids he's gonna travel to Hippopotoma and meet all these AMAZING CARTOON ANIMALS . . ."

As they spoke, Carrey felt Mao growing ever smaller inside of him, felt the demon grip loosening as his mind flashed to a YouTube clip he'd seen of the dead Mao in his crystal coffin, the spinning axis of history become a grisly souvenir.

Wink was saying, "Morris's wife, DANI, finds out he was fired. Confronts and emasculates him, forcing him on JOURNEY. He does what OLD MAN told him. Says, '*Hippos! Hippos! Hippos!*' Then a SWIRLING RAINBOW takes him to Hippopotoma, world of digitally animated JUNGLE

ANIMALS terrorized by HYENA QUEEN (think Tilda Swinton) who STEALS THEIR WATER depriving them of FISH AND CROPS and threatening their sacred mango grove, home of THE GOLDEN MANGO."

Jim's head fell into his hands, rolling gently there as Al continued, "Morris uses his ADVERTISING SKILLS to unite animals against HYENA QUEEN. They regain courage. He regains faith in self. Things go wrong. Then right. Then really wrong. Then really right. Morris Simmons has saved Hippopotoma! Sees picture of his wife. Returns home with briefcase full of GOLDEN MANGOES and FOUR SMILING BABY HIPPOS."

Al's voice went dreamy. "What happens to those babies?"

"We watch them grow up," said Wink. "Summer after summer."

"Billion-dollar franchise," said Gerry Carcharias. "Summer after summer."

"Lanny Lonstein is directing," said Al. "He's the millennial George Lucas. Guy's a digital DeMille and you're lucky he's a fan. He grew up with you, wants to make you great again. Burger King's on board for a special sand—"

Carrey was gone far inside himself. Eyes closed—

He is twelve, coming home from school with his saxophone. His father, who had his own orchestra long before, jumps up from the couch, takes the instrument, starts playing a slow and sexy version of the 1920s standard "Bye Bye Blackbird," his favorite song. Jim's mother walks up to him, speaking only with a smile. She holds up her hands as if to say, *Would you like to dance?*

He puts his hands in hers, they start spinning around the

room to the alto's whispered tones, the pair of them singing as they move, hands in hands, "*No one here to love or understand me. Oh what hard luck stories they all hand me. Make my bed and light the lights, I'll be home late tonight. Blackbird, bye bye . . .*"

His eyes water as he's pulled back to the patio where Wink says—

"Your lifestyle burns through cash. This Helena San Vicente thing. Maybe she's cool, but maybe she's not. I think you know where this is leading."

"Stop."

"Somewhere so dark they need a zillion miles of neon just to light it."

"Please," pleaded Carrey. "I don't want to do this."

"Vegas," said Al. "It's happened to better men than you."

Carrey wilted in the patio chair, missing the memory of his mother.

"The Mirage comes with a contract. Ten shows a week. You need the money, you got no choice but to take it."

"People aren't there to see you, they're just in town."

"You're living in a condo, all your neighbors knocking on your door for selfies 'cause you're still famous, you just can't afford a place with a fence."

"*I said stop it.*"

"Empty sex with call girls. They say you're special, no need for a condom. Bang! Palimony out the wazoo! Bankruptcy courts put you on allowance. You're eating meals out of Styrofoam containers from five-dollar buffets. You owe the mob money, but you lost your last cash to a sad game of keno."

"They beat you with baseball bats."

"You end up in a hole in the desert."

"Jesus!"

"There's no other way forward, Jim," said Al. "You're upsetting TPG."

"TPG? Who's TPG?"

"The Texas Pacific Group."

"TPG owns CAA."

"Like SLP with WME."

"Or UTA and PSP."

"GMO! DOA! TMI! ESP! PCP! DVD! ICU! *Heeheeeheee!!!*"

Jim devolved from acronymic eruption into mad pagan laughter, head beyond spinning, grinding, trying to process the unprocessable as desert winds blew heavy ash across the yard.

Then a screeching pitch pierced his skull; it felt like tinnitus but raised by orders of magnitude, undulating, blaring. He wondered if he was the victim of a microwave weapon as, to his eyes, Wink and Al went distant in their patio chairs, like Spielberg had suddenly racked focus on the scene. "My agents are supposed to be working for me!" Carrey ragingly concluded.

"Think of it as a partnership, Jim," said Gerry Carcharias. "The star feeds the system, the system feeds the star."

"Yeah," agreed Wink. "The star feeds the system, the system feeds the star."

Carrey turned to Al seeking explanation, received the same cold assertion:

"The star feeds the system, the system feeds the star."

"What's wrong with you guys?"

Frightened by their voided gazes, the feeling of tiny zippers being done and undone all through his skull, he got up and started retreating toward his house.

Wink and Al rose, shuffling mindlessly after him.

"The star feeds the system . . ."

"Leave me alone!"

His throat went dry. The backyard became a simmering Mojave vista.

"The system feeds the star . . ."

Forms and figures undulating, Boschian . . .

"The star feeds the system . . ."

Wink and Al reaching for him, *"The system feeds the star . . . ,"* as he fumbled his way inside, then locked the door behind him, their chanting made ghostly by the thermal glass all clouded from dust carried on the devil winds. He wanted only for water, cooling water.

He walked into the kitchen where the flatscreens were playing the local news, the weatherman Dallas Raines with his perfectly chiseled features, blond highlights whispering of teenage love, deep tan singing of weekends on the slopes at Mammoth, a Doppler-reading Dorian Gray, his job having less to do with prediction than assurance. He, like the rest of them, was a storyteller, putting a city of frightened children to bed as, more and more, meteorology described apocalypse.

"We're up in the nineties all week long. No rain in sight. That's the good news and the bad news, Los Angeles, because we got these Santa Anas rolling off the desert, and with high temperatures and fire season here you know what that means. You might wanna be hosing down the roofs tonight! And get those emergency bags ready. And now it's over to Don Chevrier for sports."

"Don Chevrier?" Carrey searched for where he'd heard this name as the giant flatscreen lost its HD, filling with grainy 1970s color footage of a man in a wide-lapelled plaid sports coat declaring, "Well, folks, the Boston Bruins are the 1970 Stanley Cup Champions as that fellow named Bobby Orr caps an amazing season with a miraculous goal in sudden death overtime."

He watched the broadcast, spellbound, Derek Sanderson passing the puck to the superhuman Bobby Orr, Carrey's favorite childhood hockey hero, who tucked it into the short side of the net, then sailed through the air like a boy in a flying dream. The replay's slow motion seemed to radiate out from the TV, slowing his heartbeats, his breathing.

The kitchen filled with the familiar smell of frying onions and chuck as his phone began to sing "Bye Bye Blackbird," a ring he'd never programmed, but couldn't resist. He picked it up, watched his thumb almost autonomously touch ANSWER.

He raised the haunted device to his ear.

"Hello?"

"Hey, Jasper!" a familiar voice, effusively friendly, a little loud, a man speaking against his own deaf ear. "You watchin' the hockey?"

"Hello?"

"What am I always telling you and your brother?"

"Take the body."

"*Take the body!* You don't let a man stand in your crease . . ."

"Dad—"

"You take 'em out!"

"Dad!"

"Heya gotta good one for ya, two guys walkin' down the street, one-a them says—"

"No."

"One-a them says, says, Heywaaa . . ."

"Dad, no."

"Says, Heeyyweeeeeeaaaulllaaghh . . ." now, from the phone, came the old hypomanic squealing that his father would leave on his answering machine after jokes begun predictably, then ended in racing aphasia that left Carrey afraid that genes were prophecy, that they would, in time, deliver him to the same place where his father, Percy, suffered. And where, in this moment, tears streaming down his face, peering through the foyer to see Wink and Al gazing pruriently at him, hot off the sight of a breakdown, it seemed he'd finally arrived.

He smoked a bowl of indica, hoping for calm, nearly finding it.

Coyotes started yipping in the canyons, the animals celebrating a feast, sending a *pfnur* through his body.

In childhood he and his cousin Tom had played a game called Bloody Mary. "*Bloody Mary, Bloody Mary . . . ,*" they'd chanted in the stairwell of his grandmother's tenement, trying to summon the spirit of a demon. Once, on the third chant a bloodcurdling scream had issued from down below them, sending a chill up his spine, raising the hairs on his head. He'd invented a word to describe the feeling. A *pfnur*. And what he felt now, against the coyotes' frenzied howling, was beyond any ordinary *pfnur*. It made him fear for his own skin. Made him recall how, years before, his daughter, Jane, would come to him at night shaken and afraid, reporting a presence in her bedroom.

A psychic had said it was the spirit of a pioneer woman who'd fallen into the ravine back in the days of Spanish rule, had broken her leg and gone into shock, rousing to find her only child, a daughter, missing, then hearing the little girl's screams against the feasting yips of coyotes in the distance.

"She has dark hair with gray in it, and she's screaming in your face," the psychic told him. "She's trying to scare you away. She lost her daughter and she wants yours."

Following this report Carrey had begun to sense the presence himself, had always imagined the spectral pioneer woman as a deranged Nancy Reagan.

Tonight, the ghost came for him.

Tossing in bed, he dreams that he's given Georgie all the children she's asked for. Not one or two, but a dozen or so. He's the kind of man who can handle it all. They are sleeping in a nursery down the hall, a huge number of infants, a litter, really. As he rises to check on them he hears demonic breaths, like from the flared nostrils of a bull—*goff-goff-goff-goff.*

Distress curdles Georgie's perfect sleeping face.

He hurries toward the nursery.

Lowers his shoulder into the door.

It opens just six inches, then meets an awesome strength.

He sees, through the slat, Nancy Reagan's unearthly black eyes, her razor-sharp teeth, bloodied off his babies' flesh. She slams the door. All he hears is infant wails, tearing flesh, tiny carcasses thudding off the walls as she discards them, gnawed bare like chicken wings. She's eating his children, you must understand, his tender children with Georgie, Georgie who left him weeks ago, who took his Frida Kahlo. Who won't return his calls—

A week became two, then a month.

Thirty years earlier at Dangerfield's Comedy Club, a bartender named Tony, a man who may or may not have killed some guys, had planted his finger into Carrey's chest and told him, sagely, "You got a divine spark. You gotta protect it."

Now he recalled those words, fearing that his terrors were a function of the spark having died.

His nights were haunted, his days without peace, fouled by clouds of ash and ceaseless construction noises. Directly across the ravine a Russian oligarch, Mikhail Svinyakov, had bought and razed four bungalows, joining the lots, building there a house whose sole reason for being was to launder his dirty money. And as Svinyakov's filthy billions were without end, so, too, was his construction. The initial phase, finished six months ago, threw up a smug black ziggurat trimmed in red steel; Carrey had thought it was over. Then work crews and heavy equipment had arrived and begun compounding the monstrosity, adding an aquarium, a disco, a ten-car garage, water features that never stopped running, and a rooftop pool whose grand colonnaded cabana paid homage to the Bolshoi, outside of which Svinyakov had gotten his start scalping tickets, a showbiz origin that worsened everything by suggesting that, in some taunting way, the sonuvabitch belonged here. Thundering pile drivers, raging drills, belching backhoes, they gave Carrey no peace.

His mind, increasingly, resembled the parliament of some ludicrous Balkan republic. There was an anti-hippos faction blaming the pro-Maoists for their failed art project. There was a Georgie Did This to Us! Party, whose intelligence held that his ex-lover had recently sold a screenplay to Kathryn Bigelow, which *Variety* was calling Oscar-worthy, running a picture of her at a London dinner party seated happily between Tom Waits and Justin Trudeau. This news roiled the whole parliament, spawning a Betrayal Caucus that was in truth but the puppet of a Jealousy Bloc, itself merely cover for an Abandonment Front that (once identified) hastily rebranded itself Need a Pizza. He had a special pie-sized slot with a thermal receiving box installed in his front gate and, through this, several times a week, received large pies with supreme toppings accompanied by sides of cinnamon sticks with extra frosting. He'd scurry out to retrieve them like a feral child, waiting until the delivery boy had driven off to avoid any human interaction, sometimes wearing a terrycloth robe, most times nothing at all. Always scampering back to the house, fearing the baby-eating Nancy Reagan. Then he'd lose all fears in gluttoning until the food was gone, his mind reset to grumbling.

There's not one cell in my body that's the same as it was seven years ago.

Where'd that guy go?

The person I was . . .

If he can vanish, what am I?

To what place, he wondered, did past selves go? Was it the same place from which, still, in the wee-est of hours, he'd receive calls from his dead father, still spewing gibberish tongues? And he'd take the calls, because how would Percy feel if he'd found a way to dial collect from the beyond and then got sent to voice mail by the son to whom he'd given all his dreams?

So Carrey would answer, "Hello?"

"*Whaffagua? WHAFFAUGUA?*"

"Dad, speak to me."

"*Afiggity cakkagey ploppo!*"

"Speak . . ."

"*AFIGGITY CAKKAGEY PLOPPO!!*"

The next afternoon a text came from Nic Cage.

Just won a sixth-century sword at Sotheby's in London. You gotta see the precision, the pride, the craftsmanship. The Saudis gotta lotta money, man. I really had to chase this fucker. It's fucking Excalibur, Jimmy. Can I hide out at your Malibu pad for a while?

Why?

I got a beef with some otherworldly assholes.

Sure, replied Carrey. *Enjoy it.*

He plopped onto his bed. Soft sheets, cool pillows. He turned on Netflix and let its warm glow wash over him, its algorithms guide him.

CHAPTER 11

And now we return to the moment when we first met Jim Carrey.

He watched a documentary claiming irrefutable evidence that the earth's alien masters would soon come to deliver the planet from its pains. He watched it in shaking wonder, the TV's streaming images soon feeling oracular, more powerful and reliable than the fracas of his own mind. He watched thick-browed hominids capture fire. He watched the face of Christ reconstructed by quantum computers. He watched a team searching desperately for the lost manuscripts of William Shakespeare on Oak Island off Nova Scotia, where the Knights Templar had almost certainly buried them along with the Holy Grail. He watched real housewives of Beverly Hills having spirited Chardonnay fights, and he saw 4K digital renderings of Pangaea and the giant creatures of the ancient seas. He saw, even, his own younger self, a sketch from *In Living Color*, "Krishna Cop," about a Hare Krishna cop who keeps reincarnating every time the bad guys kill him. He thought of those old days, of Keenan and Damon Wayans, who had given him a beautiful place to flourish in the garden they worked so hard to create; of the late nights writing with Steve Oedekerk. He marveled at how the decades had just flown by, watching his comic self die and resurrect in the sketch, again and again, ultimately achieving perfection as a holy crime-solving cow. He was left with a sense of time as insatiable, devouring even the gods with a BBC documentary about the last hours of Pompeii, the burying over of temples, the certainty of extinction that made billionaires plan Pyrrhic escapes to Mars. He was led, then, to a show called *Afterlife*, testimonials of sweet dopes who'd somehow gone to heaven and then come back to blather about it.

The pure deliverance, the rapturous hope.

Tears poured from Carrey's insomniac eyes as he watched, as he imagined the soul's flight from the body. *Let go, let go, let go*, he pleaded with himself, again and again, trying to shed his human husk. But there was never any ascension; he stayed right where he was, dissected by the YouTube algorithms that soon deduced his guiding interest, suggesting he'd enjoy seeing history's top-ten celebrity autopsy photos: John F. Kennedy, face frozen in expiration, reddish brown hair filthy with skull-brains-blood; a close-up of Michael Jackson's hand, a bar-coded tag dangling where the sequined glove once shone; Bruce Lee, mouth stitched shut like a football, sinking into coffin satin—

You're a commodity, just a commodity.

Even when you're dead, it's not their fault, it's yours, you blooded the hounds . . .

Jesus became a tax shelter.

Fred Astaire's ghost selling Dirt Devil sweepers on late night TV.

A shot of John Lennon. Face puddled on a gurney. This man, the greatest poet-songwriter of Carrey's lifetime. Born in Liverpool during the Blitz. *A working-class hero is something to be.* Splayed out for the crowd. If they could do this to John Lennon . . .

Carrey went to the bathroom, scrubbed and made himself beautiful.

He'd look dashing for generations as yet unborn, if his heart should fail him tonight.

The clock read 5:17, 5:39, 6:40. And just as his eyes were closing—

Construction resumed at Svinyakov's mansion. New drills, trucked in from fracking country, mighty rockcrushers that pound and blast, send tremors through his windows and into his skull. No point in calling the police, the Russian was within his rights. So Carrey fished a bottle of Ambien from the bedside table drawer. Shook two pills into his palm, swallowed them. A memory of Helena San Vicente here, on this bed. A reconsideration of suicide not as an act of desperation, but one of defiance. Another pill, then, finally, the gift of sleep.

He woke to the face of his daughter, Jane, and his six-year-old grandson, Jackson, who covered his mouth and nose against the foetor of night sweats and dirty sheets, declaring, "Smells like butt in here, Grandpa."

"You owe me a dollar for swearing."

" 'Butt' isn't a swear word."

"It's on the edge. What's that?" Carrey pointed to a tome in his daughter's hands, *D'Aulaires' Book of Greek Myths.*

"It's for Jackson's school. They're doing Greek mythology."

"Read it, Mommy," said the boy.

"I'd enjoy a story," said Carrey.

Jane opened the volume. This was his daughter, his beautiful daughter, whom he and his first wife, Melissa, had taken home from the hospital nursery to a studio apartment near MacArthur Park. Who'd beamed purest joy from a wicker basket as he and Melissa read Fante's *Ask the Dust* to each other on the fire escape.

Now she read to him, flipping to a bookmarked page. "Prometheus could not bear to see his people suffer and he decided to steal fire, though he knew that Zeus would punish him severely. He went up to Olympus, took a glowing ember from the sacred hearth, and hid it in a hollow stalk of fennel."

She passed the book to Jackson. "Show Grandpa how well you read now."

Carrey sat up in the bed, giving his whole attention to the boy who proudly took the book, staring intently, slowly moving through the text, "He carried it down to earth, gave it to mankind, and told them never to let the light from Olympus die out."

The words were like water to Carrey's parched soul.

"No longer did men shiver in the cold of the night, and

the beasts feared the light of the fire and did not dare attack them."

"God, that's beautiful," said Carrey, head falling back on the pillow.

Then his grandson poked at his cheek with a hesitancy that reminded Jane of the young boy's manner, earlier that month, with a stick and a dead bird. And this moment, this pitying gaze from his six-year-old heir, replayed in Carrey's mind across the coming hours, translated into a resolve that if there was no reason to exist for his own sake, or even proof that he had ever existed for any sake, there was some reason to carry on for his little girl, for her little boy.

I'll take HIPPOS, he texted Al Spielman.

What made you change your mind?

I haven't.

Let him have the last word, thought Spielman, marveling at how TPG's talent management AI had predicted that Carrey—if simply left alone and denied compliments of any kind—would accept the role in this forty-eight-hour window.

CHAPTER 12

The armored Escalade ground down a dirt path left off most maps.

The landscape shed its gridded certainties, slow-folded back into two-dimensional space, bands of ocher and blue.

The American desert is a pram of horror and wonder, the world's last unfiltered portal to the beyond, a place where heaven and hell both touch the earth.

He imagined a nervous Oppenheimer, shot in choppy black and white, chain-smoking in his worsted wools, leading the atom bomb down a sheep trail just like this one, toward the place where was unveiled, deus ex machina, history's ultimate plot device, the thing that might, to Carrey's view, with even odds, destroy everyone and everything except the data that the earth shrieks out into space.

He thought of his old tweets drifting through Alpha Centauri as the car came to a stop, churning up a dust cloud through which he saw five geodesic domes, all gleaming in the sun. He imagined them as giant eggs hatching baby serpents, the creatures slithering out, glistening with birthing goo, as a man and woman appeared from inside the central structure, greeting him with tight corporate smiles.

"I'm Lala Hormel," said the woman, a rail-thin blonde in her midforties, blue contact lenses frauding brightly above her hazel eyes. He noticed her signet ring as they shook hands, gold engraved with a screaming falcon. "I'm the TPG partner in charge of Hollywood operations."

"And I'm Satchel," said her junior associate, a pair of round glasses with prematurely thinning hair. "Satchel LeBlanc, I work with Lala."

"I'm feeling better than ever," said Carrey, as per his team's suggestion. *"And I'm ready to work again . . ."*

"How nice of you to say."

"I'm feeling so strong and excited to be back in the game."

"How good for us to hear that."

Then, an antagonistic glimmer in his eyes, speaking just a bit too loud:

"I play well with others!"

"We value that here," said Lala, taking him inside the complex, explaining, "This is all proprietary technology from our investments in Korea and Silicon Valley. We're five years ahead of the studios. That's pure competitive advantage, Jim."

Holy shit, they've taken over, thought Carrey as she walked him through the domes, each big enough for a 747.

"We've got animators, programmers, and renderers.

We've got genius sound engineers and augmented reality interfaces. We—"

United Artists got close, Laser Jack Lightning tried to do it, but where the artists all failed, a big pile of money is gonna succeed.

"Here we have uncredited but well-compensated writers adjusting the script as our mainframes analyze all chamber output in real time . . ."

I feel like the first monkey in outer space, I'll just do what I'm told, see if I get a banana, he thought as they came to a pair of air-locked doors.

"We have over a billion dollars of technology here," said Lala, ushering him inside. "A lot of baddies who'd just love to get their hands on it. The Age of Misinformation has only just begun. Now, if you don't mind—"

He was scanned for listening devices, then taken inside the control room, concentric rows of computers and workstations set behind a one-way mirror looking into a spherical beige performance space, the inner chamber. Seated at a central desk was the Millennial George Lucas, Lanny Lonstein, a pudgy redhead compensating for a weak chin with a wispy goatee. His forearm freckles sparkled in the halogen light.

"Jim, meet Lanny," said Lala. "Lanny, Jim."

"*Jim Carrey* . . . ," gasped Lonstein. At NYU he'd astonished the faculty with his deep readings of film texts, his belief that they contained a magic only revealed when a culture, like a person, gave up its soul at life's end. That they revealed this meaning through repeated viewings, like recited prayer.

"I own all the *Mask* dolls. I keep 'em in the original packaging. I've seen *Ace Ventura* two hundred eighty-three and a half times. That's an exact number. As a kid I'd watch it over and over. At NYU they told us we had to choose art or commerce. *Ace* taught me that was bullshit. *Ace* taught me you could pack the theaters while carrying out some brilliant fucking subversion."

"We were mocking the concept of the unbeatable leading man," said Carrey.

"You were eviscerating the whole Puritan ideal," said Lonstein.

"And people love animals," said Lala. "So many cute animals."

"I'd like to be alone with Jim, if that's okay," said Lonstein.

"Of course," said Lala, and left them there.

"I think cinema is, above all, a store of memory," said the director. "Did you know that the first recorded memories were Babylonian seals? Little movie reels, carved rock cylinders that they'd roll onto clay, and out would come a story, of a harvest or a flood or a hero. *Nude Bearded Hero Wrestling Water Buffalo; Bull-Man Fighting Lion*. The same man being received by an enthroned deity, apparently descended from a glowing orb."

"*Ancient Aliens*," said Carrey. "I've seen that episode."

"Yes, the Babylonians believed they had extraterrestrial origins."

They locked eyes.

"Jim. We are living through the largest mass extinctions ever. Of languages. Of species. I want to make something to speak for us after we're gone. They think we're making some movie out of a tabletop game? Let 'em think that. Let 'em call it *Hungry Hungry Hippos*. We'll know what we're really doing. You and me. We'll know that we're here, with their billions, making the first human story ever recorded. I want to tell that first story to see us through these trying times."

"What story is that?"

"*The Epic of Gilgamesh.*"

A soothing, sating aroma filled the air as Lonstein's assistant appeared with the meal that Carrey ate when he wanted to get back in shape but was not yet ready for the suffering of a real diet: two grilled nut-cheese sandwiches on spelt bread with a bottle of organic ketchup and a frosty can of naturally flavored mango LaCroix.

Lonstein watched, pleased, as the star began devouring.

"We think we're immune to massive cataclysms? Nothing could be further from the truth. Unfettered capitalism is destroying the world. It can't last."

"It yearns for its own destruction," said Carrey.

"I think celebrity does, too," said Lonstein. "Celebrity, as we know it, is part of capitalism. Unsustainable. I think that's why you all eat, at the end."

"Who?"

"Elvis. Liz Taylor. Bardot. Brando. All the real greats gorge toward the end."

Carrey paused, a long cheese strand hanging from his chin. "Thanks?"

"Don't take it the wrong way, just something I've observed."

"Michael Jackson would have been a parade float if it wasn't for his meds," said Carrey. "That was his way of getting there."

"How do ya mean?"

"Fifty years old? Fifty-city tour? Taking fentanyl to dance, propofol to sleep at night? That's showing you the same thing."

"Which is what?"

"That all personas eventually turn sarcophagal," said Carrey, plainly. "And what's the natural thing to do in a sarcophagus?"

"Die?"

"Not before you try to claw your way out."

"So let's do this," said Lonstein.

And Carrey, later on, would recall how Lanny's left hand trembled on the table, how his eyes had betrayed an almost sickly need of approval as the director took a deep breath, then belted out an eerily perfect, "*Aaaallllllllllllrighty theeennnnn!*"

He was wearing a black motion-capture bodysuit made of data-relaying fibers, and standing in the central chamber, equipped with the most precious fruit of TPG's entertainment foray: a pair of million-dollar augmented-reality goggles, one of only four in existence, a quantum leap in production technology designed to address a long-standing complaint of green-screen actors—that it was hard to imagine a tennis ball as a *Tyrannosaurus rex*.

They looked like ordinary tanning goggles, just a bit bulkier, and promised to show him the mainframe-rendered scenes in real time. "This is total immersion, the leap from acting to reacting," Lala had bragged, unpacking them. "Don't drop them."

Over half their estimated value came from projected pornography revenues.

An ultraviolet laser light scanned Carrey's torso, his face, his legs, relaying all data to the mainframes that inserted him into the digital person of Morris Simmons, a Middle American adman on a wild journey. He watched, with eerie fascination, as the black bodysuit turned into pleated shorts, a Chicago Bears golf shirt with a bulging belly. As his forearms puffed up like pressed hams. He laughed for the first time in weeks; he felt so free that he danced, first cautiously, testing the speed of the rendering engines, then gaily, even merrily, awed by delightful illusion. His fingers, always slender, were suddenly a family of Vienna sausages. He waved them before his goggled eyes, was half tempted to bite one as Lonstein's voice came through his earpiece.

"A friendly note that your fingers are not edible."

"They look delicious!"

"Just wanted to show you what this baby can do," said Lonstein, returning his digits to normal. "Okay. Let's start with scene twelve: 'Entry into Hippopotoma.' "

The chamber transformed, each beige panel generating pixels of glimmering wonder, a holographic Hippo Babylon of terra-cotta houses protected by mighty walls. The depth of the rendering was simply awesome; he believed that every brick of this city had been baked in the sun. And then he gasped at the hippos themselves. Their features were endearingly cartoonish, but their flesh was so supple, their eyes so vividly alive. He marveled at them, carrying a Dunlop nine iron, walking through a crowded marketplace of mostly barren produce stalls.

It was a scene of Black Friday bedlam, hippos battling to stuff their bags with desiccated mangoes. Then it became a proper melee. A newly arrived cart of mangoes had them gnashing their giant teeth, butting their massive skulls, drawing blood over fruit flesh, as fully savage an animal fight scene as a PG rating would allow. These, undoubtedly, to any observer, were hungry, hungry hippos.

There was no written script; the time costs of revision and the unpredictability of actors and writers from draft to draft had been deemed an inefficiency by TPG, replaced with autonomous dialogue generation—

"It's a little early for a hurly-burly!" said a voice in Carrey's ear, a voice so much like his own, and yet so much less taxing than original thought, that he almost accepted it as his true interior and didn't speak the line until prompted again. He lifted a single comic eyebrow:

"IT'S A LITTLE EARLY FOR A HURLY-BURLY!"

He'd nailed it.

Then, just like in a movie, trumpets blasted a royal fanfare and into the market came a hippo woman wearing a golden crown, the Hippo Queen, attended by five royal Hippo Guards whose presence stopped the violence.

"Good hippos!" said the Hippo Queen, voiced brilliantly by Dame Judi Dench. "We are all brothers and sisters. And we all have one enemy—" She waited a ripe dramatic beat. "Who is our enemy?"

"The Hyena Queen!" cried the crowd.

"Yes!" She gestured across the marketplace, so many barren farm stands. "She steals our precious mangoes, fouls our water. She eats our hippo babies. And her fang bacteria is so bad, if she bites you you'll lose your mind!"

"She bit me once and I woke up married to a cocktail waitress in Reno!" boomed a voice from across the square.

Carrey turned to see a bipedal rhinoceros whose swaggering gait and red necktie struck him as familiar even before all the hippos said, *"It's Rodney the Rhino!"*

This rhino bore strong resemblance to Rodney Dangerfield, the legendary comedian whom Jim had watched on the *Ed Sullivan Show* as a boy, not understanding the jokes but laughing because his father was laughing.

Who, in Vegas, forty years before, had hired a young Jim as his opening act, mentoring him, believing in him, always watching his stand-up from the wings, laughing at his goofy innocence.

Whom Jim loved and admired.

Who had been dead for fifteen years.

"Rodney?"

"Let's stay in the scene, Jim."

"Rodney's dead."

"You're not lookin' so hot yourself, kid," said the rhino as a voice in Carrey's earpiece explained, "We've licensed his essence."

"That's a thing?"

"Yeah."

"Fuck me."

"Let's get back into it. Okay? One, two, three . . ."

And Rodney the Rhino, surveying all the woebegone hippopotami, continued his bit: "I always said it. You can't trust hyenas. They'll laugh at anything!"

He pointed to Carrey.

"But this guy can save us!"

"Me?"

"Yeah, you're the one who was promised."

"No way."

"Oh yeah."

"Nu-uh."

He turned to the many hippos like they were a comedy club crowd, pulling at his necktie and rolling his eyes. "Must I always be wrong?" He pointed to Carrey's nine iron. "You're the one, I tell ya! The guy from the *Scrolls of Hippopotoma.*"

Four Hippo High Priests now appeared, unfurling a giant scroll to show a portly man with a short staff. Carrey raised his hands in protest, but as the sun gleamed from the golf club all the hippos fell to their knees, convinced of his destiny.

And if this all wasn't enough to move him, the promise of just another second or two with even the animal form of Rodney Dangerfield was.

"You're the guy who's come to save us," said Rodney. "To bring back the clean water. And the mangoes. And the kids. Because of you, we're all gonna finally get the respect we deserve! Ya with me?"

And Carrey felt the right line birthed inside of him before anything came through his earpiece. He spoke it with his whole heart: *"I'd go anywhere with you."*

Over the next month, in the semi-magical chamber, Jim and Rodney wandered far beyond Hippopotoma. They battled Marauding Lions roaring primal menace, and Rodney saved Carrey's life, goring two lionesses so gravely that the rest all retreated. Then they fought Sadistic Jackals, and here they were a team, Carrey riding Rodney like an armored tank, fending off the jackals with his nine iron, cracking jokes about how his short game had never been so good. Then they rested on a lush hillside, full moon hanging above, the landscape's every pixel evoking Kenya's Maasai Mara, Carrey laying his head on a foam block that he totally accepted as Rodney's rhino belly.

And why not?

It all seemed so much truer and richer than the gray world outside, where ashes flurried heavy from the west, fire season in the hills. In the chamber the air was pure. He realized he didn't want to leave his friend's company. He loved how his life, or its forgery, was given meaning by their companionship. Their shared, noble mission.

"That's a wrap," said a voice in his ear.

And Carrey watched the rolling hills and the dusky sky dissolve. He mourned each fading pixel, the suddenly silent birdsongs.

"Can't we keep it running?"

Across the one-way glass, in the production room, Lanny Lonstein shared a knowing glance with Lala Hormel, who flashed him a cautious thumbs-up.

"Whatever you want, chief."

They ordered their teams to stay, and set the computers to indulge all tangents, wanting to capture each moment of these friends reunited across the barrier of death.

The stars surged back to life in the chamber's sky as the valley down below them filled with a thousand elephants in silhouette.

"Sometimes they overdo it just a bit," said Rodney.

"Look, I know this isn't real," said Carrey. "But Jesus Christ I've missed you, man." He choked up. "It's so nice to hear your voice."

The rhino took offense. "How do ya know I'm not Rodney? Maybe this is just how us famous types carry on these days. Go ahead. Give me a try. Ask me anything."

"Who's your favorite joke writer?"

"The great Joe Ancis!"

"What was your favorite impression of mine?"

"The Amazing fucking Kreskin, kid! Funniest thing you ever did. Too bad nobody in America cares who he is."

"Okay, that's pretty good. But people could google that."

Carrey thought hard, wanting, equally, to stump and to trust this machine. Something personal. Between just the two of them. Private, precious—

"What did you say backstage at Caesars Palace about having sex after sixty?"

"I need a champion cocksucker, man!"

"How the fuck do you know that?"

"The difference between a person and a computer isn't so great anymore, kid," said Rodney, gently rubbing Carrey's shoulder with his horn, the sensors of the bodysuit convincingly pulsing each caress.

"It's like it's really you," said Carrey. "My God."

"Pretty swank, huh? Wish they had this before your dad died."

The cameras whirred along their cables, angling for Carrey's response. And a few of the renderers felt unease, even guilt, as they watched what followed.

"I miss him," said Rodney. "Man, Percy. That guy was hilarious."

"I feel like lately he's been trying to reach me."

"Reach you?"

Now Carrey unburdened himself, voice trembling. "He

calls my cell phone. Or something does. I answer. He starts telling me a joke, then he falls off into gibberish, this high-pitched squealing. It's exactly what he did after my mom died. He lost his way at the end."

"He just had glitches, kid."

"Glitches?"

"Yeah, glitches," said Rodney. "Take a look at those elephants down there. A couple of 'em have been beeping in and out of existence this whole time. But you know what? You can fix anything in post. And meanwhile, look at these stars. You ever seen the moon so clear? They got so much of it right." Rodney took an appreciative pause. "Just like your dad."

Carrey's eyes welled tears.

"You wanna see another little glitch?" asked Rodney, a mischievous glint in his eye. He stood, turned, raised his flap-like rhino tail. "I got no asshole! They didn't give me an asshole! I eat half my body weight every day and I can't shit."

Now they were bonded, the truest of friends. Their laughter echoed across the chamber, it seemed to go on forever, each note fully captured by the watching and listening computers.

They roamed the digital savanna like Gilgamesh and Enkidu, sharing bits of their backstories, Lonstein grinning as Carrey told Rodney of the time he'd gotten ambushed by a boy with a peashooter in a Toronto apartment block, the time, age eleven, when he'd gotten caught humping the little green rug beside his parents' bed.

Soon Carrey missed Rodney when they weren't together.

At night, in his sleeping quarters, he'd lie down on a spartan cot, watching CNN, its resolution nowhere near as compelling as the scenes in the chamber.

A billionaire casino magnate was running for president, his whole campaign a churlish collection of grimaces and playground insults. It was widely known that he kept a whole floor of prostitutes in the Vegas tower where he lived in a duplex penthouse, a situation that might have been legal in the state of Nevada if he didn't get off on pummeling them all. It began with one lawsuit, then grew into dozens, more women emerging from across the years, pictures of bruised necks, broken noses, stories of choking to the point of unconsciousness. Threats made against their lives and the lives of those they loved. Their images and accounts sprawled across the news, but where these ought to have ended the magnate's candidacy, they only fueled it. His base almost completely accepted his defense—that the women were mostly lazy millennials unfit for a challenging work environment. He was surging in the polls.

And against this all, the *New York Times* ran an article reporting that navy pilots had filmed close encounters with stunningly advanced UFOs, that the government had multiple buildings storing parts of flying saucers just outside Las Vegas, strange metals defying identification. The story fueled light Twitter comedy, then joined into the ever-louder background noise—

The world he saw on the news came to seem like a genre-fusing farce, its story lines ever less plausible, ever more dispiriting. The world of the chamber, by contrast, was all impressionist masterworks, images and plotlines manifestly finer and more nourishing than what, of late, was passing for the real.

Time behaves strangely on a movie set.

Days lurch into months.

Seasons blur together.

The sun was falling.

He and Rodney were camped by a thin river, resting by a fire. Carrey was so certain, having left the script far behind, that a shining achievement was just within their reach. They'd defeat the Hyena Queen. They'd restore all the fish to the Hippo River and all the mango groves and all the hippo children would sleep well and safe. And he'd get a big summer movie to boot. Ego and soul in rarest unison, he looked hopefully around the shadowy savanna and heard excited giggles. "Sounds like someone's having a party," he said.

"Shhh!" said Rodney, tiny ears perking up with alarm. Then he whispered, "I know what a party is, kid. That's no party, lemme tell ya."

The yipping giggles built, bouncing across the chamber, technicians peering like prison shrinks through the one-way glass. They'd been coding this scene for months, wanted to see what would win, the engineered mind or the human one, once all data was distilled and looped into the mainframes. Hyena eyes now appearing through the grass. Deep voids set with amber irises kicking back the firelight.

Two sets of eyes.

Five.

Seven.

Eight slobbering hyenas slowly taking form from the shadows, coats foul with mange and gore. Lonstein had given, and now—in homage to the original Gilgamesh, who lost his heart when he lost Enkidu—he would take.

"Rodney!" Carrey cried, right atop the voice in his ear.

The hyenas raced in from all sides, a rush of gnashing teeth and fur. Rodney, ever faithful, gathered to his feet, started swinging his great horn. He shattered one beast's skull—saying "Oopsie!"—then launched another through the air, quipping, "Is that the best you got? You fight like a buncha pink flamingos!" Then, as if to answer his challenge, two other hyenas leaped on his neck. They clawed at his eyes, bit into his ears. Carrey swung his nine iron madly, trying to fend them off, as more beasts were rendered into the scene, leaping atop Rodney, fangs finding his soft stomach, tearing into his guts, blood spraying in the firelight, Carrey wailing, at once to the Fates and the control room.

"What the fuck? It's too much!"

Lanny Lonstein marveled at his own genius, knowing he'd lose most of the gore in his final cut, but thrilled at how it had Carrey reduced to survival mode, totally convinced of the carnage, all his efforts useless against the moment's single narrative demand: that Rodney was to die, but Jim would survive, and yet be changed. "*Take me! Take me!*" he screamed, these ad-libbed lines freed from cliché by raw fear. That drove the digital engines to detect approaching climax. "*Stay with it,*" said Lonstein, directing his programmers to complete the moment with a suddenly materialized thirteenth beast, greater and more terrible than the rest, surging up from behind him: the Hyena Queen, fangs like steak knives, eyes so knowingly evil that Carrey wets his bodysuit as the hyenas feasted on poor Rodney, their cackles multiplying, filling the star with a sorrow that rose like floodwaters over what rubbled walls still stood between his experiences in the chamber and his existence beyond it.

The hyenas slowly vanished.

Rodney's rhino form remained, bleeding out into the grass. His breaths growing ever more shallow, great bulging eyes fighting to stay open.

"Rodney," said Carrey, holding a block of foam he thought of as the body of his friend.

Through this whispering he recalled a room at UCLA hospital a decade before, when Dangerfield was in his final hours, breaths short and labored, as they were now. He'd leaned close and gifted his friend a final joke: *"Don't worry, Rodney, I'm gonna let everyone know that you're really gay. That kind of thing isn't frowned on anymore."* The machines had come to life, the nurses all came running. Dangerfield had started moving his lips, trying to form words, but failed.

Rodney the Rhino's eyelids shut.

His body vanished into nothing.

The sound design cut—

No more rustling grass, just the white whir of air-conditioning.

"I want Rodney," said Carrey. "Bring him back."

"That can't be done," said a voice like his own voice in his ear.

"Bring him back, or I'm off this film."

"He's gone," said the voice, coolly.

"Bring back Rodney!"

"That's it," said Lonstein. "Gorgeous loss."

"Noooohhhh . . ."

"This is genius, Jim."

"I want Rodney back."

"He's gone," said the voice in his ear. *"Not coming back."*

"Then I'm out."

Carrey tore at the cameras on his head brace, each a

hundred-thousand-dollar prototype. He ripped them and threw them to the ground, stomped them to bits, jumping up and down on the mess of plastic and wiring like a child wrecking a Lego castle. "Bring back Rodney." He tapped on his goggles. "I wanna see him."

This only further excited the other cameras.

"I'll fuck you up, too!"

They whirred closer.

"I'm not your monkey," said a voice in his earpiece, a voice closer to his own truth than ever before, and as this scared him he changed the line:

"I'm not some puppet!"

"Control yourself," said a new voice, Al Spielman II.

"I'm in control."

"You're hopping around like a madman."

Which only deepened his rage.

He leaped up to grab at the cameras on the rigging, a $10 million cluster of technology whose contractual protections exceeded his own.

The chamber doors opened.

Out came Wink and Al, Lonny and Lala, followed by Satchel LeBlanc carrying a silver tray of crystal flutes brimming with champagne.

"What the fuck is this?"

"We're here to toast you."

"For what?"

"Extraction," said Lonstein. "Few people have uploaded so much, so quickly. The engineers have everything they need for *Hippos*. And for all the sequels."

"Sequels?"

"If you agree."

"Why would I agree?"

"Because quantum computers are *smooookkin'*!" said Lonstein, with a pathetic attempt at a *Mask*-evoking spin.

"Jesus Murphy," muttered Carrey.

"And because we can guide you," said Lala. "Not just through this film, but beyond it."

"I don't want to be guided."

"Choice is an illusion, Jim," said Wink. "Jury's in on that one. By accepting this, though, you make, perhaps, the ultimate choice. A choice that can free you to prosper into eternity. The first artist freed from time."

"The AI makes better decisions than a thousand geniuses in a think tank," said Al. "And happiness and success? They all boil down to decision-making."

"We at the Texas Pacific Group want to help you," said Lala. "To guide your brand through an endless chain of profitable tomorrows."

The chamber now filled with visions of possible Jim Carreys vastly happier, more youthful and beautiful than the actual Jim Carrey, all fixed in an unending thirty-fifth year. He spun in wonder as the scenes appeared. He saw himself yachting off Nantucket with Oprah, Tom Hanks, and the Obamas, all equally ageless, laughing at a joke he'd just told. He saw himself playing touch football with the young Bobby and Jack Kennedy in Hyannis, scoring a goal with a bicycle kick in a World Cup final, swimming among orcas off Maui, the mightiest of them jumping up out of the water, soaring over his head, its tender belly just grazing the fingers of his outstretched hand, à la *Free Willy*. Then a final tableau consumed all others, transforming the chamber into Athens as seen from the terrace of a mountain villa overlooking a perfectly restored Parthenon; he saw his parallel self in a loosely tied toga, ancient sun gleaming from his eight-pack with the brilliance of a thousand Atlantean power spheres.

"The Parthenon looks gorgeous."

"Jim Carrey paid for the restoration," said Al. "Passive income, buddy."

"The deal is historic," said Wink. "You'll never stop making money. But that's not all."

Then the room filled with the scene of a future Oscar ceremony. He was sitting in the audience, Daniel Day-Lewis presenting at the podium, tearing open a thick envelope, announcing that the best actor award goes to—

You fuckers, thought Carrey.

It felt so real.

"Jim Carrey," said the legendary thespian, not with surprise, no, but with satisfaction, his face registering joy and relief, as if a grave wrong had finally been righted, as if the fact of this occurrence made the world a more just and habitable place. Carrey spun to see all the joyful faces, wild applause exploding across the speakers.

Daniel Day-Lewis was double pounding his heart with his fist.

Sweet Christ, the bliss of this.

The soaring validation—

He walked toward Lewis, dopamine invigorating his every cell, and just as he was about to reach the Dolby Theatre stage—the mirage disappeared.

"Not reality yet," said Wink. "Still just a good dream."

"What do I have to do?"

"We've already gathered all your data. Just say the word. They can complete this film. And the next one. And you? You can get some rest. Go paint."

"I'm an artist," said Carrey. "I don't let some computer do my work."

"Tell it to Jeff Koons," said Wink. "Guy hasn't made a balloon dog in forever."

"They're pulling down all the statues of Elvis in Vegas," said Al. "Young kids don't give a gnat-shit who he is. That's not your fate. You'll last forever."

Forever. The word had a ring to it.

Carrey imagined his digital essence speeding across the cosmos, fists thrust ahead of it, Superman-style, zooming gallantly past Alpha Centauri, then through quasars and nebulae, finally beyond the dream-soaked edge of the thing . . .

"*Forever,*" said Carrey, finding it the happiest of words.

"You'll be there for your daughter, your grandson, his children."

"No more struggles," said Wink.

"No early morning call times."

The Oscar scene passed to a vision more alluring than all the rest: his bedroom back on Hummingbird Lane, a still night, no construction noises. And, at the center of the composition, his bed.

His soft, beloved bed.

"Home," said Wink. "No place like it."

"Rest, relax," said Al. "You can still work anytime you want."

"But let the future take its course."

Now a Jim Carrey perfectly identical to his own present self appeared on the bed, wrapped in his own bathrobe, face a vision of tranquillity.

So happy.

Such harmony.

So very cruelly and irresistibly possible.

He felt an eerie unity as this phantom extended its hand, beckoning him to come closer. He stepped, hesitantly, toward it, admiring the rendering work. His face, just like his face. His eyes, just like his eyes. The moonlight fell over each of them as they stood there, each form joining seamlessly with the other, the virtual and the real becoming indistinguishable, both selves whispering *Okay*, in unison, *okay*, *okay*, the cotton duvet just as fine as he remembered, the great mattress just as welcoming as it had always been as he fell onto it, exhausted, sighing deeply, almost prayerfully.

CHAPTER 13

“Fire! Fire! Fire! Please, leave immediately.”

He was at home, or so it seemed, lying in his bed.

Jophiel cowered in the bathroom doorway.

“*Shoov!*” he called, the Hebrew command for “Come!” and they trotted reluctantly to his side as he peered through the blinds, out into a jaundiced haze.

A burning eucalyptus tree had fallen onto the pool house, collapsing the roof into a pyre. “Threat inventory,” he said to the house.

“The cabana is ablaze. Outdoor temperature, one hundred fifty degrees. Please leave immediately.”

“The fires never get to Brentwood.”

“Adjacent homes are aflame.”

“The fires won’t leap over the canyon.”

"We disagree."

The digital woman had only ever spoken in the first person singular. Why this shift into the plural? How did she know about other houses? Did these semi-sentient security systems swap celebrity secrets? He rose with cracking knees, pulled on his bathrobe, and haunched down the hallway, Rottweilers at his sides, windows flickering crimson. Looking outside he saw the burning ravine, flames reaching twenty, thirty feet skyward, blasting embers into the devil winds, up over his yard, the lawn already strewn with flames.

He opened the door.

The curtains writhed like tortured spirits as a thermal blast screeched inside, searing his skin as he stepped onto the patio, the whole world like a sweat lodge. He choked on the scalding air, pulled his T-shirt over his mouth and nose, then settled into a cedar lounge chair. The fires had never come this close before. The oligarch's mansion was entirely ablaze, gulping oxygen at its base, spouting fountains of flame as the tractors and rigs that had pulverized Carrey's mornings spewed fire from their bellies. The cell networks were all jammed, but Avi Ayalon had gotten a text through, saying he'd evacuated Jane and Jackson from Laurel Canyon, but the police and fire departments were blocking the roads into Brentwood; Avi advised him to take the Range Rover and meet them up north.

"Tell Jane I love her," Carrey replied, but the message kept failing to send.

Down at the Russian compound, a fuel truck met the flames, its tires popping as prelude to the gas-tank explosion shattering the glass on the mansion's northeast façade. *How very beautiful*, thought Carrey, transfixed. *Let nature have her way, erase this eyesore, cleanse the land and return it to the wild things.*

A pale apricot glow to the north, greater fires there, exquisitely rendered. Music flowed from one of the burning houses, arpeggiated notes filling the night with a plaintive grandeur; it sounded like a Philip Glass score. The last he knew he was in a geodesic dome in the desert, settling down for a digital nap. Had Wink and Al dealt him into the disaster genre? Was this reality? He unlocked his iPhone and opened Twitter, where trending news headlines seemed to verify the crisis.

Fires Beyond Control.

Only 5% Contained.

#FireSelfie was trending, people competing to livestream their adrenaline-flushed faces from as close to the biggest blazes as possible, daring each deathward, many vanishing into the smoke, all for the likes of total strangers.

The eastern winds roared, fanning the central ravine fires to sixty feet, glowing embers wafting across Carrey's lawn, over his house. He held up his arms, totally covered in ash. He saw his reflection in the glass doors, the flaky sediment covering his hair, his shoulders, too. He seemed like an elderly version of himself, grayed by time. He smiled, imagining himself blowing away, joining with the dust. He was calm, resigned, almost Buddhist in tranquillity. His Mao preparations, his deep dives into historically dubious, yet still terrifying, documentaries, had filed down death's fangs. He'd lived through the eruption of Mount Vesuvius.

This was nothing.

Then, leaping from the fires, shattering all calm, a mountain lion sprinted straight at him, incisors bared, gaining fifteen feet with each bound. Carrey's inner peace dissolved in a scream. Jophiel launched to defend him, steel fangs gleaming, countercharging the great cat, all animal bodies meeting in a tangle of claws and muscle as, beyond them, a fire tornado swirled up from the hulk of the Russian house and began moving toward the Hummingbird estate.

"*Shoov!*" cried Carrey, but the dogs ignored him.

"*Shoov!*" he repeated, again ignored by the Rottweilers who'd clamped their teeth into the mountain lion's neck, refusing to let go even as the great cat buckled and bled.

Finally, despairing, Carrey gave the one command that would override their programming: "*Ahava!*" he said, the Hebrew word for "love."

It worked.

For the animals, as for the man, the memory of a mother's love was overriding.

They turned from the wounded cat toward the great house as the fire tornado swirled closer to them with unexpected speed. The dogs raced but were overtaken, midstride, by the firestorm.

Carrey ran inside, thinking first of himself, then of his exquisite art. His Picasso, one of the guitar series, a seminal cubist work unveiled at the 1915 Armory Show. His Basquiat, *Flash in Naples.* His gorgeous Hockney, *Alliums.*

I have to save them for prosperity, he thought, then paused, shocked and appalled at the Freudian slip. *Prosperity?* Is that what had been running his show? He gave the thought a second take, revising it toward a more noble motivation: *I have to save them for posterity.*

But he couldn't sell the line—the first take was better.

"Siegfried's Funeral March" from *Götterdämmerung* came over the home's audio interface, selected by the security system, which, sensing its plastic components beginning to melt, thought it time to say farewell. Against rising brass and strings, Carrey recalled a treasure more precious than all others: Charlie Chaplin's cane, won at auction in 1995 with his payday from *Batman Forever*.

It was, upon purchase, his most sacred object, affirming his arrival, fulfilling his very spirit.

Chaplin had not merely impressed but formed him. Showed him how any gesture—a kiss, playing with some bread rolls—can be freed from the mundane, imbued with magic. Charlie Chaplin was always turning caterpillars into butterflies. He had used comedy to reveal, and not flee, the truth of the human predicament. He'd roller-skated blindfolded over the void, like a planet circling a black hole. He filmed a factory worker sucked into a machine, fed through its cogs and gears, assailing an age that turns people into things. And Charlie Chaplin had battled the bleak world with—what? Not a knife, not a gun. A cane. Gentle, gestural, the baton of a maestro. Chaplin's cane, with no disrespect to Hockney, Picasso, or Basquiat, was, in this moment, what Jim Carrey most wanted to save.

And intending to do just that, he walked against the broiling heat into his living room, grabbed the delicate object from its Lucite brace, clutched it to his chest, and made for the door, when with an awful crash, the tallest of his weeping willow trees fell through the roof, splitting the support beams, trapping Jim Carrey between his overturned glass dining table and a nest of burning vines.

Still, he clung to Chaplin's cane. Still, he hoped for escape, to crawl out to his Range Rover, parked safely on the street. As the fires soared. As his central air system, set to maintain an internal temperature of sixty-eight degrees, drew on generator power and sent a final burst of air through the house, whipping the shattered home into a proper inferno, Carrey began to barter with the cosmos for salvation.

He'd repent, he swore. He'd renounce all earthly delights. If it was fun, he'd avoid it. He'd change his name to Francis, or Simon Peter. And if the cosmos wanted to throw in some special power or skill, like healing the sick or talking to birds, something to distinguish him from others in this new field of endeavor (and also maybe a small group of followers, nothing huge, but dedicated believers), well, all that would be appreciated.

Unnecessary, but appreciated.

"Save me," he prayed, cowering. "Please."

The flames lapped higher; the roof hissed and groaned.

The heat was baking his eyeballs.

Another blast erupted by the front door; he assumed it was the oil tank exploding.

I'm gone, he thought. He closed his eyes, a sailor yielding to the deeps, waiting for some final narrative-completing vision that wouldn't come. *This is it*, he thought, *death*, *slow drifting into nothing*.

Then, as happens to heroes in myth, and in cinema—he heard a saving voice. Feminine and fearless, tender yet strong as steel, a cool, wet towel on the mind, singing the sweetest of songs, his name: "Jim? Jim Carrey?"

Was this a hallucinated angel, come to take him into the great forgetting?

"Yeah . . ." He sobbed, fearfully. "I'm here . . ."

"Where?"

"I'm in the new solarium," he gasped, looking up through the torn ceiling, a final joke. "You can't miss it."

Then, through the smoke, the choking stench of burning plastics, he saw them, the Daughters of Anomie, an elite group of radicalized war veterans, all missing at least one limb, all come to save him from his world.

"My house," said the star, deliriously, as the tallest of them lifted the dining room table off of him with a single awesome power squat. "My house!"

"Let it go."

"My things!"

"Rejoice in the lightening of your load."

"Who are you?" Chaplin's cane held tight against his chest, he puzzled over these women in their oxygen masks and aluminized fire suits.

"We're the DoA."

"The Daughters of Anomie?"

"Relax." They fitted a respirator on his face, picked him up by the limbs, carried him from his would-be grave, out into the foyer. He studied the waves of fire rippling across the ceiling above their heads, glinting off their titanium limbs. Then, outside, he saw the fire tornado dancing madly, a zillion embers rising like the city's every selfish prayer, up into the night.

Dear God, please take this cellulite from my thighs, that I might know beach readiness . . .

Holy Lord, that I might fly private until the end of days, and so be closer to thee . . .

They carried him through his front gates, out onto Hummingbird Lane. They laid him in their Humvee, a hybrid model bought from *Soldier of Fortune* magazine. Carrey shivered as they unzipped their fire suits. Most had shaved their heads, marine-style. Their arms were strong and toned in olive tank tops, shoulders broad and powerful, like an Olympic volleyball team. Even their prosthetics seemed advanced, superior.

One woman wrapped him in a fire blanket while another pulled aside his bathrobe, jabbing his left buttock with a syringe.

"What did you give me?" asked Carrey, suddenly woozy.

"Just a little happy sauce, all natural from the poppy fields of Topanga Canyon," said the woman who'd injected him, Bathsheba Brenner. She had joined ROTC at Harvard, an act of service to prepare for a career in government, then, as a Green Beret fighting ISIS in Iraq, she decided that terror was the new activism.

A sedative ease oozed over Carrey as the car screeched away from his house, radio scanning police and fire frequencies.

"*The Getty's fucking burning!*"

"*Tanker to Bonhill, tanker to Bonhill . . .*"

"*I've got thirty men pinned down here and—*"

The radio cut to terrified screams as the Humvee reached Sunset. Before them, taillights stretching for a thousand hopeless yards, then vanishing into a Netflix-red haze.

Carrey's lungs burned. He retched up a plug of ash-heavy snot. A titanium hand offered him a bottle of water. He looked up into the delicate face and twinkling almond eyes of the hulking commando who, as a man named Salvatore Marinelli, had been an aimless dog-track gambler and who, as a woman named Sally Mae, had found renewal in organic gardening and ethical bank robbery.

"Yeah, suck it down," said Sally Mae, winking playfully.

All up and down Sunset Boulevard police struggled to maintain order, laying down magnesium flares, explaining to a sinewy bleach blonde in head-to-toe Fendi that, her claims to the Jif peanut butter fortune notwithstanding, she'd have to wait this out with the rest of them. "We're all even now, bitch."

Up ahead a family abandoned their Subaru, father hauling suitcases, mother carrying a wailing infant, their little boy holding his toy lightsaber at the ready, like he might protect them all. His mother reached to cover his eyes as, tearing through the traffic just behind them, came a man wearing only an IKEA bag with holes cut for his arms and head. He squeezed his scrotum like it was a clown horn, yelling *"Honk! Honk!"* as he weaved among the cars. People briefly forgot their predicament, stretching up their phones, flooding the already overloaded satellite system with Instagram shots of his bouncing septuagenarian genitalia. Then the air stilled before rushing up the escarpment where the fires roared ever hotter, ever higher. Carrey looked across the street to the Brentwood Inn. Its trysting residents were visible in the windows, some hurriedly dressing, placing calls to the loved ones they'd been betraying just moments before, a few staring horrified down Sunset as a jet of purple propane flames shot up from the street like it was a giant Bunsen burner. A shock wave rolled through the cars.

"It's the gas mains," said Willow, a West Virginia trucker's daughter who'd joined the marines for college money, had twice saved her unit in Fallujah before losing her right leg to an IED, and joined the Daughters after the medical bills bankrupted her family.

Chunks of flaming asphalt rained down on the Humvee's roof.

"Shit," said Carla, a strikingly beautiful black woman, a sergeant's daughter and West Point graduate who started each morning reciting lines from the *Iliad* while doing a hundred one-armed chin-ups. The loss of her left arm to an Afghan mortar attack had ended her combat career and plunged her into a clinical depression. She'd met Bathsheba on Twitter, had found her will to live restored by the younger woman's theory that they could still serve America's spirit by preparing for its political system's inevitable self-destruction. "They're all gonna go."

Agonized screams, people burning in their cars, seeding chaos and havoc. Those with enough horsepower made for the median strip, the sidewalks. A Ford pickup on monster wheels knocked over a series of parking meters like bowling pins. Carla joined the demolition derby, slamming hard into a Kia just ahead of them, issuing commands.

"Bathsheba. Flash grenade. Right between the Yukon and that Sentra."

Carrey watched Bathsheba pull the pin free with her teeth, admired the juxtaposition of her soft, pink lips on the dark military steel, the carefree grace with which she lobbed the grenade from the side window.

"We prefer nonlethal measures," said Bathsheba to Carrey as they made their break. "Saw enough death in the desert wars." She peppered a stubborn Mercedes with rubber slugs from a 12-gauge, shattering its back windshield as Carla gunned the Hummer up on the Kia's hood, crushing the car to foil as they rolled onto Kenter.

"Christ!" said Carrey, afraid, confused. "What are you doing?"

"Strictly speaking?" said Sally Mae. "This is a kidnapping."

"In the middle of a fire?"

"Gates open, doors unlocked. We never let a good crisis go to waste."

"Why me?"

"'Cause we like you, Jim. We really like you."

"You kidnapped me because you like me?"

"We've found that, if done right, kidnapping can be a positive experience for everyone," said Bathsheba. "We started with Silicon Valley guys as a way of financing ourselves, keeping pace with the latest in prosthetics while also protesting big tech's ceaseless predation on our privacy and dignity."

"It felt right at first, but they got crazy tedious," said Carla, swerving to avoid a Volvo. "Big entitled babies. They start screaming the moment you take them. So you gotta duct-tape their mouths, which triggers bullying memories. Then they start shaking and pissing themselves."

"So you gotta hog-tie them, and that just makes it worse 'cause guys on the higher end of the spectrum hate being touched," said Sally Mae. "Some got so anxious they couldn't perform for us."

"Perform for you?"

"After capitalism eats itself, we'll have to rebuild," said Bathsheba. "For this we'll need good seed. A man like you can plant that seed."

With these words a twanging boner took form beneath his bathrobe. Trying to keep his head in the apocalypse, he thought of his Brentwood neighbors, soon to be forced from their estates. Where would they all stay, when every five-star hotel was booked? There were stories, in years past, of people checking into the Ramada Inn, fighting over slivers of melon and tiny croissants at the continental breakfast. A sobering thought, and one that had its desired effect, his arousal subsiding as Kenter became Bundy; then they turned onto San Vicente, charging over the median strip of burning coral trees toward the Brentwood Country Club.

The Humvee roared up a craggy access lane, then onto the course, kicking up chunks of highly valuable earth as it churned up the fairway.

"This'll get us clear," said Carla. "Then it's back roads to Topanga."

"Topanga?"

"We've got a safe house there."

They joined a slow-moving convoy of SUVs that had smashed through the club's chain-link fence from San Vicente, now a vein of fire.

Carrey pressed his face against the window—

FOUNDED IN 1947, said the club's greeting sign, before vanishing into the flames. Ash and embers murmurating in the ruby sky. They passed a Buick SUV, its chrome rims amber with reflected fire. A redheaded girl in the back seat recognized Carrey and started waving excitedly. Her guilelessness was touching. He replied by curling the corners of his mouth toward his eyes, then arching his eyebrows up at a sinister angle that grew and grew until the girl recognized this as the face of the Grinch and lost all fear of fires in her giggling. They ripped across putting greens, forded an anemic stream, drove, finally, past a sand trap where someone was still golfing, trying, again and again, to smack his ball up onto the green, to complete his game. Carrey craned to see the maniac, recognizing him as his manager of twenty long years, Al Spielman II, seemingly at war with the earth itself, smacking, cursing, each swing just burying the ball deeper into the sand.

"Wait, I know that guy."

"What guy?"

"That guy."

"There's no guy."

"Stop the car!" said Carrey, who for all their differences still cared for Spielman, wished him well.

"You seem to misunderstand the captor-captive power dynamic," said Carla, pulling clear of the trap, leaving Carrey to watch as a black smoke curtain billowed across the fairway, erasing poor Al from sight.

"We change," said Sally Mae, setting her titanium hand on Carrey's shoulder, the mighty woman's empathy so deep, it seemed that he could feel it flowing through her alloy fingers. "Sometimes we do leave people behind."

The radio crackled to life, a warped static that surged and subsided, fragmented and re-formed, over and over, metamorphosing, each time, toward the sweetest music Carrey had ever heard, notes whose healing power surpassed even that of the sacred solfeggio tones he had piped into his hyperbaric chamber.

"Change the frequency," said Bathsheba, and Willow did, but the music reappeared, as if paired to the vision that now appeared in the western sky, a single shining disk.

It seemed, at first, a star magnified by a raindrop on a window. Except for how playfully it flitted along the pattern of a perfectly equilateral triangle. And how much larger it was, even in the distance, than any normal star. How its light didn't glimmer so much as pulse.

"What's that?" asked Bathsheba, pointing up.

"Drone?" guessed Willow.

"That's a giant fuckin' drone."

"Maybe a weather balloon?"

"What are you, Operation Blue Book?" said Carrey. "That's a fucking UFO. Cyborg commando women and fires and calls from my dead dad and now a fucking UFO? Who's doing this?"

"Who's doing what?"

"Ignore him. Just drive."

"It could be TPG," mused Carrey.

"Who's TPG?"

"TPG owns CAA. And they own my digital essence. And probably yours. They got a hundred giant mainframes out in the desert. This could easily be happening in one of them."

"A computer simulation?"

"Why not?"

"'Cause we just pulled you from a burning house, asshole," said Carla. "We're real goddamn people. People who've suffered and lost and been changed by suffering and loss."

"Our pain proves that we're real," said Bathsheba.

"Ever feel the limbs you lost?" asked Carrey.

"Don't go there."

"But you do, right? Phantom pain. In legs and arms that have been gone for years. Sometimes people feel things that aren't there."

"Give him another injection, Bathsheba."

"I actually think he's making sense."

Carrey's iPhone vibrated in his pocket.

"Gimme that," said Sally Mae, then saw the caller's name.

"It's Nic Cage," she announced. "Should we let him take it?"

"I dunno," said Bathsheba. "He reinforces oppressive tenets of systemic patriarchy."

"Actually I think he's hot," said Carla. "And his deeply expressionistic acting perfectly captures the madness of our age. It's no mistake that his technique draws from Germany in the twenties. He's a seer."

"I more than agree," said Willow. "Cage is like the Chuck Yeager of the dramatic arts, breaking through barriers once deemed impassable."

"All right, all right," said Carrey. "Can I have my phone please?"

"You're a goddamn hostage," said Willow. "We'll control the communications."

"I dunno," said Carrey as Cage rang to voice mail. "If TPG's buying up digital essences, they probably got Cage's and they'll just keep torturing us until we take the call. They'll throw awful things at us. They'll take away the people we love and—"

"Give him the phone," said Sally Mae as Cage called again. "He's spiraling."

"Fine," said Carla. "Put him on speaker. And no dicking around."

So Sally Mae accepted the call, flooding the Humvee with the atonal horror of Nicolas Cage singing gaily from the beloved Christmas carol "Do You Hear What I Hear?"

"Way up in the sky, Little Lamb! Do you see what I see?"

"Nic?"

"A star, a star, dancing in the night!"

"Yeah, we see it," said Carrey, eyeing the spacecraft. "We're all looking right up at it."

"I've seen this before, man! In my Malibu Memory Retrieval."

"I know, Nic. I was there."

"Where are you now?"

"Right now? I'm with the Daughters of Anomie."

"The feminist commandos? Fucking cool!"

"Yeah, they're all right," said Carrey. "Anyway they're kidnapping me, we're going to Topanga."

"Shya, you'll never make it," said Cage. "Topanga Canyon's a kiln. You don't belong up there unless you're fucking ceramic. And this flying saucer? I know these guys. I've seen their gross snaky faces. They've been following me across the globe, I bought ten houses to get away from these squirmy motherfuckers, but they just kept showing up. I spent so much dough refurnishing. It really stank."

"Ugh," said Bathsheba. "It's all about him."

"Take that back!" spat Cage. "Whoever you are, you take that back!"

"I won't."

"Look, I'm known for playing the reluctant hero, but don't think you can kick me around. Shit's about to get"—Cage inhaled then on his end of the phone, for his own reasons, struck five dramatic and angular poses before booming operatically—"RAAAAAWWW! And the government won't listen to me 'cause apparently buying a black-market meteorite puts you on some kind of fucking list. So I haven't chosen this, okay? This is a weight that's been thrust upon me. Crushingly . . ." His voice quavered, softening the hearts of the Daughters of Anomie. "Come to me, Jimmy," Cage concluded. "All other roads lead to death."

A burning knot of palm fronds fell onto the windshield.

"Where are you, Nic?"

"At your house up in Malibu."

"Why?"

"You said I could stay here."

"When?"

"Last month."

"I meant for a day or two."

"Yeah? Well, necessity is the motherfucker of invention, man. Come to Malibu. Take the old Pining Path to Santa Monica, then drive up the beach from there."

"What's the Pining Path?" asked Bathsheba.

"A system of back roads to the beach," said Carrey, who had taken this route during his brief but joyous affair with Pamela Anderson in the summer of 1996. "Lovers used them during the days of the morality code, to avoid being seen as they left town."

"The tide's coming in now," said Cage. "The water will keep you safe. It's your only option."

"Topanga's burning," confirmed Willow, checking fire feeds on Twitter.

"Then we don't have a choice," said Sally Mae.

"Hurry," said Cage. "And Godspeed."

So they drove down the fairway, past the blazing clubhouse, out through the smoldering front gardens. Then they turned onto Baltic and took the old Pining Path, weaving through neighborhoods of frightened people hosing down their lawns, gathering all their valuables. Soon they reached the Santa Monica Pier, planks and pilings straining under hundreds of evacuees. Medics triaged burn cases; restaurants handed out meals. The famous Ferris wheel was empty but still spinning, purple neon slicing through the smoke. They muscled for a mile along the Pacific Coast Highway, then, up ahead, saw the rear edge of the Topanga fires. Even Willow, who'd killed seventeen during the battle of Fallujah, gasped to see the hills all garish tangerine. "It looks like a napalm strike," she said.

The traffic was locked all down the highway, forcing them on foot. They cleared out of the Humvee and walked onto the beach, trudging heavy with weapons and ammo, past stray dogs and horses, soaring palms burning like torches atop the escarpment, lighting their way.

Then, amid a city in grievous pain, struggling against the rising surf, body strained beyond capacity, Carrey collapsed of exhaustion. So Sally Mae, who as a free safety for Staten Island University could bench-press four hundred pounds, scooped him up. He wrapped his arms around her neck, felt her augmented breast against his cheek. He closed his eyes, drifting into sleep for just a moment before startling—

"Georgie?" he gasped.

"She's safe. She's in Puerto Rico with Lin-Manuel Miranda."

"How do you know that?"

"I follow both their Snapchats. Now relax."

Then the firelight refracted off the woman's titanium prosthetics, into Carrey's dilated pupils, stretching and feathering into full-grown angel's wings.

—

Just outside Malibu, they saw what had stopped the northbound traffic—a sixty-car wreck where the canyons ran nearest to the sea. And as the sirens screamed in climax, an Exxon tanker truck gave up an eardrum-blistering blast, gas flames vipering in all directions, engulfing, once again, a casino bus dense with carbonized bodies frozen in struggle, mouths agape midshriek, faces twisted in pain, hands seized in clawing actions. There'd been a rush to the ocean; the strongest had made it to the rocks at the top of the beach and died there, in a pile. The rising surf had cleared a sliver of safe passage just beneath it, wet sand defying flames. And here the sea carried away the dead, accountants, plumbers, schoolteachers, and artists, breaking waves turning them to common slurry. Carrey clung to Sally Mae as she carried him over the surf, seeing people from his past among the cremains as the waves rolled in and took them away.

There, curled in a tight U, in a khaki suit and brown tie, he saw his uncle Jim, for whom he'd been named, a jeweler who, for his Catholic confirmation, had given him a penknife engraved with an ancient saying, THIS TOO SHALL PASS AWAY.

The surf rolled in, pulled away—

He saw, half buried in hot pants and a star-spangled tank top circa 1989, the early fitness guru Richard Simmons, hands clutching a bag of powdered-sugar Donettes.

The surf rolled in, pulled away—

Another body, eyes pure fear, a platinum wig dangling from bobby pins, Helena San Vicente, tossed by the tide, and then swept away.

Carrey's old faith now rose over all later existential musings, his lips suddenly making prayers like the nuns had taught him, "*Hail Mary full of Grace . . .* ," something deep inside still believing that these words could conjure real magic, could summon the virgin mother of an Aryan man-god to protect and guide him. He prayed with tragic hope, at once telling himself that the Daughters of Anomie were the avatars of angels and wondering why his mind was wired to believe in a soul. He prayed not once but many times, as Sally Mae carried him over the heartbreaking sand.

The Malibu Colony's lights came into view, among them those of his own house, where Nicolas Cage, standing watch on the second-story sundeck, sighted them all through binoculars. "Dare forward!" he cried, thrusting his hard-won medieval sword toward the heavens. "All that you were sure of, you must now leave behind. The hour of contact is upon us. Time to see all sides of the diamond."

CHAPTER 14

The patio was fringed with razor wire, piled with sandbags.

Carrey entered his house exhausted, stomach cramping from the miles-long walk, throat and lungs burning from smoke inhalation, but he would find no immediate peace. A crate of Uzis sat on the kitchen island. Over in his breakfast nook, Sean Penn, Kelsey Grammer, and Gwyneth Paltrow were all seated Indian-style, struggling to assemble a shoulder-fired missile system whose many components lay scattered around a crate marked ARMED FORCES OF ANGOLA.

"Stinger reprogrammable microprocessor is a dual-channel ultraviolet tracking seeker and proportional navigational guidance missile system," Gwyneth read from the instruction manual, sipping a glass of rosé. "The spectral discrimination of the seeker detector material, when super-cooled by the argon gas in the battery coolant unit . . ." She searched among the scattered components, then, with a playful smile, picked up a tiny steel bulb, wondering aloud, "Is that this thingamajigger?"

"No," said Willow. "That's the oscillation modulator." She walked over and joined them, taking parts from the pile, expertly snapping them together, making more progress in a few minutes than they had all night. "Where're the rockets?"

"In the bathtub," said Gwyneth.

"What?" said Carrey. "The fuck are you doing?"

"We're preparing for battle," said Kelsey Grammer, wearing an outfit entirely stolen from the 20th Century Fox wardrobe department: a Napoleonic overcoat, a World War II–era steel battle helmet bearing four Patton-esque stars. And something of Patton's spirit possessed him as he looked up at Carrey and, borrowing from Kubrick's *Full Metal Jacket*, snarled, "Why don't you jump on the team and come on in for the big win!?"

"That's good," said Carrey. "You got that down."

"Why, thank you!" said Kelsey, relieved. "I felt good running the line in my head but—until you hear it out loud?—you just don't know."

"We were watching the fires with Natchez when his place burned down," explained Sean Penn, wearing Vietnam battle fatigues. "His third eye saw something his other two couldn't handle. Guy's on heavy benzos, not taking it real good. He's been making the same sound for two days now."

"*Mmmm . . . !*" groaned Natchez, catatonic on the sofa.

It was now clear to Carrey that Nicolas Cage had exceeded all reasonable definitions of beach home borrowing; had, rather, effected something far closer to wartime requisitioning. Someone had thrown a bale of razor wire on the daybed. Crates of hand grenades were piled atop the dining room table, a flamethrower leaned precariously against a thirty-pound gasoline tank. A bank of laptops purred on the kitchen island, a number of half-eaten vegan chicken wings scattered among them.

"Fuck you do to my house, Nic?"

"Like John the Baptist," said Cage. "I prepare the way."

"What's this gunk on all the windows?"

"Silicone shatterproofing."

"Why would the glass shatter?"

"'Cause we buried landmines in the side yard."

"Fucking hell, Nic! You know I'm anti-violence."

"Even Arjuna had to heed the call."

"Don't you throw the Bhagavad Gita at me!"

"*Mmmm!*" again Natchez moaned, like a bear many days in a trap. Carrey turned to see the stricken guru's eyes bulging in their sockets. "*Mmmm!*"

"Something in there's trying to get out," said Cage, then turned to the Daughters of Anomie. "So, you're the leftist commandos?"

"Ecoterrorists," said Carla. "It's a distinction with a difference. We could sack Exxon's world headquarters with the hardware you got here, and probably have some left for at least a raid on Monsanto. Where'd you get it?"

"El Chapo," said Sean Penn. "He owed me a favor. What's your story?"

"I was One Hundred First Airborne, Korangal Valley. Willow and Sally Mae here were both marine snipers, eighty-seven kills between them. And Bathsheba ruled half of

Baghdad before the scales fell from her eyes. How 'bout you boys?"

"I once played a two-star general," said Kelsey Grammer. "It was primarily a boardroom comedy, but *Variety* said I projected real authority."

"I was in *Thin Red Line*, *Taps*, and *Casualties of War*," said Sean Penn, stubbing out a cigarette on his forearm. "Took basic training for all those roles."

"And you were great in them," said Carrey. "Powerful performances."

"I wouldn't know," said Penn. "I can't watch myself."

"The point is we'll need to: we can hold our own," said Cage. "And I've spent the last year in deep research, monitoring transmissions from the Boötes Void."

"Fuck's the Boötes Void?" asked Sally Mae.

"It's the Great Nothing," said Carrey. "I've seen this on YouTube. It shouldn't be there. And yet—there it isn't. A massive stretch of empty galaxy."

"Yeah," said Cage, eyebrows popping wildly. "Or at least that's what we've thought! But now we know the emptiness was just a ruse, the stealth technology of an awesomely advanced civilization. They've been transmitting information, it's just so highly encrypted it flows right through matter. These are the bastards who've been following me my whole fucking life . . ." His voice broke with pain. "I fought these reptiloids a thousand times! Across eons and multiple lives. Not an eternal recurrence, naw, that'd be too kind. As a kinda torture. Along the way, I had a pretty good film career."

His tears, at least, seemed real, a description maybe of his frustration with typecasting or maybe a sincere reaction to this story he'd adopted as a personal faith while all other faiths crumbled. Carla felt real empathy for this man, for all men, as a silly species of wayward children playing at specialness.

"Nic's last claim, to past lives, is not scientifically verifiable," said Gwyneth Paltrow. "But the rest checks out. We've captured the transmissions. Amazingly complex. They cloak themselves by bending light. Only a dynamic recursive neural algorithm can unbend it. Thankfully, I've learned to write those while running Goop."

"You learned algorithms from running a lifestyle website?" said Carrey.

"I was motivated by the website," said Paltrow. "I learned at MIT."

"You went to MIT?"

"Absolutely," said Paltrow. "You can do anything online. But that's unimportant. What matters is this: the hour of contact has arrived."

With a sound of tearing Velcro, Cage produced a remote control from inside his trench coat. He cut the house lights with one click and opened the living room's retracting ceiling to the night sky with another. Then the Oregon ecoterrorists and the Hollywood actors gathered close in the darkness, gazing up in wonder at the glowing orb.

"Maybe they're friendly," said Carrey, "like neighbors coming over with a fruit basket?"

"'Friendly' is a word they forgot long ago!" said Cage, doing an Elvis-inspired karate kick. "Gwyneth, you wanna show them?"

Gwyneth Paltrow logged in to the computers, explaining, "I'm tasking a satellite loaned to me by my good friend Elon with scanning the space around that disk. Don't be shy. Come closer."

They gathered around her monitor. The screen filled with an image of the sky above them. "This is our world as it currently seems," said Gwyneth Paltrow. Then, with a flurry of keystrokes, the image changed drastically. There was no longer just one glowing object, but many, all around it, legions of light balls hovering right over their heads.

"This is our world as it *actually* is. We count over five hundred of these craft. More arriving by the hour, gathering over Tokyo, Sydney, Paris. And almost every other major city on the globe."

She zoomed in on one ship, the images, at resolution, showing its perfectly streamlined form, beyond any human power of construction.

"Who are they?" asked Carrey, voice suddenly boyish.

Again from the sofa came the agonized *mmmm* sound, formed by a psychic landslide within the person of Natchez Gushue who, whole body seizing, slowly extruded the word of his horror: "*Monsters.*"

Then, in a great failing pulse, the images of the saucers dissolved from the screens, leaving behind just an unremarkable night sky.

"They know they've been seen," said Bathsheba.

The next morning Carrey woke early and lay in bed, scrolling through his iPhone.

Twitter reported news of UFOs over twenty major cities.

NORAD had scrambled fighter planes up and down both coasts. The pope was broadcasting a Prayer for Peaceful Encounter from the Vatican, where theologians worked furiously to reconcile scripture with the visitation, debating whether the spaceships were piloted by angels or demons. The Scientologists had no such quarrels. For them the saucers were ultimate validation. They were promoting a viral Instagram tile that said RON WAS RIGHT and calling senior members to their headquarters in San Jacinto, where a neon-lit UFO landing circle had been constructed, a buffet of champagne and truffled mac and cheese laid out, a thousand chairs arranged for an outdoor screening of *Battlefield Earth*. And while Carrey could accept every mad bit of this news—he was, after all, a man who had once spent many nights trying to free his soul from its presumed residence in his upper thorax—he was disturbed by what followed. An ad consumed his screen—

It started with trombones playing sliding scales, honking each note like a sneeze as the camera went close on a familiar nose. A nose dripping mucus, and owned by a digitally perfect Marlon Brando, set in eclipse lighting to suggest the character of Kurtz from *Apocalypse Now*. He blew hard into a Kleenex, opened it to ponder its contents, then turned to address the viewer directly.

"The horror! THE HORROR! The horror—*of nasal congestion*. I'm Marlon Brando. I did some pretty good acting when I was alive. Many considered me the best. But I'd have been even greater if I'd had Mucinex."

With the popping of a pill he was instantly healed, cheeks in high color, song welling, mightily, from where only phlegm had been just moments before.

He took a deep breath, turned, velvet curtains parting behind him to reveal a packed Broadway theater, everyone cheering and throwing roses. He gracefully picked one up, held it to his nose, smelled it. Then a cut from Brando to a bottle of Mucinex in its own tiny spotlight at stage left, a single rose landing perfectly in front of it as the ad cut to video of light spheres dancing over Jakarta, riot police swinging billy clubs, brutally repressing a crowd of ten thousand terrified souls. Carrey pocketed his phone, slightly more depressed by the digital whoring of Marlon Brando than the plight of the ten thousand Jakartans.

He walked downstairs.

Gwyneth Paltrow had taken the guest suite. Sean Penn and Carla were sleeping on air mattresses, Natchez Gushue and Willow on the living room couches. Carrey had been trying to cut down on caffeine for several years but now that struggle, like so many others, seemed part of an abandoned world.

He made himself a coffee, stepped out onto the porch.

Kelsey Grammer and Bathsheba had drawn morning guard shift, but somewhere along the way had traded vigilance for wonder. Their Uzis lay forgotten in the sand as, holding hands more like schoolchildren than lovers, they stared awestruck beyond the waves where the front line of an alien armada hovered little more than a mile overhead, barely disturbing the ocean's surface, emitting a rose-gold glow against the water, this light falling brilliantly over every grain of sand on the beach, seeming to calm the waves and the fires in the hills. It filled Carrey with an abiding peace as it washed over his face, accompanied by the sweetest sounds he'd ever heard, the hovering spaceships emitting a divine harmonic that passed right through you in healing waves, freeing you from all fear, all shame, all dread . . .

Carrey felt the dissolving of an inner weight that had grown so heavy he'd forgotten it was there. He felt a deep and connective presence in this moment, no dissonance between soul and body. It was a harmony so totally consuming he hardly noticed the animals lined up all down the beach. Horses set free from Malibu stables. Zebras and ostriches escaped from private zoos. House cats and dogs, birds flown down from the hills: all had gathered to the shore, great and small necks alike craning up at the armada, chirping, braying, eyes closed, like ur-beasts beseeching Noah or retirees on morphine at an assisted living center, depending on one's view of the arrival.

"The light pleases them," said Kelsey. "It pleases us, too."

"It's like Prozac." Bathsheba laughed. "And late June."

Carrey angled his head to receive a maximum dose of the magical light. He thought of the Atlanteans, vanishing into otherworldly glows.

"The animals aren't afraid," said Bathsheba. "Why should we be?"

They walked up the beach, followed by paparazzi angling for dream shots of celebrities, animals, fires, and flying saucers all at once, barking inane questions: "Hey Jim, whaddya think of the flying saucers!?"

"Is this really what you want to be doing at the end?" asked Carrey.

"What else would we do?"

The images were selling for so much money they didn't stop to consider that money would soon be worthless. They flashed away as the actors and ecoterrorists strolled past the Malibu Colony homes, patio pools, and hot tubs become wildlife refuges. Stray llamas sipped from Sting's waterfall, while a family of emperor penguins bobbled and splashed in his Jacuzzi. "You're ruining the splendor," snapped Kelsey Grammer to the paparazzi. "And you're harassing these noble animals."

"Those guys bothering you?" boomed an avuncular voice from down the beach.

Carrey turned and saw Tom Hanks. Tom Hanks flanked by a trio of private firefighters and a duo of burly security guards, yes. But still: Tom Hanks. It was impossible to hear him and not feel some restored faith in human goodness.

"Mornin'!" said Kelsey. "And a fine one, at that!"

"It's like the first dawn!" said Hanks, gesturing to the animals lined up down the beach, basking in the sweet light, the alien armada just beyond them. "Or the last one. Either way I feel like a billion bucks. Hey, is that Jimbo?"

"Hey Tom," said Carrey, warmly. "You stuck it out?"

"Fire department got overrun in Mandeville." Hanks shrugged to acknowledge his extensive private bodyguard. "Had to fight it out ourselves."

"Private security is the death of democracy," said Bathsheba. "A return to the Hobbesian state and an affront to the people's dignity."

"Who's that?" said Hanks.

"That's Bathsheba," said Carrey. "She's been radicalized."

"Good for her," said Hanks. "Wanna come have breakfast?"

Here was another major star, an actor of his caliber, and in other ways beyond him. Carrey had long marveled at Hanks's mastery of the industry, his easy sashays down corridors of power. Had Tom Hanks sold his essence, too? If so, that was at once reassuring and disconcerting. On the one hand, it meant it was probably the right business play. On the other—

who was the star here? Because with Cage involved, and Penn and Paltrow and Kelsey Grammer, and all the Daughters of Anomie (who could easily be Millennial actresses unknown to him despite massive Instagram followings), well, that suggested many harvested essences had been smooshed together, the film a headcheese of digital personas. And as Carrey had read no contracts, had essentially traded his spirit for the promise of a nap, well—true horror now fell over him, deepening as they walked to Hanks's sprawling veranda—what if they'd given him a supporting role?

"Honey, we got guests," yelled Hanks to his wife, Rita Wilson. "It's Jimbo and Kelsey. And this one," he pointed to Bathsheba, closed his eyes. "Bathsheba! Can we get you guys something? Coffee? Mimosas?"

"A cappuccino would be delightful," said Kelsey Grammer.

"Mimosa," said Bathsheba.

"Jim? *Jim?*"

"Coffee . . . ," said Carrey, absently. He wasn't paying attention, was entranced by laughter coming from down the veranda. His heart raced; he felt rare nerves as he turned to see, sitting on a wrought-iron patio sofa, filming the orbs with a digital camera, a titan of his industry, eternal wunderkind, father of the modern blockbuster, and now, undeniably, a prophet of some kind—Steven Spielberg.

Spielberg looked up, face wild with joy, turning the camera on Carrey as he approached, whispering like he was narrating a film.

"And the Lord said, 'I will destroy man whom I have created from the face of the earth; both man, and beast, and the creeping things, and the fowls of the air, for it repenteth me that I have made them . . ."

His camera went close on Carrey's face as the star surveyed the armada.

They spanned the horizon now, a thousand ships, maybe more. As the optics zoomed, Carrey felt all existential panic subside. Where was he? He was where he'd always dreamed of being, before Steven Spielberg's camera. Planted, fixed, affirmed, not just by its presence, but for how its aperture overrode the chaos of the world, fixed the scene, the moment. He imagined himself not as he was but as he appeared in Spielberg's eye, and in this imagining felt possessed of definite form. "Enlivened." That was the word. And there was another, just beyond it: "completed." Reality and fantasy had converged, almost entirely, and here he was, in the viewfinder of the great secular mythmaker. Enlivened, yes. Completed. No need to search for words, to wow with comic genius. He'd prepared for this, in hours of late-night TV watching. He was ready.

"Genesis meets Revelation," said Carrey, nodding to the gathered animals, the iridescent ships. "The beginning completes the end."

"Beautiful," said Spielberg, then, with a giddy chuckle, "And isn't it also possible, Jim, that the end offers a new beginning?"

"I've never seen you so happy."

"My dreams have come to life."

"Is there any difference between life and dreams anymore?" asked Carrey. "Have you seen this Brando commercial?"

"Mucinex gave the grandkids fifty million," Spielberg said ruefully. "We've been posthuman for a while, I guess. Doesn't matter now. Come see."

Carrey sat and peered through the lens, zoomed in close

on the nearest ship. It was so perfectly formed. Spielberg panned along the craft. No joints, seams, or rivets. A slender miracle radiating light.

"It's like a Brancusi."

"I don't know what Brancusi is," said Carrey. "But I'm sure it's very nice."

"I'm just saying that they must value beauty to make such gorgeous machines." He looked to his wife, Kate Capshaw, approaching with a tray of her famous challah bread. "Oh wow. Here it comes!"

"Challah!" boomed Tom Hanks, taking a piece of the warm bread from the tray. Spielberg pulled back for a two-shot as Hanks handed Carrey his coffee, then settled into the chair just beside his and, clearly playing to reclaim what must have been a deeply gratifying monopoly on the master's lens, said—

"We've had darn good lives! We did darn good stuff! We're all flying down over the Hudson River now. We're coasting past the moon in a wounded craft, low on oxygen. But I'd rather be here, with you guys, with Kate's warm challah bread, than in that bunker with Leo and Toby and those lingerie models." He spoke with a lump in his throat. "Rather be here, tossing around a Nerf football. Frying up some burgers and hot dogs. Lighting sparklers. With Jimbo. And Kelsey. Steve, Kate, Bathsheba. Than running from this thing. Whatever it is. Wherever it's from." He fought back tears. "Just want to say that."

"They're beyond our knowing," said Rita Wilson, rubbing his arm. "It's okay."

Spielberg's camera lingered on them: portrait of a husband and a wife.

"I never expected humanity was really gonna matter very much," said Carrey. The camera panned to him. "To look for any meaning in it is a ridiculous thing. The vastness just laughs at you. How's it go? Matter makes up three percent of the universe. The rest is dark energy or dark matter or whatever? They don't know. They were never gonna know. Things grow and die. Fungus on a tree. Lavender in a field. What's the meaning of lavender in a field? I'm okay with the meaninglessness. I'm okay without meaning."

"But we made our own meaning, didn't we?" said Hanks. "We gave it to each other as a gift."

"I see what you're saying," said Carrey, with a shrug.

Spielberg pulled back for a low-angle two-shot of the A-list stars, neither wanting to argue, each appreciating the other's viewpoint.

"Why didn't we all get together sooner?" said Hanks. "While there was time?"

"Ask TPG," said Carrey.

"Who's TPG?" asked Rita Wilson.

"TPG owns CAA," said Kate Capshaw.

Spielberg panned down to the silver tray, where the crumbs of his wife's challah bread danced ever more wildly as the spacecraft's tones grew louder. Hanks turned toward the sea, eyes flaring with fright, watching as the ships moved. Then, with the others, he looked back to the table, where, amid the music, all the sweet bread crumbs had self-arranged into a perfect, vibrating geometric form, which awed them even before, in a gasp, Spielberg identified the pattern.

"It's the Tree of Life."

Then the bread crumbs scattered into disarray as the alien

harmonics met interference from nearby speakers, a manic voice booming:

"CHECK ONE-TWO! CHECK! YO—YOU AIN'T GOT THE ANSWERS! YOU AIN'T GOT THE ANSWERS! EVERYBODY, LISTEN UP."

The animals let out startled wails.

"I AM THE ALIENS' EMISSARY TO ALL MAN-KIND!"

"Who is that?" said Jim.

"Kanye," said Tom Hanks.

They all left the veranda, plodded up the sand alongside the paparazzi to find Kanye West standing on the sundeck of his sleek modern beach house, wearing a pair of silver-mirrored contact lenses and a titanium crown set with emeralds in the form of an Adidas logo. He preened and posed for the news drones, stretching his arms up toward the sky, as if to bless and welcome the alien fleet. Spielberg, Hanks, and Carrey drew little more interest than a group of passing llamas as, from inside the house—preceded by full camera crews from FOX, CNN, TMZ, and E!—came Kim Kardashian. Wearing a pearl tiara and a silver bustier with flying-saucer breast cups, she held a frightened child in her arms, caressing him as Kanye played to his iPhone camera, livestreaming to the billions for whom he was, by that late and raving hour, earth's most viewed extraterrestrial news correspondent.

"You need not be afraid! They speak to me in supernatural verses! I am one with their jam!" said Kanye, tapping his titanium crown. "This is what's happening!" He gestured to the frightened baby squirming in Kim Kardashian's arms. "The alien angels hath laid with Kim. They filled her womb up with the Star Child!"

Kim Kardashian held the baby up for the cameras. He wore a gold lamé onesie from the Baby K child's clothing line of which, at the age of one, he'd been elected CEO by a unanimous board vote. The company had just been sold to Qatari investors. The baby, now one and a half, was worth $700 million.

"Why were you chosen for this?" asked the CNN reporter.

And all prior history and logic felt to Jim Carrey like a garbled dream as Kanye explained, "In another dimension I'm a dodecahedron named Cake. And I was gonna kill the aliens, but I didn't. So they honored me here. Told me I'm the Archangel and Kim's the Star Mother. Gave us the Star Baby."

"It's very humbling to say the least," said Kim Kardashian.

"How did they give you the baby?" asked the CNN reporter.

"They entwined our DNA," said Kanye. "Synthetically."

"How did they contact you?"

"They called me."

"From where?"

"Palm Beach."

"I thought they spoke to you through your crown?"

Then Kanye West, drawing upon his full powers as a freshly minted Archangel, commanded the flying saucers to disintegrate the CNN reporter in his place. When that didn't happen, he burst into tears.

"These are higher intelligences," said Spielberg. "They'll either love us unconditionally or coldly annihilate us. One thing is sure. They don't explain themselves; they don't hold press conferences."

A light drizzle began to fall.

The glow from the ships passing overhead brightened as all cell phones and televisions—any screen that streamed data—pulsed to life, all receiving the same broadcast.

It began with a title screen, A BRIEF INTRODUCTION TO PLANETARY CANCELLATION, which dissolved to a live shot of a figure beyond ethnicity, beyond gender, a taupe-skinned study in pleasing aesthetics, guaranteed to evoke affinities across all cultures. Counter to Spielberg's assurances, Tan Calvin would now explain himself.

"Earth has been one of our most beloved and longest-running programs," said Calvin. "Eden was beautiful, but dull as dog shit. Doldrums! The program wasn't working for us as viewers or for you as characters. We introduced conflict. When Cain bashed Abel's head in, we knew we had something. Of all the spheres, our people tuned in to yours. The fall of Babel was so good we gave it a sequel, this time with twice the towers. Holy wars: of all the programs across all the galaxies, earth was the first to discover that oxymoron. And some would like to watch you atomize one another, but the ratings board, and certain professional codes, won't allow that. And so I'm here. I have come to take you home, and in these remarks I shall inform you of the best practices for a planet in your situation." The rain fell harder as Calvin continued, "I am putting out the wildfires in California to show you that, while mighty beyond imagining, I am kind. Take it as a token of good faith as we conclude this deeply gratifying programming experience."

The spaceships froze above them, a great craft hovering just down the beach, others arrayed in a perfect grid, one every five square miles. And through the mist falling down off the hills, shooting down from every ship with triumphant blasts—blasts like angels' trumpets—came pure beams of the same golden light Carrey had felt that morning but now so much stronger, filling the world as music played from the ships, the same healing frequency but now with definite harmonies, like Barber's "Adagio" raised to a cosmic power healing all wounds in fast time. It soared as the rose-gold shafts thrust down from the spaceships; Tan Calvin imploring—

"Walk into the happy light. Be free, be cleansed. Freedom from concerns. From bills to pay. From grief and sickness. No bodies full of pain. No one to impress. No loss of any kind. Only cleansing light, forgiveness. This is our parting gift to you: eternal aching bliss."

Kim Kardashian, Star Baby in her arms, left sobbing Kanye to be the first human assumed. She kicked off her high heels, jumped off the patio, and, remarkably fleet of foot, she dashed toward the light field, a dozen cameras following. She stepped inside the glow, fell to her knees, and began to moan. Then her moans turned joyous.

And she began to rapture . . .

"She's going up ass first!" said Kelsey Grammer.

It was true, Kim's early ascension was a bit wobbly. But then she learned to work the beam, floated heavenward like a true angel, pressing the Star Baby to her breast, spinning with ecstasy, followed by the cameras that broadcast the moment worldwide; #starmother, #starbaby, and #followthatstar began trending as *Homo sapiens* embraced its own demise. First went the lonely, the empty, the ill—also surprisingly large numbers of those who had seemed to be living perfect lives, but had, in fact, been secretly, totally miserable. Images spawned and multiplied, the rapturees' faces suggesting that not only was this painless, it felt awesome. Within moments, worldwide, millions were rushing for the lights, crowding the Champs-Élysées, prison guards rapturing alongside inmates as orbs hovered over penitentiary yards, whole families ascending from the Rio favelas, disregarding all prior faiths to embrace Calvin as, if not quite a messiah, a reliable manufacturer of miracles.

In Malibu the stars were mesmerized, watching in disbelief as Kim Kardashian hovered thirty yards between the ocean and the saucer. So many were eager to join her, to cast off the millstones of their invented selves. Some raced so fast into the lights that they missed the last piece of Calvin's offer, didn't see how his tongue flickered, lizard-like.

"To those who resist, to them shall be great suffering. Children gnawing at their mothers' entrails. Bodies roasting over slow fires, then bodies eaten raw. Then hunger and cold, all shall know. Horrors not yet seen by man. Until he is no more."

Looking up from the broadcast, Carrey saw Spielberg speaking on his phone.

"Ready the Amblin Twelve. We'll be there in an hour."

"What's the Amblin Twelve?"

"A spacefaring escape pod, Jim," said Spielberg, guiltily. "Beyond a certain point, toward the end, it was the only really fun thing for us billionaires to spend money on."

"Can I come with you?"

"Sorry," said Tom Hanks. "It's a real compact module, and Oprah needs a seat for her emotional-support animal."

"What about throwing around the Nerf ball? What about grilling hot dogs?"

"We'll bring videos of those things. And treasure them,"

said Hanks. "Anyway, it was great brunching with you, finally. Okay, we gotta skedaddle."

"Let them go," said Kelsey Grammer, consolingly, as the Spielbergs and Hankses traipsed down the beach. "Each must meet the end on their own terms."

And, for both men, the sting of exclusion gave way to spinning wonder as other celebrities poured from all parts of the Colony, tearing for the light, decades of auditions and rejections filling all with a fear of failing to make the cut. Lindsay Lohan went up like a kite on an April breeze, crying "Yippee!" before colliding with Diana Ross. Then they grasped hands, steadying each other, maneuvering to accept Keanu Reeves. All linked arms, singing one last crowd-pleasing refrain of Ross's 1970 hit "Reach Out and Touch (Somebody's Hand)," soaring up like skydivers in rewind.

But the greater ecstasy was Kelsey Grammer's.

He walked into the beams with Bathsheba and felt, deep within him, that at last, with this svelte twentysomething commando, he'd found it, pure love. Holding hands, they swirled skyward, and words rose from within Kelsey, truths of love gifted to Juliet by Shakespeare, lines of such beauty that men had forgotten their genders entirely while speaking them at the Globe Theatre, lines that he'd longed to speak since Juilliard but had always been denied him by the strictures of his day.

"My bounty is as boundless as the sea," he said as they daiseyed over the Pacific. "My love as deep; the more I give to thee, the more I have, for both . . . are infinite."

"That's so beautiful," said Bathsheba, tears filled with golden light.

"You really think so?" said Kelsey. "I thought I was pushing."

And then they were Twizzlerized.

Maybe, thought Carrey, this was all Lanny Lonstein's masterpiece.

Or maybe he was in a luxury nuthouse, pissing through a tube. Or maybe he was overdosed in a Vegas hotel, this nightmare but a final blabber of the dying cerebral cortex. The surrounding world offered no explanations, no proof or disproof. It was content, smugly so, to simply be. He recalled a Bible passage about when the stars would fall from the sky, later seeing on YouTube that, indeed, this would happen, the galaxies would spin so far away from one another that all would be cold and dark. What was wilder than that? Or bleaker? Oblivion was coming for them all, worse than any tsar's army. Here, above him, were strong ships leaving port.

Why get fussy about the owners, the destination?

The light pulled him toward it.

The music called, too.

Carrey felt all inner beasts quieting as he dared his foot inside the light field's outer edge, then passed his whole body through. This was real.

Only this.

The little children shooting up like bottle rockets.

The grief-heavy souls struggling up like week-old helium balloons.

All concern was fading now.

The smoldering hillsides, the distant city, sad shadows. The only place was here, the only time now, as he stood on the sand, awaiting his ration of the miraculous. A giddy tickle spread across his every cell as Cher and Dolly Parton whizzed by overhead, both singing Leonard Cohen's "Hallelujah." A deep wanting to join them . . .

And just like that, his feet left the earth.

Weightless with joy, freed of burdensome memories, delighted by happy ones, which became his total awareness. Grilled cheese sandwiches. Chasing a puck across a frozen lake. His mother in high color. Healthy, jolly. Instigating dinner-table food fights. It was understood, when she made her special cherry cheesecake, that half was to be eaten, half to be thrown. Glistening airborne cherries and her melodic laughter, which, he realized now, had become his own. His brother, John, had matured early, was fully developed by age ten; Carrey and his sister Rita would ambush him in the shower, finding him in full pubescent bloom, mortified as they pointed and sang, "*Hair, hair, long beautiful hair . . . !*" Performing in the living room, aged eight, jokes landing, his father turning to the guests, saying, "He's not a ham, he's the whole pig!" Waiting on the balcony of their apartment to see his father driving home his new car, a brown Vauxhall, to Carrey's young eyes a marvel of engineering and achievement; the car in which, one summer, the whole family drove four hundred miles to see the Sleeping Giant, an island in Thunder Bay that looked like a resting Indian chief. Drawing as a boy, cartoons he made, a man called Marvin Muffinmouth. A train to Sudbury, six years old, drawing Marvin Muffinmouth, walking up the aisle of the car, showing Muffinmouth, proudly, to the other riders. The kitchen table where, age two, he'd contorted his face, again and again, resisting a spoonful of pureed cauliflower, sending his family into hysterics, discovering a gift, and a weapon.

You must understand that Jim Carrey and all the others on that beach, they were very happy, meeting better ends than nearly all of the hundred billion souls who'd come and gone before them. Better than death by Spanish steel. Better than most of them deserved. And for Carrey it all grew better still as he heard a voice calling him back. Linda Ronstadt. She was thirty-six again, a Mexican princess. "*Volver, volver,*" she sang, suddenly right beside him, holding his hand. "*Come back, come back,*" she whispered as he laid his head against her chest. As he became, for the first time in decades, entirely unbothered. He was the space of contact between his cheek and Ronstadt's skin. He was Ronstadt's fingers in his hair. He was the music of both their voices, singing "*Volver, volver . . . Come back, come back . . .*"

Then a sharp clawing around his ankle as, down below, on the fifth try, Nicolas Cage, Sean Penn, Willow, and Sally Mae succeeded in lassoing him with two hundred yards of climbing rope. There followed an angry, violent tugging as they yanked him away from his bliss, as if Carrey were an updrafting zeppelin. He resisted, seeing the rope as a slithering boa constrictor, kicking and flailing, struggling mightily back to Ronstadt, toward the candied nothing that lay beyond her embrace.

But finally they landed him, dragged him thrashing from the light field and pinned him down on the sand. "*Linda,*" he bawled, again and again, pained by his broken rapture as they carried him back to his house and laid him out in his bed.

CHAPTER 15

Entering the rapture beam was euphoria, and being yanked out left Carrey's mind frail and fuzzy, able to grasp only the faintest wisps of experience, present and past.

Natchez Gushue's bone-white body bobbing in a bathtub, vertical slashes down the wrists.

The ammonia stench of smelling salts.

A plastic spoon full of macaroni and cheese.

Then some clarity returning: Linda Ronstadt was lying beside him. She'd been watching him sleep, it seemed. He admired her teeth, as he had decades before, the incisors slightly angled in. He'd forgotten this. So much that had once been so precious, he'd completely forgotten.

"What are you?"

"I'm a memory," said Ronstadt. "A remnant, I'm not real."

"Memory's a kind of reality," he said. "Better remembered than forgotten."

It was raining outside. The room smelled like warm caramel and orange blossoms.

"One day," she said, with her impish smile. "One day, if you live long enough, you'll find that more people have forgotten you than still remember you. Maybe at a gas station. Maybe getting coffee. Even those who know you will just know old pictures. You'll be given over to the big forgetting. And free."

His clothes were ragged, soiled. She helped him take off his shirt and curled beside him. She laid her head on his chest, and they fell asleep that way, the rain getting heavier outside. And as they rested, systems around the world failed.

Broadcast booths emptied.

Militaries devised and abandoned plans of defense.

The have-nots shish-kebabed the heads of the haves into grisly totem poles.

Tan Calvin had learned that apocalypse was best composed in counterpoint, the honeyed visions of rapture most powerful when set against stark scenes of civilizations twitching out their last. Time moved along normally for those near the light fields, the billions lining up for miles, drawn to oblivion, but for those who still valued living, it dragged. As mere days seemed to pass in Carrey's Malibu bedroom, savage weeks tore through the wider world. Jim and Linda watched it all on his iPhone, Calvin's planet-ending broadcast streaming on every platform, a sleek video feed set to an otherworldly funeral dirge. It was the greatest show anyone had ever seen.

They saw the vice president of the United States, a smarmy Methodist preacher with the most insincere face to ever disgrace a human skull, announcing his ascendancy to the Oval Office following the casino magnate president's abdication. The casino magnate, said online commenters, had given the aliens America's nuclear codes in exchange for the promise of endless extraterrestrial pussy and a luxury condo development in the Andromeda Galaxy. Pool footage showed the first family rapturing in a private light field, rising up into the ships. The vice president was now in a Cold War bunker, the full Congress behind him. But as he laid his hands on the Bible to take the oath of office, a detachment of marines declared loyalty to a senator from Wisconsin. Automatic gunfire rang out. Blood sprayed across the camera lens. Screams and mauling—

And so like this, earth's final inhabitants were forced not only to watch their own erasure, but to find it totally addictive.

"It could have been so different," said Carrey. "What a big canvas we had to paint on. And this is what we composed?"

Then came a nuclear launch by the Japanese, whose atomic weapons program had been the collapsing world's best-kept secret. But the missiles just skipped off the light fields, some of them bouncing into the sea, others zipping upward, exploding in the thermosphere, a failed display of might that took the rapture from a merely popular product to a sizzlingly hot one. Why fight a man who was impervious to a full-on nuclear attack? And who was offering a painless path to sweet oblivion? Families filled the streets of towns and cities everywhere. Apartment buildings emptied into whistling hollows. The rain fell harder, the sky pulsed ruby beyond the windows.

"I'm hungry," said Carrey. "I've never been hungrier."

The sun grew dim.

He and Ronstadt were eating grilled cheese sandwiches,

watching TMZ drone coverage of Laser Jack Lightning and his followers assaulting a saucer hovering over a Coffee Bean & Tea Leaf in Venice Beach.

The Scientologists, while imperfect, had been more correct about the basic nature of the cosmos than any other religion. They wore magnificent gold spandex bodysuits, woven of a material that blocked out both the rapture light and hostile thetans. They fought with plasma blasters specially developed for them by Raytheon, the only human-made weapons, it seemed, capable of penetrating the light shields. Which really pissed Tan Calvin off.

Thirty seconds into the assault and a ghastly breed of killer robots swarmed out from the saucer, all shooting crimson death rays. The Scientologists were overrun. John Travolta had long ago commissioned a special battle wig for the major role he believed he was destined to play in this intergalactic showdown, a rainbow-strobing, fiber-optic pompadour whose frontal swell was so menacing that its designers had privately dubbed it "hair-o-shima." But even Travolta's hot new look was no match for Calvin's killer robots. Deeming the battle lost, he fled to the waterfront, a wounded man slung over each shoulder. Only Laser Jack Lightning was steadfast. A final close-up showed his leading man's face all courage and ferocity as he blasted away, unyielding, declaring, "*Every part I've played has trained me for this moment!*" He vaporized two of the sentinels, crying exultantly, "*It's beautiful, man!*" grinning from ear to ear in the face of death. "*It's BEAUTIFUL!*" Then in a crimson flash he was gone, broadcast cut to static.

"Why does it have to end this way?" Carrey asked Ronstadt, watching.

"You'd prefer what—a flood?"

"It'd feel more meaningful. To me, at least."

"It's all accidents, Jim. The whole world, the whole universe. A life. Accidents. It's not personal, not any of it. If it wasn't this, it'd be some asteroid. Or the heat death of the sun."

She smiled, kindly.

"It's ending," he whispered, resting his head on her chest. "What do we do?"

Then, like a nesting doll, Ronstadt's memory shared a memory.

"Remember when we went to Tucson?"

"Yeah."

"When I was little my grandmother took me to a church there. It was all this beautiful pink stucco. And the choir sang so gorgeously. It was run by Benedictines. I didn't believe the hocus-pocus, but they weren't dumb. Saint Benedict lived after the fall of the Roman empire. It was the start of a thousand years of darkness and lies. Repression. A whole world ending."

"So what did they do?"

"They went up into the mountains, into the caves. They settled for finding some peace in their own minds. They lived off scraps of kindness."

He struggled to keep his eyes open.

"You were good to me."

"We were good to each other."

Their breaths found common time, his mind's many fists unclenching as he fell into healing slumber. When he woke up, she was gone. He rolled his head from the pillow to see

Cage, Sean Penn, Carla, Sally Mae, and Willow standing above him, faces covered in battle paint.

The smell of burning rubber wafted up from the beach.

"Where is she?" said Carrey, concerned only for the loss of Ronstadt.

"You've had a trauma, man," said Sean Penn. "You're not alone. Nuclear exchange on the Indian subcontinent. Two million dead in a morning. We're living in a world that's blowing itself to pieces as fast as everybody can arrange it."

"The Russian army was wiped out defending Vladimir Putin's secret mansion on the Black Sea," said Cage. "The U.S. Congress turned to cannibalism after learning their emergency food supply went bad in 1981. The Chinese politburo is all living in a submarine. It's down to us."

"Don't *us* me," spat Carrey. "I want Linda."

"That's the rapture beam talkin'," said Cage. "Shake it off. Fight's coming."

He tossed Carrey a sleek silver pistol.

"What's that?"

"Plasma blaster. Travolta brought them."

"I'm nonviolent."

"Violence is our way of life now."

Carrey opened the blinds and peered outside. Travolta and the Scientologists had fled from their battle, landing on the beach in an inflatable raft with an outboard motor, refugees in their own city. The saucers had departed. Just a few were left up the beach, maybe a dozen still hovering over downtown Los Angeles.

"They started leaving yesterday," said Sean Penn. "Sent out an electromagnetic pulse, took down the whole power grid. Wiped out all the bank records. We're all beginners again." This last part made him smile. "Mop-up crews were sighted up by Oxnard, moving down the coast."

"They'll be here by morning," said Sally Mae.

"The same guys who took out Laser Jack?"

"Worse than that. These are Striders. Each twenty feet high, covered in scales sharp as Ginsu knives." Cage held up his hand. "What a burden, to be chosen."

"Why'd you pull me out, Nic?" said Carrey. "I was ready to go up with Kelsey Grammer and Bathsheba. With Cher." He leaned up out of bed, grabbing Cage by the collar. "I was out! Goddamn you! I was out. What the fuck do we even do now?"

"Now we fight," said Sean Penn. "That's what remains for us, here. No more lives of comfort, no more pampering. The human animal, back to hunger. We fight for our very survival."

"We fight for jasmine tea," said Gwyneth Paltrow, entering from the en suite bathroom in a vintage YSL beret, face painted with green and black combat stripes. "We fight for memories of pear-and-arugula salads in Bridgehampton. We fight to reclaim a world filled with so much joy your only concern is laugh lines on your face, maybe a little neck work, at a certain point."

"We fight," said Sally Mae, interrupting, "for a world reborn free from inherited privilege, rapacious capitalism, body shaming, congenital fame, predatory lending practices, and government-protected pharmaceutical cartels. A world where privacy is a right, not a word."

"We fight to avenge the Laser Jack brigades," said John Travolta, appearing from the hallway. He'd fully recharged his battle wig; its fibers surged angry waves of yellow and red. His gold spandex bodysuit had shrunk several sizes in Carrey's dryer, and it squeaked as he entered the bedroom. "We fight for disco fever and rigorously enforced intellectual property rights."

"Jimbo," said Sean Penn. "Are you with us?"

Carrey knew his line even before it arrived in his head. He picked up the Scientologist plasma blaster, caressing it with a gesture that might have seemed overwrought in simpler times but was perfectly suited to this hour of planetary climax. In the voice of a seasoned hitman accepting one last job to put his daughter through college, he said, "Yeah, what the fuck."

The Daughters of Anomie were the only ones with any real combat experience.

In Iraq and Afghanistan they'd seen how an advanced civilization could be defeated with wits and cunning and after discussion had chosen the Malibu Country Mart—a high-end outdoor shopping mall—as the most advantageous combat setting.

"I don't care if you took basic training for Hamburger Hill," said Carla as they gathered around a hastily drawn map of the mall. "I don't care if you were a mighty warlord in one of your fucking past-life regressions."

"I *battled* the warlords," said Travolta, protesting. "We were the only ones who could help."

Carla reached her titanium hand under the table and flicked his left testicle through his gold spandex bodysuit. "Suppressive!" said Travolta, wincing in pain.

Ignoring him, Carla continued, "You listen, you take orders. It's the only way we make it."

"Yes, ma'am," said Sean Penn, lighting a fresh Camel off his old one.

"I want Nic Cage, Sally Mae, and Jim Carrey on this antiaircraft gun above the Chipotle. Watch the hills. Start firing when you see them. Lure them in, then abandon and fall back. But you fire until the very last. Draw them down onto Cross Creek Road. Right into our Claymores."

"Make those alien cunts confetti," said Gwyneth Paltrow, clapping her hands. The battle paint was changing her. "Dance to the music of their agony."

"It'll definitely slow 'em down," said Carla. "That's when Paltrow, Sean Penn, and I all launch white phosphorus grenades from Urban Outfitters. Distract them, turn their flank. Then Willow, Travolta, and the Scientologists? You light 'em up with plasma blasters from Taverna Tony, the Greek restaurant."

"Ugh, Taverna Tony's my favorite!" gasped Travolta. "The fried halloumi? So worth the calories."

"Yeah?" said Carla. "Well, tonight they're serving grilled alien. They'll be caught in a cross fire. As Carrey, Cage, and Sally Mae close in from Chipotle—more plasma blasting, clearly—cutting off all escape. A classic Taliban trap. This is how I lost my arm and leg."

She hiked up her pants to show them all the titanium leg. It revived their spirits, some proof that the powerless could prevail over the powerful, so inspiring the actors that they now competed to own the moment with a line for the ages.

"Let's make some alien widows," said Sean Penn.

"Let's turn 'em into mincemeat and masticate 'em!" said John Travolta.

"Let's pour some salt on these SLUGS!" said Nic Cage.

"Let's kill for killing's sake and rejoice in how it changes us," said Gwyneth Paltrow. "I wanna play Slip 'N Slide in their fucking guts."

"I don't know if this is real," said Carrey. "But I can't afford to doubt it."

The night sky was muddy red.

The rain poured down in sheets as they hauled armaments across the Pacific Coast Highway and began to turn a shopping mall into an extraterrestrial slaughterhouse. They planted Claymores all down Cross Creek Road, smashed out the windows of Taverna Tony and Urban Outfitters, and stacked both storefronts high with sandbags, making them gunners' nests. With makeshift pulleys they hoisted Cage's antiaircraft gun onto Chipotle's roof, lumbering not just under the weight of steel but the compacted grief of all who'd come before them, people who'd done their part to keep the human candle burning, the martyred millions of Cambodia and Pompeii, the nameless dead of all the wars edited from history books for digressing from central narratives. Carrey thought chiefly of this last group as they huddled under the tarp, because he knew that, with no one left to tell their story, it was to this group that they'd belong if their lives ended here. Cage scanned the hills with his binoculars. Sally Mae sat at the guns, rolling up her shirtsleeve, unlatching her prosthetic arm from its socket. A titanium bolt was fused into the bone beneath the stump, the skin around it chafed and raw from hauling and lifting. As she rubbed the scar tissue with lotion, Carrey felt a withering fear consume him.

"Are you afraid of it?" he asked Sally Mae.

"Afraid of what?"

"*It.*"

"THE BIG SLEEP!" Cage shouted, against the rain.

"Oh. I dunno. I've seen people take it both ways."

"Whaddya mean?"

"Some of the toughest guys?" said Sally Mae. "They start crying, calling for their mothers. And as they pass they get a look in their eyes, like they see something horrible coming, like a reckoning. They're scared. Then others, they'll surprise you. They go out real calm and serene."

"But they all end up the same," said Carrey. "All gone, all forgotten."

"Yeah," said Sally Mae. "All gone. Forgotten."

"I ain't afraid," said Cage. "I've lived and died a thousand times."

"That's what you tell yourself," said Carrey. "I think the death fear's just so strong the ego does anything to block it out. We hide in grandiose stories. Superheroes, God-men. Fame is a mind plague; we thought it'd make us immortal as it ate up our precious time."

His whole striving life now seemed so distant. Had any of it mattered? He'd exhausted himself—for what? He thought of a puffer fish he'd seen on the BBC. A pathetic creature, little fins, bulging eyes, poppy-seed brain. Unremarkable in every way. Except that, way down on the seafloor, it wiggled in the sand to make a stunning geometric pattern, perfectly proportioned, intricate as any mandala. All to attract a mate, to pass on its genes. Was there any real difference between them? The fish, too, had a talent. But was, presumably, untroubled by anything like the panicked vertigo that came over Carrey now, huddled against the sandbags, heart pounding in his chest.

"I'm in a fragile place, guys," he said. "Not sure I'm gonna be much of an asset here."

A crimson light flashed over the hills. Cage was busy with his knife, scratching his name into the tar-tiled roof. Carrey took his binoculars and scanned the ridge. More flashes. Brighter, closer. He panned down to Taverna Tony. Travolta was in an argument with Willow, evidently refusing to huddle with the others, insisting on the dramatic choice of standing with one foot heroically planted on the sandbags, à la *Washington Crossing the Delaware.* Carrey swung his sights across the way, tight on Sean Penn, crouched in the bunker that had been Urban Outfitters, lighting up another Camel. Then the cigarette dropped from Penn's lips and his eyes ignited with the same fear that sank Carrey's heart as, swinging the binoculars up toward the hills, he saw them.

"Sweet Jesus . . ."

An alien mop-up crew.

They were worse than giant robots. And worse than giant serpents. They were giant robots piloted by giant serpents, a synthesis of scriptural and science-fiction horrors, Tan Calvin's people in unmasked form, awful snaky guys, just as Cage had seen, piloting gleaming alloy exoskeletons, bipedal warbots painted with insignia representing all the worlds they'd destroyed, hieroglyphs of apocalypse swirling across the bodysuits that might have been described as futuristic if our heroes, after glimpsing these foes, still believed in the future as a meaningful concept.

"Who's making up grandiose stories now?" said Cage. "Light 'em up, Sally Mae!"

"I'll give the orders here," Sally Mae said. "Both you bitches get ready to reload me."

They hurried into position, Carrey standing over the crate of artillery shells, Cage ready by the breech of the gun, Sally Mae trimming and calibrating as the Striders neared, gaining twenty yards with each step, closing in five hundred yards, four hundred—

Three hundred.

Two hundred—

Sally Mae opened fire, raking the formation, hitting two directly. The machines just shuddered, then took their own aim. And out came the death rays. A hail of killing crimson light, each beam a foot in diameter, hundreds coming now from the Striders, filling Jim Carrey with terror. This was where he'd die. But the volley went wide, crashing into Mr. Chow. Giving them a second chance.

"Reload!" cried Sally Mae. Carrey lifted the artillery shells from their crate, passing each carefully to Cage. Never in his life had anything felt so arrestingly vivid as this simple act. The present, at last, unpolluted by thought for the past or the future.

So breathtakingly real.

"That's it, Jim," said Sally Mae. "You're doing great."

Aiming at the nearest Strider, she fired off the volley that would betray their position: seven shells howling through the night. The first three shots landed, disabling the devil bot's shields. The fourth and fifth went wide. But the last one hit, turning this enemy into a fountain of greenish flames.

The other machines now locked in on the gunner's nest, raining death rays on the Chipotle.

"Move!" said Sally Mae.

They hurried down the access hatch, raced through the front door, following the mighty woman onto Cross Creek Road. The Chipotle was ablaze, and through the smoke of burning meat and rubber they saw the first of the Striders enter the shopping village, triggering the buried Claymores. They ducked as thick white blasts shattered the storefront windows, their ears ringing. The Strider's knees buckled, then it crashed to the pavement, sending out a bone-rattling shock wave. The remaining machines paused, scanning about for this newest threat, when, from Urban Outfitters, came a war cry unheard since Little Bighorn, issued then from the Lakota, now from Gwyneth Paltrow, who, with Sean Penn and Willow, opened fire with rocket-propelled grenade launchers. Unlike the rest, Gwyneth experienced no combat fear. Only pure berserker spirit, a unified animal instinct chanting from a wild place beyond the human heart: *dominate, kill, survive.* She aimed for the downed Strider, lining its pilot's pod up in her sights, launching three grenades at this creature who, while hideous to human eyes, had people who cared for him back in the Boötes Void, memories of weekends in the Sombrero Galaxy joined with others in a giant, slithering mating ball, memories that played within his mind as Gwyneth Paltrow's first two grenades shattered his pod, as her third sailed right through, burning into his slickened belly before exploding him into caustic slime.

The other four Striders refused the trap.

Crimson death beams shot through the smoke-engulfed street. Sean Penn, Carla, and Gwyneth Paltrow struggled to sight their weapons, calling desperately to Willow and the Scientologists.

"Where are you? We're getting slaughtered here!"

Only Willow had kept her cool, peppering the machines with a stream of plasma blasts. The others had fallen to infighting. Travolta's two soldiers—Harley Sandler and Hurley Chandler—had been on the outs with each other ever since Sandler beat Chandler for a minor role on *Days of Our Lives*. Now they were bickering over who would shoot which alien first.

"Shut up, you two!" scolded Willow.

"Don't command my men," said Travolta.

"Tell them to fire! Return fire!"

"That's it," he said, summoning powers of concentration he'd mastered over years of study. "I challenge you to a staring contest."

"What's wrong with you?"

"We'll see who the real leader is."

"We're being blown to hell!"

"You blinked!"

The whole restaurant flashed brilliant crimson as the death beams homed in on their discord, raking Travolta's chest, punching clear through Willow's skull, bisecting Sandler's and Chandler's torsos, cauterizing the flesh and organs such that these poor souls didn't die but persisted in stumpified form, their puzzled shrieks harmonizing over the tympanies of the alien cannonade. With what life they had left, they tried to elbow-walk to safety, staring up eerily, as they went, at the walls of Taverna Tony, painted with a mural of ancient battle on Trojan plains, Bronze Age heroes fixed here in the city of celluloid: Achilles, Ajax—and Diomedes. Whose spirit now rose up within Nicolas Cage, an Italian, after all, descended of Trojan stock. And a man who sensed that his hour had arrived.

"I'm going in," said Cage. "They'll all die if I don't."

"Don't be crazy," said Carrey. "They'll blow you apart."

"Naw. Told ya, Jimbo, I'm immune to the death rays."

"That's a grandiose story!"

"Grandiose stories are all we have left," shouted Cage. "That and my sword, Excalibur." The Striders were bearing down, turning their rays on the Urban Outfitters.

"Remember that well I told you about?" said Cage, eyebrows popping. "Well, they just pulled up a bucket full of hell."

"I love you, Nic," said Carrey. The end was close for them all; Cage had a right to the final moments of his choice. "I respect you as an artist. As someone with whom I shared dreams in this town a million selves ago. Aim well, my brother."

"We did all right," said Cage, with a smile. "You gonna use that plasma blaster?"

"Probably not," said Carrey, and handed over the weapon, for which he had no special love anyway. Then, certain of his destiny, wolf rising in the heart, Nicolas Cage burst out from the cover of the Chipotle's smoldering shell, firing both plasma blasters through the rain and smoke, walking toward the approaching devil bots, coattails blowing in wind, his mind reeling as he went with the thrill of all genres fusing at the end of the human narrative. He was Buck Rogers. He was Doc Holliday. He was Saint Michael slaying the dragon. He was Perseus bearing down on Medusa and he was Nureyev leaving his deathbed to conduct *Romeo and Juliet* one last time, and his face channeled all of these as few faces could. "*Fuck the critics! Fuck the tabloids! Fuck you bastards for hounding me across space and time!*" he screamed, charging that which any reasonable person would have fled and, maybe by force of sheer will, maybe by accident, maybe, indeed, by destiny, he was immune to the crimson death rays. They didn't slice through him as he drew closer but rather diffused within him, the result of a slight mutation in his DNA, a tiny structural difference in his cell walls that simply shrugged off the wavelength of the beams—just as some tan at the beach, and others burn. His aim was true, he'd rehearsed this scene a thousand times. He fired dense plasma blasts into the pilot chamber of the nearest machine, and it froze as the direct hits killed the pilot at his controls.

"*Woohaa!*" he cried, sighting Gwyneth Paltrow, Sean Penn, and Carla through the smoke, grinning with the thrill of death defied, turning his plasma blasters now on the closest of the three surviving monsters. Overwhelming its shields, absorbing its crimson fire with little more than a twitch down his spine, he giggled, gaily, aiming for the knees, disabling the Strider as Sean Penn and Carla took down another with phosphorus grenades.

Leaving only one, the squadron's alpha—Cage's horrible, eon-spanning nemesis.

He drew close to the deathbot, twenty feet high, and its pilot, in his mind, the demon who had followed him through so many sweat-soaked nights.

"You drove me from my homes, my life," said Cage. "Why? What love I might have known, what tenderness, across time, but for your demented hauntings. For what? The cosmos is brutal enough without people like you taking others' suffering as entertainment. No more. It ends tonight."

He raised his plasma blasters. "Final reckoning, motherfucker."

He fired into the cockpit, watched by his waiting victim, the terrified reptiloid captain, who cried, in his own way, as Cage shot up the edges of his pilot's pod, shattering its polymer shell, who struggled and spasmed in his harnesses as earth's atmosphere poured chokingly over him. And who managed to send out a distress message as Cage raised up Excalibur to deliver the blow that would, Cage believed, liberate earth for millennia to come.

Down came the sword, gashing open the serpent's abdomen. Cage didn't stop there. He hacked and stabbed, mutilating each organ as if afraid it might respawn the demon, while Gwyneth Paltrow played at figure skating in the flow of guts dripping from the body—a pair of actions that may have offended the gods of battle.

"Guys," said Jim Carrey, eyeing the ridge. "It's not over."

It wasn't. Now, down from the mountains, came not six but at least a hundred alien mop-up machines. And not Striders, but Super Striders, each forty feet tall, crushing trees and rocks as they moved down toward the little shopping village, heeding the alien captain's distress call. Chilling music sounded from every atom as they approached, the last movement of Calvin's requiem was his final insult, an alien muzak version of Doc Pomus's "This Magic Moment," its tragic, supernatural banality draining the last traces of hope from their souls as out, now, came not crimson but raspberry death rays, the result of a slight tweaking of frequency, Calvin's people having adjusted to the news of Cage's immunity. In all his visions, all his dreams, Nicolas Cage had never ever seen a raspberry death ray. And now he realized that a few glimpses of the future do not form a complete picture.

"They figured me out!" he cried. "We gotta move!"

He fled with the rest as these new beams rained down, as the friends, who only moments before were planning a new world, now sought just basic survival.

Each Super Strider bristled with twenty cannons, the pilot pods all covered with protective shields, slightly beaked, suggesting giant plague doctors.

The survivors raced down Cross Creek Road, death rays following them in flight, raspberry reflecting in the rain. Then, hissing like a viper, a ray caught Gwyneth Paltrow's leg, severing it just above the knee. Her debutante's scream was the final cry of a certain kind of humanity, declaring the world as they'd known it a lost civilization. Carla scooped her up and carried her down the shopping mall street. They ducked into a side alley. Paltrow stared with awed horror at her wound, veins cauterized, charred femur tip just poking through the flesh.

"My leg is gone, my leg is gone . . ." she gasped. *"It's awesome!"*

"We're gonna get you a new one," said Sally Mae, jabbing a morphine syrette into Gwyneth Paltrow's thigh.

"We're pinned down," said Sean Penn. "No escape."

"Can't we gank a ride?" said Cage, nodding to abandoned cars up the alley.

"Useless," said Sally Mae. "Those are all fancy. Computerized. Fried in the electromagnetic pulse."

"How 'bout that one?" said Carrey, pointing to an old Triumph motorcycle, vintage, from the late 1970s. "Looks analog to me."

"It's worth a shot," said Sally Mae. "Can't fit more than three of us, though."

They hurried toward the motorcycle. Sally Mae played with its ignition wires. The engine sputtered and faltered, three times. Then its headlight blazed to life.

"Come on, girls," said Sally Mae to Paltrow and Carla. "Time for some tactical retrograde. By which I mean let's haul ass."

"Really?" said Carrey. "Suddenly it's ladies first again?"

"It's a woman's right to change her mind," said Sally Mae.

"This is how it has to be," grumbled Sean Penn, squinting against the smoke of the Camel hanging from his lips. "Gwyneth's wounded. Sally Mae, you're the best fighter—they'll need you. And Carla is with child."

"What child?" said Carrey.

"My child," roared Penn. "She's with my child."

The women climbed onto the motorcycle, Sally Mae at the handlebars, Carla holding up a morphine-dazed Gwyneth Paltrow behind her, turning to Sean Penn as he placed his hand on her stomach and made a final request. "If I die, tell our child I went peacefully. With grace. Tell our child that, in my last breath, I thought of its first breath. That this connects us. Tell her every time someone blows cigarette smoke in her face, it means I'm there. Watching over her."

"I will," said Carla, tenderly. "I promise you."

"Tell the kid about me, too," said Cage. "Tell everyone, actually. Say I died after killing an alien in combat with my sword, Excalibur. And you don't have to, but you could throw in the part about me being immune to the death rays. Make sure to say I died kinda falling to my knees with my arms in the air, in slow motion, like Dafoe in *Platoon*. That's all I ask, in exchange for my sacrifice."

"What about you, Jim?" said Sally Mae. "What do we say?"

"Should we say you killed a dozen alien Super Striders?" offered Carla. "A one-man Alamo?"

"No," said Carrey. "I had a modest combat record."

"Tell them Jim had a hundred heads and a hundred arms," said Gwyneth, druggedly. "Say it took a hundred aliens to kill him and he never ever *ever* gave up."

Carrey didn't totally dislike this idea. What if each of the heads had its own expression? Wasn't that close enough to his truth? That'd be something, a one-man carnival describing the artist who contains multitudes, the one man as all men. Didn't he want some part of the record? A starring role in the *Book of Regenesis*? If he made no claim, he'd be a footnote. Doubts and confusions scurried like mice across his mind as death rays fell up the alley. No time now for funeral speeches, only for messages in bottles.

"Just find my daughter," said Carrey. "Find Jane, tell her I love her."

"Okay," said Sally Mae. "And now we gotta move."

Carrey looked to Penn and Cage, both practiced in war and action genres, and yet, like him, wholly terrified of what lay ahead, the three men sharing a look of assent hardly original to this moment, the same exchanged by boys charging the no-man's-lands of the Somme a century before, a recognition that each was placing his life, his every caress, his every August evening, into fortune's indifferent hands. And then Jim Carrey, Sean Penn, and Nicolas Cage, the last standing titans of Hollywood—mortals made colossal by worship in the marketplace—they charged down onto Cross Creek Road, plasma blasters firing against the raspberry hail, the Super Striders pursuing them, taking the bait. They drew away nearly all the fire, creating a window of opportunity in which the Triumph screeched down onto the Pacific Coast Highway, speeding north as, instincts switching from fight to flight, the leading men ran like panicked livestock.

Penn was first to fall. A Super Strider shot a raspberry ray clear through his right arm, cleaving it at the joint. The limb fell into the mud. There was no cover in sight. He crouched and took the still-burning Camel from his severed hand, lifting it defiantly to his lips and pulling a final, sating drag as a second death ray sailed through his beating heart. He died thinking of his child, a boy or a girl, it didn't matter, it would be born feral and free, would do its part for the rebuilding of the world, the creation of a new moral system across the hard years to come. Sean Penn's consciousness was safe in this bliss even as his body crumpled to the ground, seared and scalded by the Super Striders now just a hundred yards away, cannons blazing.

They took Cage as their next target, jockeying to smite him as a carrier of immunity, their death rays finding him as he bounded across the street. How many get to choreograph their final seconds? He died just as he said he would, turning to face their swarm, laughing at them, even, because if the worst threat they had was oblivion, that was fine by him, an endless vacation from the torments of being. He fell in slow motion, arms stretched toward heaven, face a vision of Christly surrender. *You did things that hadn't been done, that others were afraid to do*, thought Carrey, watching Cage's body hit the ground with an excruciating wheeze.

You gave me courage.

He thought of the Pietà, Jesus laid out in the Virgin Mary's arms. Voices from some catacomb inside of him prayed to her, asking for safety, for velocity, and, failing these, for a death as exquisite as Cage's.

Then he was turning the corner around the Café Habana, its concrete shielding him from the fusillade, his whole being crying out for a return to the place where—thrashing, frightened, struggling to breathe—a squirming species began its story five hundred million years before, a genre-bending tale of fantasy and comedy, action and adventure, murder and magic.

He ran like running was the last language left, eyes set on the sea.

CHAPTER 16

The Super Striders made a game of wrecking the shopping mall, sheer wrath rejoicing in itself, death beams falling through the night mist, bombarding the stores, a temple sacking, to some view: John Varvatos, L'Occitane, Lululemon, all burning.

All signs and names turned to carbon, given over to the winds.

Jim Carrey ran with the vision of a dying Nic Cage still clawing at his heart.

He ran from annihilation, toward the hope of escape, face covered with grease and strange blood. He scurried across the highway, then down an access lane toward the beach, where, charging out from a driveway, right into his path, came a large and frightened beast, a creature fled from some eccentric's private zoo.

A rhinoceros.

He froze in its gaze, and it froze in his. A moment of interspecies appraisal in which Carrey felt his heart flush with hope at the scintilla of a chance that this was his old friend Rodney Dangerfield. That Lonstein had been guiding them toward this, the old duo reunited, using one-liners and sheer pluck to turn the tide against the Super Striders.

"Rodney?" he whispered.

And listened hopefully for an answer as the animal's eyes went wide. Then it grunted, flared its nostrils, and charged. Carrey fled down the road, toward the rear gates of a beachfront mansion, leaping over them and falling into a hedgerow as the raging rhino crashed its horn between the gates' steel posts. The beast struggled to dislodge itself, but the steel had cut deep into its skin. It made terrible cries, sounds like from a broken kazoo, nothing human in there. The Super Striders were on the highway, strafing the oceanfront mansions, impacts spawning heat devils across the night.

And now the star recalled the single rule he'd learned watching chunks of human history on YouTube and Netflix: in dire moments one must flee and not look back. He ran down to the beach, scanning its breadth for some mode of escape. But this was a rich man's paradise: no motorboats, no sailboats, just paddleboards and lounge chairs, American leisure, in its ultimate hours, not so different from lying in state.

Then in a flicker of raspberry light—

He saw the rubber dinghy that had carried Travolta and his men up from Santa Monica. He charged down the slick low-tide sand, pushed the craft toward the water, blood in his throat, groans and grunts forming the last prayers as naturally as they had the first. The killers were on the beach now, raspberry death raining all around as the boat hit the water, as Carrey yanked on the outboard motor's pull cord.

Once, nothing.

Again, desperate, nothing.

Turning, he saw the death squads. Some danced in celebration, their gleaming alloy beaks shaking with apparent laughter. Others had stopped their exoskeletons around piles of charred bodies, slithering down from their captain's pods to feast on human barbecue, broadcasting their conquest to delighted viewers back home. And it wasn't clear to Carrey if they were vomiting from secondary mouths or ejaculating from unseen sex organs, but thick sprays of black fluid spurted from their lower torsos as they bucked in gorging peristalsis.

And here, we must pause to note, Jim Carrey was different from others who'd left everything behind in flight. There is some comfort in being eradicated by your own kind, a knowledge that this was part of the species' compact, that the blade could have swung the other way. A solace that, however meager, is unavailable to those slaughtered by aliens. He soiled himself in fear and yet welcomed his stench, a human stench; he found it comforting and familiar as the Super Striders tightened their cannons on his stretch of the beach. As, sobbing and pleading, he yanked on the outboard motor. *Again, again, again—*

Then, finally, barely, it came to life, vibrating hope through his every cell as he climbed into the raft, ducking low, gunning for the only safety available, that of open water.

He lay flat, like in a bed, afraid to move, telling himself that each elapsed second brought him safety. He prayed to his remnant gods for preservation, but without sufficient faith to dare looking back for nearly an hour. Then two miles out into the Pacific, shivering in his shit and his fear, he lifted up his head to glimpse the coastline. It had become a dancing pyre, the Malibu Colony in flames; his home, too, with Chaplin's cane inside, gone with the person he'd been and the world that had formed him. There are, it has been sung since Troy, tears for things, and mortal things do move the heart. He cried now, for Sean Penn and Nicolas Cage, for Sally Mae and Carla, whose fates he'd never know. For his daughter, for his grandson, wherever they were. He cried, even, for Wink and Al, and despite all the grievances between them what he'd have given to have them in the boat, to help him plan, to console and encourage. Well, maybe not Al, whose overeating would be a problem in any resource-constrained environment and could even lead to cannibalism. But Wink, yes, definitely Wink, who at least had played the good cop. Who had believed in him when others didn't. Who had combat experience, who had seen men die, just as he had now, and what a miracle it was, Carrey marveled, that Wink had retained any humanity after all the loss and pain that he now knew as well, the sorrow that filled him as he motored farther out to sea, the coast becoming just a rim of burning villages, a dying filament—

Oh fallen world, he thought, lines coming to him as naturally as in the desert production chamber. *You cried out to the stars to free you from your loneliness, and they did, but they took all else as well. And what am I now?*

A man and his world are entwined. You can't demolish one without injuring the other.

Who had he been?

A god of the cultural marketplace.

What was he now? A creature on a dinghy ten miles off the California coast, his vast estate reduced to just a single rucksack left behind by Travolta. It contained two canteens, a first-aid kit, and a dozen Cookies 'n' Cream Laser Jack Lightning–branded yogurt bars, wrappers printed with Jack's chiseled torso in silhouette. As he admired the sculpted abs, Carrey's memory flashed to *The Last of the Mohicans*, or at least Daniel Day-Lewis's whitewashed portrayal of that man, not just allowed but applauded in a bygone cultural era. Maybe these yogurt bars and the sudden vision of healthy native persons was a cosmic invitation, he wondered, a brief flush of hope. He'd find an island, get in sick shape. He'd be just like the last Mohican. In a way, he might even *be* the last Mohican, insofar as all humans have a common ancestor.

How did that movie end?

It seemed vitally important to know, a narrative model to guide him. But he'd seen so many movies. The endings all blurred together. Did the Mohican get shot by the French? Or did he have a baby by a waterfall? Carrey needed so badly to know, closing his eyes, beseeching the full smorgasbord of possible creators for an affirming memory, coastline fading to nothing.

And then he was floating in total darkness.

Panicked, he turned the dinghy toward his best guess at east, madly gunning the engine, hoping each fuel-draining throttle would recenter his world. Here was a man who was decades removed from visiting a gas station, who assumed a functioning GPS on every dashboard. Who cursed John Travolta for leaving him a day boat with a fuel tank only big enough for tooling around the marina as the gas ran low and the engine sputtered. Who punched his own face and screamed until his voice broke and nothing came out, enraged to lose his only bearing.

Important to put out good energy, he told himself, slumping exhausted into the dinghy.

Vital to affirm, to manifest, to go to sleep with positivity and gratitude, communicated warmly to the cosmos. It came to him, a single buoyant thought:

TPG owns nothing now.

He woke beneath a hazy sun, head throbbing. He pissed deep amber off the dinghy, into the endless gray-blue waves, ripples doomier than prison bars.

He was thirsty, just half a canteen left.

Two swigs, three if he was careful.

You could distill water from the sea, he knew. He'd watched this on survival shows. It had to do with molecular bonds. It was a matter of persuading the salt to fall out of love with the water, and it involved a tarp and an old plastic bottle. Or maybe a magnifying glass. He'd seen it, but the details had trickled off his mind.

So much information, toward the end, had trickled off the mind.

He drank just enough to wet his swelling tongue, ego madly searching for something with which to fight despair, settling, finally, on the vaguest and so least assailable of hopes—

Trade winds.

Memories of a Twitter infographic. The oceans were a living system. And he was part of that system, this was certain, he knew, having just pissed into it. And that system was part of greater systems spanning a creation which, give or take the odd death squad, was basically kind and benevolent, or at the very least indifferent.

Trade winds.

He visualized them spiriting him up north, to Oregon. Saw himself coming upon the Daughters of Anomie's deep forest paradise. He saw Sally Mae and Jane wearing crowns of moss. He saw his grandson, Jackson, growing strong, poised to lead in the pure new world. But then the vision fell apart. He saw the happy village raided. He saw starving decades, barren fields, pitched battles over stores of gasoline and Spam, the world returned to primal maulings. He felt the skin blistering on his forehead.

He was no longer thinking about trade winds.

He was curling himself into the rim of shade that fell from the dinghy's side, tucking his head low, rubber craft rising and falling on the swells.

He was vomiting over the side, stomach acid burning his mouth.

He was swallowing down his last water, body demanding it, bile stinging his lips, his chin, his tongue. He was dizzy, washing his face clean in the sea, gargling the water, then gulping it down, powerless against the demands of his thirst.

He was asleep, dreaming of swallowing sandpaper.

He was awake, nighttime now, his thoughts dragged like granite slabs on sledges.

The ocean was more than still; it was polished obsidian.

The stars shone crystalline and bright, all reflected perfectly on the water's surface, the thick central band of the Milky Way completing its spiral around the boat, a sacred wheel, infinite time and space freed from any axis. He dared his head over the side, expecting to glimpse infinity, seeing, instead, a haggard, unshaven creature, eyes hollowed by hopelessness.

He spat at the ghoul, then turned to see he wasn't alone.

Perched across the dinghy was Ted Berman, host of BBC's *Pompeii Reconstructed: Countdown to Disaster*. "I've seen many ruined civilizations," said Berman. He wore his appropriated Indiana Jones outfit, complete with thrift-store fedora, and spoke in his convivial TV-host manner. "But I've always wanted to come here, at the end of it all, with the last man, Jim Carrey."

"Berman?" said Carrey.

"The mind, deprived of sleep and nutrition, cedes higher functions and seeks a soothing exit reel," said Berman, as if addressing an unseen audience. "Each epoch has its own gods and beseeches those gods as it ends. Jim Carrey, here, is not so different from the last Pompeians. Kanye West, though manic, was possessed of real genius. What God remains, at history's end, but abstract forms?" He produced a ram's horn from his knapsack.

"What's that for?" asked Carrey.

"We're passing through a thin place," said Berman. "A zone where worlds touch."

He raised the horn to his mouth and blew a plaintive note, a low wailing, the sound of a suddenly sentient lamb lamenting its slaughter. He held it until his face reddened, until the veins bulged on his neck and all the stars in the unified field of water and sky began to vibrate, then to swirl—

First, in chaos.

Then, toward an intricate pattern, an incandescent flower with endless petals, each ten million light-years long, a sparkling mandala across the heavens, and Carrey listened like a schoolboy learning of flight as Ted Berman explained, "This is the shape of all that has been. All the lives that have ever been lived. And the light that shines from them is every dream and every memory, every hope and every wish."

"Yes," said Carrey, warmed. "It's just like that."

"And it's always been there. It just needed the appropriate quiet to reveal itself."

Berman blew his horn again, a slightly higher pitch. The flower petals turned to blazing fractals swirling in perfect Fibonacci spirals and Carrey gasped raw wonder as Berman, with all the authority vested in him by a BBC gig and a bachelor's degree from Cornell, said, "This is the true shape of time, an endless spiral of spirals."

And Carrey gave a raspy giggle to think that he'd ever worried about the constraints of a human life span. About his waistline. That he'd ever spiked an avocado smoothie with couture amino acids. That the mystery of time's endlessness had been hidden from him all his days, waiting for someone to cajole it into view with the proper notes of music sounded at the proper point on the spiritual meridian.

"We've learned so much tonight," said Ted Berman, putting down the ram's horn. "And now, I'd like to say a few words about our sponsor: *Slim Jim's meat sticks and beef jerky snacks*."

"Huh?" asked Carrey, confused. "What about time and—"

"Slim Jim's meat sticks and beef jerky snacks are bold, spicy, and made out of the stuff men need," said Berman. "Satisfy your hunger and snap into a Slim Jim today!"

And then, from his backpack, he produced no fewer than ten of the beef jerky snacks, holding them up, fan-style, like winning poker hands. "Jerky, Jim?" he said.

Forgetting all communion with guiding geometries, Carrey leaped on him like a wild bobcat. He tore the Slim Jims from Berman's clutches, ripped away the plastic wrappers with his teeth, planted his canines into the juicy meat, gnawing, chomping, feeding, sucking, guided by an inner roaring until that roaring quieted, and then he fell asleep, belly full, animal cells fed.

He woke without a memory's faintest glimmer, pain shrieking through his hands.

With horror, he saw the flesh was gone from his fingers, ripped away, as if by piranhas. The bones were bare, blood smudged, nerves and tendons severed, dangling loose. He screamed, then winced in screaming, throat burned by stomach acids. It hurt, even, to swallow.

He curled fetal, shivering-shock, whimpering.

Use your brain, use your brain, use your brain . . .

Where was he?

At sea. In a boat. What was this kind of boat again?

Dinghy.

Hardly a word, so onomatopoetic—

Dinghy, dinghy, dinghy . . .

He was Jim and he was in a dinghy . . .

Asserting this basic truth, he felt one with the pitching craft, Jim and Dinghy, Dinghy-Jimmy, *Jimsy-Dinghy, Jinghy Dimmy*, he said, giggling, *Jimsy-Dinghy, Dimsey Jinghy*, and he laughed so hard he spat a plug of blood-streaked bile into his palm. He stared at it, saying, *Snivaloggh*, again and again, *snivaloggh, snivaloggh*, laughing like laughter was never a business.

He lay on his side, coughing up plugs of *snivaloggh*.

He hadn't retched so violently since he was a boy with the scarlet fever, or the flu, or whatever it was . . .

His memories were reels of celluloid, slowly dissolving. He panicked. He rushed to review and preserve them. He closed his eyes, searching through the vaults of the self for frames of what he was. But the damage was beyond repair, the rooms and holds flooded with salt water, the memories lost, except for one . . .

When again he looked up, his father, Percy, was sitting beside him, wearing his navy suit, the only suit he'd ever owned, and his favorite blue velour clip-on bow tie.

"You're okay, my boy," he said, gently taking his son's wounded hands, all pain subsiding as he whispered into his ear: "*There is one spirit guiding all things. The universe, one verse. The stars and the sea and the wind through the wheat fields. And us, you and me. Once through flesh. Now through memory. See? I'm in you and you're within me.*"

"We are each other."

"Yes. We're not separate, not how it seems."

Carrey smiled to think he'd ever thought he was a person

at all. What a ludicrous delusion. What colossal labor. How exhausting, to be a self. To keep the Ponzi fed, with words, with feats, with playing at exceptionalism. He went to hug his father, but the phantom was gone. He was alone, head dangling over the side of the half-deflated raft, eyes clenched shut against the sun.

Desperate for proof of sustained being, he probed the inside of his mouth with his swollen tongue, popping a molar loose from his gums. Which didn't bother him in the least, because he was utterly sure, as he let the tooth fall from his mouth into the sea, that whatever this body was, it wasn't him.

Here, in circumstances beyond dire, his mind, as in a confession, revealed the truth of what he actually was, and as his was the only mind in the world, and its perceptions of reality in that moment the last recorded impressions of his species—the woods and the tree falling silently in it—his feelings in the dinghy were, by full force of all the logic they seemingly defied, the grand totality of all human truth, the final strand of a battered species' narrative. And the truth, dazzling and majestic, is that he was not a man in a stolen rubber skiff.

He was everything. Which was hard to define, the mind, at that point, drawing off last traces of final calories. But he was wholeness, and wholeness was him. He felt it so totally, the integration, interaction, and reconciliation of all things. The space in which all occurs. Wholeness freeing, occupying, his entire mind, a soothing word, absent of jarring syllables, a soft exhale. Wholeness, not separate from the stars, totally and joyously—

The snowcapped Himalayas. The island of Manhattan before the fall. The Mississippi River and the glaciers that carved the Great Plains. And time, too, all of it. And all beyond it, truth and falsehood and light and dark and Dick Van Dyke falling over an ottoman and lovers sharing first kisses in convertible Thunderbirds on hot summer days and wishes blown on dandelions by children in those blessed spaces of time where people looked to the future with hope and the rings of Saturn and distant galaxies and soft-serve ice cream, a tear of joy brimming in the eye, the last bit of water remaining in this body crawls slowly down its cheek . . .

Soft clouds were now passing over a slightly less menacing sun, down on the temporal plane, above the tired and broken body, drizzle rousing what life remains in that husk, water and light . . .

He reached for a name that no longer mattered, the sound he had known himself by.

And a voice that seemed to come from the rain whispered—

Shhhhhhhh . . .

Acknowledgments

A special thanks to all those who helped us along the way: Dan Aloni, Ann Blanchard, Paul Bogaards, Ray Boucher, Jane Carrey, Percy Carrey, Ruth Curry, Jeff Daniels, Jackie Eckhouse, Linda Fields Hill, Gary Fisketjon, Eric Gold, Ginger Gonzaga, Alex Hurst, Chip Kidd, Debby Klein, David Kuhn, Marleah Leslie, Tom Leveritt, Sonny Mehta, Jimmy Miller, Nicole Montez, Tim O'Connell, John Rigney, Dawn Saltzman, Jackson Santana, Gemma Sieff, Jean Vachon, and Boing!

A NOTE ABOUT THE AUTHORS

Jim Carrey is an award-winning actor and artist.
Dana Vachon is a writer who lives in Brooklyn.

A NOTE ON THE TYPE

This book was set in Janson, a typeface designed by Nicholas Kis (1650–1702).

Composed by North Market Street Graphics, Lancaster, Pennsylvania
Printed and bound by LSC Communications, Harrisonburg, Virginia
Designed by Anna B. Knighton